RISE OF THE KING

RESTLESS KINGS BOOK 1

BELLA MATTHEWS

ASIN: B0948FN7V3

Editor: Jessica Snyder, Jessica Snyder Edits

Copy Editor: Dena Mastrogiovanni, Red Pen Editing

Cover Designer: Jena Brignla

Photographer: Michelle Lancaster, Lane Photography

Model: Lawrence Templar

Interior Formatting: Savannah Richey, Peachy Keen Author Services

Mom ~ No stronger heroine ever existed.
Thank you for teaching me to stand up for myself and go after what I want.

Your heart knows the way. Run in that direction.

— RUMI

PLAYLIST

- Kings & Queens – Ava Max
- Wild Ones (feat. Sia) – Flo Rida, Sia
- Kiss Me – Ed Sheeran
- Legendary – Welshy Arms
- Play with Fire (feat. Yacht Mo…) Sam Tinnesz, Yacht Money
- Smells Like Teen Spirit – Malia J
- Try (Ya Gotta Get Up and Try) – joc.sco
- Human – Christina Perri
- Closer – Kings of Leon
- Everybody Wants to Rule The World – Lorde
- Nothing Else Matters – Metallica
- Beggin' – Mmanskin
- Back To You – Selena Gomez
- Unsteady – Erich Lee Gravity – X Ambassadors, Erich Lee
- Royals – Lorde

https://bit.ly/RotKPlaylist

PROLOGUE

SAM – AGE 16

I'VE ALWAYS KNOWN ONE DAY I'LL BE KING. MY FATHER HAS been telling me this my entire life. And when Vito Beneventi speaks, you listen. Pop is the head of the family. Not just my family—*The Family*. His father was in charge before he died, and I'll take over after Pops dies. It's the way of our world.

Most of my life can be broken down into befores and afters.

Before my mother died, she wanted my brother and me to be sheltered from this life. She was born into it. She knew what to expect, knew she couldn't protect us. But I heard my father and her argue about it anyway. Mom knew my life was planned out the minute she gave birth to a boy. But still, she tried to keep my little brother and me as far from harm as possible.

Eventually, she accepted my fate.

That's when she started telling me, as the big brother, my job was to always keep my baby brother, Sebastian, safe.

She made me swear it on my life before she died in a car accident a few years ago.

After she died, Pop started pulling me into this life a little

1

at a time. By the time I was fourteen years old, I was doing a little bit of everything for everyone. I cleaned cars. Picked up dry cleaning. I was the food delivery guy. Whatever was needed by one of *The Family*, I was supposed to make it happen.

I was a glorified gopher.

Learn everything.

Be able to do everything.

It was my first step in my eventual ascension.

It wasn't until my sixteenth birthday a few months ago that my father told me I'd start training with my mother's brother, Uncle Nick. My uncle is a guy who has a smile for everyone. But that smile hides the monster inside. He's brought me with him on his collection runs for the last month. I've watched him smile while we collect money that's owed. He asks about everyone's family by name. He knows what sports their kids play. According to him, this makes the job easier. Shows the guys they're dealing with someone who knows where they live and who they love. And those guys never miss a payment for the very same reasons.

Until they do.

Until they can't pay us.

Then Nick unleashes that monster.

I've watched him make men twice his size cry for their mom.

But today is different

Today, he's brought me to an empty warehouse. Inside is a man who's been beaten. His eyes are swollen shut, and dried blood cakes his naked chest. He's dangling by his arms from a meat hook that's attached to the ceiling when we enter.

I look around quickly and clock seven of my dad's men scattered around the room . . . waiting. "What's going on,

Nick?" I step forward, needing to understand what's expected of me.

He puffs on his cigar and leans against the wall before answering, "Hold tight, Sam. Your father will be here soon."

No sooner do the words leave his mouth than my father walks into the room. Dressed from head to toe in a tailored black Italian suit and leather shoes, he looks every bit the boss he is. "Jesus Christ. Somebody cut him down."

Order given, he crosses the room toward me, muttering something about dramatics and then stops in front of Nick. "We sure it's him?"

Nick nods once as I watch the terrified fuck fall to the floor in a lump, crying.

Pop's icy glare is momentarily locked on mine. "Come with me, Sam. Say nothing."

I don't answer. I just follow as we move to stand in front of the broken man on the floor. His eyes are two small slits amidst swollen flesh, but they're both focused on my father. "Please, Vito. Please . . ." he begs, sobbing. "They were going to kill my family. Please."

"So instead, they killed mine. I should gut your wife in front of you. Make you watch while she takes her last breath. But that would be granting you a goodbye I never got." My father's voice doesn't shake.

There's no hesitation.

It's cold, calculated, and it elicits the exact reaction he's looking for, judging from the piss trickling down the guy's legs. My father pulls his prized revolver out from inside his coat and hands it to me. "This is the man who sold out our family, Sam. This is the man who caused your mother's death."

I don't hear anything else my father says. When they told us our mother had died in a car accident, no one ever said it was related to *Family* business. I suspected but never knew for sure. A haze of rage threatens to take control of my body as I move next to the man on the floor, put the gun flat against his temple, pull back the hammer, and shoot. A spray of red blood hits the floor seconds before his body follows.

Some things you're trained to do.

Other things you're born to do.

This is the first life I've ever taken.

It won't be the last.

ANASTASIA – AGE 10

My mom looks over her shoulder every time we leave our house. Her shiny, black hair always bounces when she turns her head, and her pretty brown eyes look around everywhere we go. She doesn't think I've noticed, but she's done it for as long as I can remember.

She still walks me to school every day. It's only a few minutes' walk from our home. A few of the kids from our neighborhood walk together without their parents. But not me. No . . . My mom says I'm not old enough to walk alone. I honestly think my mom would be happy if she could strap me in a baby carrier and take me with her everywhere she goes.

I'm not even allowed to go to any of my friends' birthday parties. I get invited, but she always says no. She never lets me go to anyone else's house. Maybe she watched one too many murder shows on TV. She's always said the world is dangerous, that it's a scary place, and we have to be careful.

I thought she was just paranoid.

But that was before today.

After school, we went to Mom's friend George's house. I love it there. It's a big cabin in the middle of the woods. It doesn't look that big from the outside, but once you're inside, it's enormous. George lives there with his wife and their daughter, Sierra. She's a few years older than me, but she gets to do even less than I do. Sierra homeschools and rarely leaves their property.

According to Sierra, her dad is even more paranoid than my mom. When we come over, Sierra and I usually bake for fun while the adults go into the basement and do whatever they do. I never knew what the adults were doing down there.

We've been coming to this house for as long as I can remember.

Sierra was my first friend.

But today was different.

Today, I didn't get to stay with Sierra.

Today, I didn't get to bake the turtle fudge brownies we were planning on making.

Today, I learned what Mom and George have been doing in the basement all these years because today, they included me.

Mom told me that George was going to teach me something important. She told me I wasn't allowed to be scared. That I had to listen to everything George said very carefully. That I had to be her big strong girl.

Today was the day I learned to shoot a gun.

They walked me down the steps of the basement and through a dimly lit long hallway before we reached a metal door with two large locks on the outside. Once we were on the other side of the door, George unlocked a cabinet bigger than my bedroom which was filled with all sorts of guns. Some of them looked longer than me. Others were small. A few were shiny and others scratched up. Two were even pink. He said they were Sierra's.

George picked out one of the small pink guns then guided

me over to a special lane with metal walls on either side. There was a piece of paper with a bull's-eye in the center hanging down from a fancy metal hanger that moved at the touch of a button. Mom stood behind George and me . . . watching.

George spent a lot of time going over gun safety.

Treat every gun as if it were loaded.

Never disrespect the power and responsibility that comes with holding a gun.

Never point your gun at something you're not willing to destroy.

If you're going to shoot, shoot to kill.

Mom stepped up and shot a few rounds. Her shots were perfect. Dead center. Bull's-eye. She didn't hesitate. She wasn't scared. Her hands didn't shake.

The acrid scent of the gunpowder didn't seem to bother her, even though it stuck in my throat. The loud bang reminded me of fireworks on the Fourth of July even with a set of earplugs muffling the sound.

She appeared to be enjoying herself.

When George placed the small, cold gun in my hand, its heavy weight surprised me.

I was even more surprised by how much louder it was when I fired my first shot with George standing behind me, his arms supporting mine.

I'd heard the noise when Mom and George were taking turns demonstrating for me. It was jolting then, but it was different this time.

Louder.

Scarier.

George promised with enough practice, it would get less scary.

With enough practice, it would be easier.

With enough practice, I'd never have to be afraid.

I don't know what he thought I was afraid of.

After an hour in the basement, it was dinnertime. Mom led the way back up the stairs and into the kitchen. But George stopped me as he was locking the gun back in the cabinet. "You did well today, Anastasia. I want you to promise you'll remember what I'm about to tell you. Are you paying attention?"

I nodded my head as he placed his big hands on my shoulders and waited for him to impart the final rule.

"When I was with the Rangers, we were taught to shoot center mass." He motioned toward the center of his chest. "'Aim little, miss little,' they said." George squatted down so he was at my eye level, then continued, "That's not what I'm going to teach you."

George drew a "T" with his finger across his forehead, right above his eyes and then straight down his nose. "This is the T-Zone, Anastasia." He tapped the spot between his eyes. "If you ever have to shoot someone, you shoot them here. That's the shot. That's final."

I don't know who George thought I was going to be shooting. But when I looked up at him, thinking I should be scared of what he was saying, I wasn't. "Can I come back and practice again, George?"

His eyes sparkled back at me. "You're going to come back every day until I've taught you everything you need to know."

AMELIA

PRESENT DAY . . .

AT SOME POINT, I'M GOING TO NEED TO SUCK IT THE HELL UP and buy a car. It's not even that far of a walk from my apartment to Annabelle's house, but I think my eyelashes quite possibly have snowflakes frozen to them as I try to blink. Why the hell didn't I wait at home for Belle to pick me up? Oh, that's right. I'm stubborn.

I've been in Philadelphia for six months, and I've let myself make exactly one friend.

Not that I had many before I left Washington.

I came to Kroydon Hills because I knew it would help me feel closer to my mom. She always talked about the town where she grew up. How much she loved it here. What a great place it was to live. Close enough to the city to get lost, but small enough to still have a main street. She always talked about coming back here. But that was before cancer stole her from me.

Before a lot of things were stolen.

Annabelle Hart owns the ballet studio down the street from Sweet Temptations, the bakery I own.

Although now, she's Annabelle Sinclair. She married the quarterback for the local pro football team, the Philadelphia Kings, a few days ago. That's why we're meeting today. It's Christmas Day, and they have a game this afternoon. Belle invited me to watch it with her family in their private box.

9

Family. Sometimes I feel like I never really had that.

My mother loved me. But she lied to me my whole life.

About who she was.

About what she did.

I just didn't know it until she died.

To say that I have trust issues could be the understatement of the millennium. But when you were raised to never trust anyone but your mom, and then she dies, trust doesn't come easily. Add to that what happened after her death. After my stepdad. After I found out the truth.

Nope. I refuse to think about that now.

Not today.

Belle isn't like that.

She doesn't want anything from me.

She's the first new person I've trusted in years. She stops in my bakery before she opens her studio, so I basically see her every day. I guess she's worn me down because now I laugh more than I have in a long time. Smile more too.

I guess you could say my typical state is resting bitch face.

Belle's parents are gone, so it's just her and her little brother, Tommy. And honestly, it's even harder not to fall in love with him. He's the coolest kid I've ever met.

And it's really only a few minutes' walk from my place to hers. As I round the corner of her street, I'm relieved to see her car is still here. I was worried today would be the first time Annabelle Sinclair was ever on time for anything. But as I walk up the driveway, the hairs on the back of my neck stand on end, and a shiver travels down my spine.

Both the driver's side and back doors of her car are open, but no one's inside. Tommy's stuffed T-Rex is in the car, but he's not. Tommy never goes anywhere without Rex. Belle's Mary Poppins bag is lying open in the driveway.

Discarded.

She keeps her entire life in that bag. And that bag is always attached to her.

What the hell?

I take a quick glance around the ridiculously suburban street, white picket fences included, and notice a big, black Hummer, that may be her friend Bash's car, parked across the street. After closer inspection, I realize it's also empty and looks completely out of place among the high-end family cars parked in the neighbors' driveways.

George's voice whispers loudly in my memory, *"Trust your instincts."*

That damn voice has saved me more times than he'll ever know.

All those years of training.

Of watching and listening.

Of making sure that, if I needed to, I was ready to deal with the worst mankind had to offer.

My instinct has me pulling my snub-nosed revolver out of my purse. It's a .38 Special and has gone with me everywhere since I left Washington.

It fits in my purse or my pocket.

Small and hammerless, there's no chance of it catching on my clothes.

Perfect for concealed carry.

These are the things that matter if and when you ever need to use it.

George helped me get this one when I left home to come here.

His connections got me a fake ID that can pass any amount of scrutiny.

He helped me get a lot of things after Mom's death.

Just as I'm about to walk up the brick path to the front door, I hear a scream coming from the side of the house and immediately change direction. Even with my hackles raised, I still half expect to see Belle having fallen and hurt herself. Something that would have caused her to scream. Something that could be explained.

What I see when I get to the open kitchen door will haunt me for years.

A woman, a customer of mine named Leah, is holding a gun in one hand and a knife in the other. Something about Leah has seemed off these past few weeks. Belle and I have talked about it, but she dismissed it. She convinced me Leah was just a little different. A little needy.

Crazy but harmless.

She's typically posh and put together. Her dirty blonde hair, that's usually bouncy and blown out, hangs greasy around her shoulders. Dark, smudged circles under her eyes are stark against her pale skin.

Judging by the way she has her gun pointing at Belle, I should have listened to my gut.

I'm not going to make that mistake now.

There are two men in the room. Sebastian Beneventi and a tall man who looks like Bash.

No one has noticed me yet.

When Leah's gun is pointed in Bash's direction, the other man speaks up in an alarmingly commanding voice. "You're aiming a gun at my brother. You don't want to do that."

I guess he's Sebastian's brother. I've only heard of one. I'm not sure if he has more.

Leah laughs. She actually laughs. Hysterically.

"Oh, yeah? And who exactly are you supposed to be? The cavalry? It doesn't look like you're in any position to tell me what to do, now does it?" She swings her gun between the other Beneventi and Bash, who's blocking Belle from the path of the gun. "One of us has a gun in this room, and it's not any of you."

"You have no idea who I am, lady, or the slow, painful

ways I can make you beg for death before I finally give in and kill you." This was apparently the last straw for Leah because she lunges for this guy.

Bash tries to block the weapon-wielding psychopath from whoever this guy is and takes a knife to his side in the process. I can't tell how deep it is, but blood is pouring down his side, staining his grey hoodie.

This is what I was trained for all those years ago. Safety. Protection.

Damnit. I never wanted to need to use a gun again.

But I guess I always knew I'd have to.

The tall stranger lunges to take Leah down, but Belle gets to her first when she swings a three-foot animatronic T-Rex at her head, causing her to stumble but not fall.

When Leah turns around frantically and points the gun at the gorgeous man who's not Bash, I don't think. I don't hesitate. I go back to my afternoons spent in the shooting range in George's basement in the woods.

When a life is on the line, don't go for center mass.

Don't take the chance they can still get their shot off.

Go for the kill zone. The T-zone.

Aim. Squeeze. Shoot.

I fire one shot, and she goes down.

I don't double tap because I don't have to.

She's dead.

Tears fill my eyes as I hold back the vomit threatening to escape.

Oh my God, I just killed a woman.

Any semblance of calm flees my body as those words begin to sink in.

It wasn't the first time I'd shot someone, but I learned from my previous mistake.

This time, I shot to kill.

With trembling hands, I place my gun in the pocket of my

jeans and dash past Leah's dead body that's lying in a growing pool of blood on the floor, then drop to my knees in front of Belles. "What the hell happened? Are you alright?"

She looks at me with wide, scared, tear-filled eyes and clasps my hand for a moment. "I'm fine. Help Bash."

Sebastian is part of the tight circle of friends Annabelle has tried to bring me into. "You're not fine, Belles," Bash growls, pulling his blood-soaked hand away from his side and then looks around the room. "Where the hell is Tommy?"

"I'm up here," Belle's twelve-year-old brother, Tommy, yells as he starts down the steps. "I heard something." His ever-present noise-canceling headphones are hanging around his neck.

With her body bruised and broken, Belle looks at me with a newfound fear in her eyes. "Amelia?" she rasps, and I nod, knowing what she's asking. Tommy has autism. I'm not sure how much of what's happening he's aware of, or watched happen, but he definitely doesn't need to see the woman I just killed lying dead on his living room floor.

"Got it." On shaky feet, I stand and move to meet Tommy on the stairs. "Hey, Tommy boy. Let's go wait outside, okay?" Looking around the chaos of the room, I lock eyes with Sebastian's brother, who's moved to block Tommy's view of the dead woman on the floor.

The resemblance to Sebastian is uncanny.

"What's wrong with Bash?" Tommy asks innocently from the bottom of the stairs.

Bash groans, "I'm okay now that I know you are too, Tommy boy."

Everyone loves this kid.

"Yeah." I take Tommy's hand. "He got a boo-boo." Once I've got Tommy angled away from where tall, dark, and handsome is blocking Leah's body, we make our way to the front door.

Tommy and I sit down on the front steps, and I start to go through a mental checklist of what I'm about to be hit with as he presses a button on his iPad and pushes his headphones back up, engrossed quickly in a Christmas movie.

Sometimes I wish I still had the innocence of a child.

But then I remember that I never got to be innocent.

How did this happen? I just served this crazy woman coffee two days ago.

She seemed off but not lethal.

When the door opens back up, Bash and his brother help Annabelle outside and into the white rocking chair next to the front door.

Rising, I study the stranger. "Who are you?" This guy's giving off dangerous vibes.

Not directed toward us, but there's something there.

"Sam Beneventi. Who are you?" He cocks a dark brow.

Ahh . . . So he is Bash's older brother. Which means my initial thoughts were pretty close. Bash's family *is* the Philadelphia mafia. Sam Beneventi has the dangerous, sexy stranger thing going for him in spades. But I'll be damned if I'm going to let him know that. Instead, I tell him, "I'm the girl who saved your ass."

"Yeah . . . right. So, what's the story?" Sam looks around at the three of us.

I take a deep breath and center myself before I answer, "The story is the truth. I was coming to meet my friend to go to a football game. I heard shouting, so I went to the side door. It was wide open. I looked inside and saw her slash Bash across the stomach, then aim a gun at tall, dark hitman here."

I didn't think. I reacted.

I did what needed to be done.

But now that I'm looking ahead to what comes next, it's starting to hit me.

Dealing with the cops.

Knowing my new identity has worked for years is one thing. I've got bank accounts. I've got a driver's license. I've got all the things you need to establish a new identity, thanks to George and his connections. But we never planned on me having to deal with the police. I look around at the three of them and realize they're waiting for me to finish. "Well, you all know the rest. She aimed it at him, but I'm faster and have a better aim." I look at Belles. "It was self-defense."

"Why did you have a gun?" Belle's skin is pale, like she's about to pass out.

"Where did you learn to shoot like that?" Bash asks.

"Self-defense" is the last thing I say before red and blue lights flash and an entire police department descends, coming to a stop in front of Belle's house.

SAM

WHEN YOU COME FROM AN ITALIAN FAMILY LIKE MINE, Christmas isn't the big holiday. Christmas Eve is. My father's house fills up with people waiting to eat what my nonna has spent the entire day cooking and the day before that, prepping. Everything is made fresh, from the hand-rolled pasta to the seafood I pick up from the market in South Philly that morning. We have at least fifty people at the house for The Feast of the Seven Fishes before everyone heads to church for a candlelit midnight mass.

When the night ends, it's with just a few of us opening one present each back at Pop's house. That was a tradition Mom started before she died, and we've never given it up.

Dinner is for *The Family.*

But after mass is for actual family.

What's the difference between the two?

The Family means my father's organization. The mafia.

My father is the head of *The Family.*

Actual family is much smaller.

Me, Bash, Pop and his mother, our nonna, are all the family we have.

I'm loyal to *The Family.* But my family are the only people I love.

Christmas Day is more laid-back. Bash and I meet at Pop's for Nonna's leftovers and to open a few more presents.

This year, he and I were going to watch the Kings game at the stadium from the coach's suite. Bash lives with one of Coach Sinclair's kids and is good friends with the other two, so this wouldn't be the first time he's seen a game this way, but I try to steer clear of his world for the most part.

It's safer that way.

Today was supposed to be easy.

Fun.

I wasn't expecting to be driving my brother home from the hospital after he got twelve stitches for a stab wound he got while we saved the ballerina's life.

"Asshole. I'm not that hopped up on pain pills. I know where you're going, and you passed the exit for my house." Bash is a whiney fucker when he's in pain. "Whatever. Fine. Take me to your place for the night. You gonna give me a sponge bath too?"

I ignore the tantrum he's throwing and keep driving.

"You gotta at least do me one favor." He leans his head back and closes his tired eyes.

I glance over at him out of the corner of my eye as I take the exit for my condo. "I don't have to do anything. You've already been a big enough pain in my ass today." This fucker knows I'd do anything for him, and he wields that weapon well. But he's testing my patience.

"Shut up, asshole." He fucking smiles, knowing I'm going to do whatever he needs.

I've kept him away from the business side of *The Family* his entire life. I never expected to be in a situation like we were earlier today with Sebastian by my side. And I'll kill someone before it happens again.

He doesn't belong in this world. He's going to do better things with his life.

"What do you need me to do? Call Murphy and tell him he's gonna have to sleep in his own bed tonight?" Bash and his buddies are a little too codependent, but they're good guys.

Bash wheezes out a laugh. "Fuck off. We're roommates, and he sleeps in his own bed with his girlfriend every night." I catch him looking out the window instead of at me. "Be serious for a minute." His voice is scratchy. Exhausted. "I want you to check on Amelia. I'm worried about her."

"Snow White? She looked like she could handle herself, man." Not that I wouldn't mind handling her, if I'm being honest.

"Why are you calling her that?"

"Did the crazy chick hit you in the head too? She looks like that cartoon movie Mom used to love. Black hair. Milky white skin. Red lips. Great rack."

"Did Mom drop you on your head? Snow White didn't have curves. She had a bunch of dwarves. And animals that cleaned her house." We pull into the parking garage beneath my building, and he slumps in his seat.

Snow White had a tiny little waist and a great rack in the movie and in real life, but I don't argue with my brother. "You need help getting out of the Hummer?"

"No. I just need you to go check on her. Make sure she's okay. She's alone, man. From what I've gotten from the girls, she has no family, and Belle is her only friend. I don't know what's going on with the cops. Or if she has money for a lawyer if she even needs one." My little brother is always trying to take care of everyone else. He's gonna be a doctor and save the world one day.

I round the car and open his door for him. "Come on, Bash. Let me make sure you're okay first, and then I'll check on her." I support him with an arm wrapped around his waist as he leans on me. He doesn't need to know the computer guy working for me is already getting me her information and I've got a call into one of my guys at the police station.

You don't make the shot she did without being an expert.

That wasn't a fluke.

That was skill.

And if she's in my city with that kind of skill, I need to know who she is and why she's here.

Two hours later, I'm parked in front of Sweet Temptations, the bakery Amelia owns in Kroydon Hills, waiting for her to get home when my phone rings.

A quick look tells me it's my guy who I tasked earlier with looking into Amelia. "Yeah."

"She just left the station. Should be coming your way in the next few minutes. No charges. It was a clear case of self-defense. The gun was registered. She's licensed to carry." I hear his fingers tapping against the keyboard before he whistles out a long breath.

And then silence.

I fucking hate silence. "Speak."

"They ran her prints. It's standard procedure." There's a hesitance in his voice, that makes me grind my teeth.

"I don't have time for this shit, man. What came back with her prints?" I see a car pulling slowly down the street before it comes to a stop in front of the bakery, and Snow White gets out. She looks around, clocking her surroundings before walking up the stairs on the side of the building.

"Nothing came up out of the ordinary. At least nothing the cops found." Mike has his ways of always getting the information I need. When I don't answer he adds, "I dug a little deeper, though, and the information just stopped. She has no history."

"What the fuck does that mean, asshole? Tell me you've got more than that." I need to know what she's hiding.

Preferably sooner rather than later. It's getting fucking cold sitting out here.

"Amelia Johnson didn't exist until a few years ago. Before that, she had a different name. Anastasia Rivell. She checked out and went off the grid. That's when she changed her name."

"Get me all the information you can about who she used to be. Call me when you have something for me."

The lights in the apartment above Sweet Temptations turn on one by one.

Doesn't this girl know secrets are easier to hide in the dark?

AMELIA

I'VE JUST PLACED A TRAY OF MY FAVORITE GO-TO COOKIES IN the oven when the alarm on the metal staircase outside my building is tripped.

Screw this day.

I don't get visitors. Ever. And I'm too old to believe a fat man in a red coat is coming to see me with gifts aplenty today. Whoever is outside is probably not friendly.

And definitely not wanted.

I lift the purple hat that serves as the lid on my oversized Dopey the Dwarf cookie jar and remove my gun before moving to check the security monitors set up in the second bedroom of my apartment.

What the heck is Sam Beneventi doing here, and why is he knocking on my door?

When I don't answer the door fast enough for him, he knocks again.

Louder this time and with more force than necessary.

With a shake of my head, I call out, "Hold your damn horses," and take my time. Once I get to the door, I leave the chain in place, and crack it partially open. A cold burst of wind whips through the opening, and I wrap my favorite comfy sweater tighter around myself. "Why are you here?"

"Well, hello to you too, Snow White." Sam attempts to reach through the cracked opening and release the chain, but I smack him away. "Let me in, Snow."

"My name is not Snow White, Beneventi." I push on the

door, trying to shut it when he blocks me with a foot in the opening. "Move it or lose it."

Sam's foot stays firmly planted between the door and the jam. "Open the door. You're going to want to hear what I have to say."

My eyes trail from his feet to his face. "I'd let you in if you'd move your foot, genius. I can't unlatch the chain unless the door's closed."

Sam huffs out a sound of annoyance in a puff of cold air before pulling his foot back.

Of course, I take the opportunity to slam the door in his face, and for a hot second, I contemplate not reopening it. This door is reinforced steel. You're not breaking it down with Italian leather boots on your feet.

But I decide to be a big girl instead, and after I put my gun in the waistband of my jeans under my sweatshirt, I let the mafia prince in.

Suddenly I'm feeling a bit like Little Red Riding Hood opening the door for the big bad wolf.

Or maybe just the idiot who opened Pandora's box.

Either way, this feels like a bad move at the end of a bad day.

The timer goes off in the kitchen as Sam walks through my door, looking around and taking it all in. From a stranger's perspective, my apartment probably doesn't look like much. It's small and above a bakery. But I own the bakery and the building, allowing me the privacy I needed and the ability to modify it however I wanted.

No questions asked. No nosey neighbors.

It's my safe space. I can breathe here.

Until Sam walked through my door. His enormous presence sucks all the oxygen from the room, taking up all the space and leaving me crowded where I'm usually lonely.

"What is that incredible smell?" The look of hunger on his

face tells me he may eat me if I don't feed him a cookie immediately.

Maybe he is the big bad wolf disguised as a tall, dark, and annoyingly handsome hitman.

You'd think I'd be afraid right now.

You'd be wrong.

Stupidly, I'm intrigued. George would be so disappointed.

I pull the hot tray of gooey chocolate chip cookies out of the oven and place them on the stove top to cool before turning back to Bash's brother. "Why are you here, Sam? You don't know me, and today's events don't change that."

I amend my earlier statement.

This exquisite man smiles at me, and I realize there's no maybe about it. He *is* the big bad wolf. And a lesser woman would have given anything to be his Little Red Riding Hood for the night. But I need to get him out of here.

"You're a prickly little princess, aren't you?"

"I'm sorry. Prickly what?" I level him with a glare. "Listen to me carefully. I'm no princess. So whatever fantasy you're rocking on that chiseled jaw of yours has got to go." His smile grows obnoxiously wide.

Oh no. "That panty-melting smile isn't working on me. Not even a tiny singe. So put it away and sit down." I point to the saucer-sized chocolate chip cookies. "You have to wait for them to cool a little. So talk. Tell me what you're doing in my apartment on Christmas night, instead of at the hospital with Bash and Belle."

I may not be at all interested in getting involved with any man, let alone this one, but I certainly can appreciate how scorchingly hot he is. Movie star hot. I don't remember the last time I've felt a real attraction to a man, so being attracted to Sam is irritating the hell out of me. Which means instead of allowing him to study my face after that little tirade, I move across the room and grab a spatula from the drawer to take the cookies off the tray.

I may call myself a coward as I turn away, but at least I'm a coward whose emotions won't be on display.

"Panty-melting smile, huh?" Plump lips pull back, framing bright white, perfectly straight teeth. A strong jaw and the most beautifully blue eyes I've ever seen that are framed by long black lashes are topped off by a head of gorgeous thick brown hair. I mean seriously . . . it's just not fair.

"Shut up." I push the plate of cookies in front of him. "Do you want some milk with them?"

Sam looks around my apartment again, then raises his hands. "Hold on. Time-out. Why are you feeding me cookies and milk? And how the fuck did you have time to bake anything?"

I pour us two glasses of milk and pass one to Sam before leaning against the counter and picking up a cookie. "I'm a pastry chef, Sam. It takes me less than five minutes to mix a half batch of cookies and eleven minutes to cook them. Not a biggie."

I watch that mouth bite into the cookie and hold my breath until he moans.

Actually moans. "Oh my God. This is the best thing I've ever eaten."

Not gonna lie. That reaction never gets old. "Thank you. Now would you like to tell me why you're here?"

Cobalt blue eyes look up at me, assessing. "I think you know why I'm here, Amelia."

"I really don't." I blow out a frustrated breath. "I've spent the last few hours at the police station, and I've already answered enough questions meant to throw me off my guard to last me a lifetime. I told them everything I knew. So, if you have something to ask, ask it." I steel my spine and cross my arms, ready to be pissed off. To throw him out of my apartment, and go the hell to bed, ending an unusually awful Christmas. But an image of Belle flashes in front of me, and I soften. "Wait. Before you ask me anything, how are Belle and Bash? Are they both okay? I mean, the cops at the station said they were fine, but I still should have asked you that as soon as you barged in here."

Sam dunks his cookie in his glass of milk, and I resist the urge to gag.

Why do people do that?

It ruins a perfectly perfect cookie.

And leaves cookie bits in an otherwise perfectly good glass of milk.

I am not a fan of cookie floaties.

Why would anyone want to drink chunky milk?

"Sebastian is fine. A few stitches. A few pain meds. He'll have a great story to go with a good scar to use to get himself laid. Ballerina is still in the hospital, but she's going to be fine. The babies are fine. You should call her. She was asking about you earlier."

I give him a curt nod, appreciative of his answer, but still annoyed by his presence. "Thank you. Now what do you want?"

"Where did you learn to shoot like that?" he mumbles around a mouth full of cookie.

I scrunch my face up, disgusted. "Seriously? Chew before you speak next time."

Sam makes a big show of chewing, and exaggeratedly swallowing. "Don't deflect, Amelia." Another dunk.

"I'm not deflecting, Samuel. I'm refusing to answer your question when you haven't answered mine." I pull the plate of cookies out of reach as punishment.

"Sebastian asked me to check on you. He wanted to know that you're alright. He was worried."

Huh. Of all the things he could have said, that was not

what I was expecting. And it makes me strangely uneasy. "I'm fine. You did your good deed. Now it's time for you to go."

"Not how this is gonna work, Snow White. I answered yours, now you answer mine. Where did you learn to shoot like that?" His long arm reaches forward as his fingers pull the plate back to within an easy reach. "And don't tell me it's a long story 'cause I've got all night." A chocolate morsel falls from his lips as he asks, "Got any more milk?"

I spin around, annoyed, and grab the jug of milk from the fridge. "A good friend of my mother's taught me. He was a big believer in being able to protect yourself. I own the shop downstairs and sometimes have big bank deposits on me. I carry my gun everywhere I go." I've learned out of necessity that the best way to lie is to cover it in a truth. A partial truth never feels as bad leaving my lips as an all-out lie.

I top off his glass of milk and slam the fridge door. "Happy?"

Sam sips the milk as he eyes me over the glass. "Okay, listen. I'm tired and not in the mood to beat around the bush. It's been a long fucking day. So how about you tell me the real story, Anastasia?"

My gun is out of my waistband and trained on Sam before he takes his next breath.

SAM

"Put the gun down." Okay, so it might not have been the best move to scare the Disney princess with the crack-shot aim. But in my defense, I'm fucking tired. It's been a long two days, and I want another one of her cookies. Or possibly to find out if she tastes as good as her cookies. I could easily come up with something equally delicious to do with a bit of chocolate syrup.

Amelia takes another step forward. "Oh yes, let me put my gun down because the scary bad guy tells me to trust him. Sounds like a great idea."

I don't think anyone has ever spoken to me the way she does.

She's not scared of me as much as I think she's scared of what I said.

With both hands raised, I take a small step toward her. "I didn't say trust me. I said put the gun down. I'm not here to hurt you." I know this woman is a perfect shot, but her dark eyes are shaky. She's scared, and for the first time possibly ever, I don't like that I put that fear in someone's eyes.

One more small step forward and I disarm her.

It's risky, but I slap the gun away from the aim it has on my body, angling it toward the wall. Then I grab her wrist with my left hand and break her grip with my right before I spin the gun toward her face.

Her shoulders shake, and tears gather in her onyx eyes.

Once I pull the gun away, the magazine gets ejected, the chamber racked, and the bullet resting inside popped out.

After the weapon is cleared, I pass it back to her and pocket the ammo. "Never let someone walk close to you when you're holding a gun. You've got to know that with the way you can shoot." Then, putting space between us, I move to the other side of the counter and pick up another cookie. "I meant what I said. I'm not here to hurt you."

"How?" Her confidence from earlier is gone, betrayed by the quiver in her voice. "How do you know that name?"

I stay put on my side of the counter, giving her space. "I have a few guys on my payroll. After your impressive shot earlier, I asked them to let me know what happened at the station. They ran your prints."

"I didn't give them my prints. I wouldn't have been here baking if I had. I would have been packing." Her skin turns ashen. "Oh, God. I have to pack. I have to get out of here." She's no longer talking to me.

Killing a woman earlier didn't send Snow White into shock, but knowing they ran her prints does.

"Amelia. Why did you change your name? Who is Anastasia Rivell?" It's time to start pushing. Time for the answers I need.

"She's someone I left in Washington. I left her there and started a new life." Amelia starts moving around the apartment, checking the locks on the windows and closing the curtains. I watch her grab another gun from under the table next to the sofa and check to see if it's loaded. "It's not safe here, Sam. You need to leave. Tell Bash I'm fine. Tell Belle she was the first real friend I've ever had. Tell her, one day, I'll come back and meet her babies."

"Amelia," I call out to her, not moving. Not wanting to add to her frenzy. "You don't have to be scared of me. No one else knows who you are. The cops bought your story. They aren't digging deeper. My guy made sure of that. You risked something today, wanting to protect the ballerina and maybe even Bash. I'm not going to let anyone hurt you."

Where the fuck did that come from?

I don't protect people. That's Sebastian's thing.

"This is bigger than you, Sam." She sits on the arm of the couch that appears to have come from a secondhand shop. It fits the eclectic thing she's got going on in here and gives me a slight feel for the woman in front of me.

My guess . . . she likes warmth and comfort.

She may seem no-nonsense.

But I don't think that's the real her.

That's just what she portrays to the world or at least to strangers like me.

She lifts her head and blows away an errant lock of her dark hair. "It doesn't involve you, Sam." Then, gun in one hand, she wipes her eyes with the white sleeve of the t-shirt she's wearing under the Philadelphia Kings football jersey that's swallowing her small frame. "I just . . . I didn't . . ."

Very slowly, I walk toward her. "Why did you have to change your name? Did someone hurt you? Did you hurt someone? If I'm going to help you, I've got to know what happened." There goes that word again. When did I decide I was helping this woman?

Wide eyes slowly rise to meet mine. "I haven't heard that name in a long time. I haven't been called that name in years . . . I left it behind. I left Anastasia on the other side of the country after my mom died."

I take another step closer, being careful not to startle her. "Why did you leave Washington?" One more step and I'm standing next to her.

"I've only ever told that to one person," is whispered. As if she's not answering me but telling herself.

Lost in her own world.

She seems to shake herself out of whatever thought just tortured her before standing and adding, "He would be so disappointed in me right now." Amelia crosses the room and places her hand on the door.

I catch a slight tremor betraying the false bravado she's trying to present. "I really do appreciate you letting me know, Sam. Thank you. Now, could you please leave? I have to pack."

"You don't have to leave." Christ. Why do I want her to stay? This woman is going to be a pain in the ass. "Tell me what has you scared. I can help."

She runs her now-shaking hand through her dark hair, pushing it away from her face. It hangs down past her shoulders. A beautiful shiny black strand falls right back in front of her eye. "Yeah, Sam? You can help me?" Sarcasm drips bitterly from each clipped word. "You don't even know what you could be up against." She laughs quietly at first, before full-blown, hysterical laughter begins reverberating around the room.

"Amelia . . ."

"You want to know what I did?" Her shrill scream echoes throughout the room, and her wild eyes lock on mine. "My mom died. And instead of comforting me, my stepfather tried to hurt me. There I was. Twenty years old. I'd just lost my mom, and my stepfather—whom I'd never particularly liked, but up till that point, I had no reason to distrust—decided the best way to comfort me was to have sex . . . with me."

"What the fuck?" Those damn protective instincts come roaring back to the surface, and I want to kill her stepfather.

"It didn't happen. I said no. I tried to stop him, but he wouldn't stop, so . . . I shot him. But I aimed for center mass, and he moved. I didn't make that mistake today." Tears well in those dark eyes, and I want to fix it all . . . for her.

31

That fact alone should make me back up.

I should walk away.

I did my good deed.

I checked on her.

I warned her.

Now, I should leave.

But something has me asking for more. "That's why you left? That's what has you so afraid?"

She looks away for a beat, wiping the tears that have begun to fall onto her cheeks. "That horrible excuse for a man lived but went to jail. I buried my mom. Cleaned out her house and found a bag full of money. So I took it and went to the only person I could trust to get a new identity. I wanted to leave everything behind. I wanted to be untraceable. Good thing too because that person I could trust told me that my mom and stepdad had been muling drugs for the Canadian cartel. See, stepdaddy dearest was a pilot, and Mom was a flight attendant. So that bag of money I stole to start my new life . . . That was the cartel's."

Amelia shifts from foot to foot.

Uncomfortable.

She absently chews on her thumbnail, looking up at me through impossibly long, black lashes. "I don't have any idea why I'm telling you all of this."

"Because you need to talk to someone. Because you know I can keep you safe. So what happened next?"

"At that point . . . the point when I chose to leave and take the money . . . I'd been told. Warned. At that point, I knew who the money belonged to, and I still took it." Her eyes never leave mine as she gets angrier. Her pale skin burns a fiery red, and her tears stream down her face, unchecked. "But here's where it gets even more complicated. A few months before my mom died, she told me something, something she'd never told me before. My mother was pregnant with me when she moved to Washington. And she moved because she saw something she shouldn't have and agreed to help the FBI. Apparently, we were in witness protection, and I never knew it because I never knew a different life."

She angrily wipes away the tears that are falling unchecked. "I had to leave. My stepfather was the only person who ever knew the truth, and I'd just put him in jail. What could he have done with that kind of information? What could he have done to me?" She looks at me like I have an answer. And suddenly, I wish I did.

When I don't offer anything, she continues, "I wasn't giving him that chance. I left. And I never looked back. I thought I was safe here. I was completely across the country. I left Anastasia behind, and Amelia was born." She carefully runs her thumb over the pearl inlay of her gun. "I've been so fucking careful. Damnit. I touched the damn water bottle. So fucking stupid." She stomps her foot down in a rage, and the guttural sound that rips from her throat sounds more like it came from a wounded animal than this tiny woman.

Fueled by agony and regret.

For reasons I may never understand, I want to make this better for her. "Amelia, I'm going to touch you. Do not shoot me."

Her eyes trace the trail of my hands as they slowly reach for her shoulders.

I need to ground her.

To keep her here instead of in the past.

"I need you to understand that my family owns this city. You are not going to be hurt as long as you're in Philadelphia. Your fingerprints have been wiped. No one will ever know. I can keep you safe."

Suspicious eyes look up at mine. "Why? Why would you do that for me? I have nothing to give you in return. And I'm not going to sleep with you. I don't use my body to pay my debts."

I force myself to laugh off the last comment. "Lucky for you, I don't take unwilling women to my bed, Snow White."

Amelia shakes herself out of my hold. "Why, Sam? Why help me?"

"Because I want to. Because I can." I think about it for a moment, having no other real answer. Meeting her untrusting eyes, I add, "You didn't hesitate earlier, and I'm not hesitating now. Stay, Amelia."

AMELIA

TWO YEARS LATER . . .

YOU'D THINK GETTING COMFORTABLE WHERE YOU LIVE WOULD be a good thing.

Building relationships.

Putting down roots.

All the things most people strive to attain.

You'd be wrong.

Getting comfortable is just another way of saying you're becoming complacent. Complacency kills.

George taught me that.

Building relationships makes it that much harder when you have to grab your ever-present go bag and get the hell out of Dodge. Or in my case, out of Kroydon Hills. I know I'm being paranoid. I really do. But that doesn't make the conversation I'm about to have any less real. Or the go bag sitting in my back seat any less necessary.

Sam Beneventi kept the promise he made to me nearly two years ago.

He's helped me stay off anyone's radar.

Off the grid and out of trouble.

My security systems have been upgraded.

I've essentially got my own personal group of bodyguards for how often Sam's crew stops by the shop for coffee. My assumptions were right. Sam's family business is less than legitimate. But who am I to judge?

He's helped me stay safe, and he's never asked me for anything in return. In the weeks following the shooting at Annabelle Sinclair's house, he started dropping by my shop for a cup of coffee and what has since become his favorite double chocolate chip cookies. Although he'll never admit it, Sam Beneventi has a sweet tooth. And I've thoroughly enjoyed feeding it.

I guess you could say a friendship, albeit a forced one, developed from there. This tall, dark, and devastatingly handsome man who probably exists in so many people's nightmares somehow became my closest friend. He may also exist in a few of my daydreams, but that's another secret I'll take to the grave.

Because of our shared circumstance, I was able to talk to him about things I couldn't share with Belle. Or with anyone really. Not because I didn't want to, but because I don't want to put their lives in danger.

No matter how much I wished there was a way I could share more with Belle.

With the girls who I now loosely call friends.

In all these months, Sam has never scared me.

Sure, I've worried for him when he'd share what he could about things going on in his world. But he's never made me worry for my own safety. Until he called me thirty minutes ago and asked me how quickly I could come to his restaurant.

Nothing good ever follows a call like that.

Tonight is one of those muggy September nights I've come to realize is common for the East Coast. The damp air feels thick and heavy against my skin even though the scorching temperatures started to drop when the sun went down a few hours ago. Just my luck, the air conditioner in my car crapped out on me yesterday, and I really don't want to tap into my emergency fund to fix it right now. When I finally gave in and bought a car, I went sensible. A car that wouldn't stand out in a crowd. Now I'm wishing I'd listened to Sam and gotten something a little newer.

Who knows? After this meeting, I might not care about how hot my car is.

I might not be in this state much longer.

I've known where I'd go next since I decided to move to Kroydon Hills.

Always be prepared.

My lawyer has very specific instructions should I have to leave.

He knows what to do.

He just doesn't know who I really am.

To him, I'm Amelia Johnson. And that's all he gets to know.

It might seem silly to own a shop when I constantly have one foot out the door, but I didn't care. I wanted something that was mine. I wanted to be my own boss. I never wanted to have to be told what to do again, and buying Sweet Temptations did that for me. I know I most likely won't get to stay here much longer, but it was worth it.

I'm not really looking forward to Kansas. But it's the next stop on my tour.

It may sound silly, but I've wanted to go there since I was a little girl, addicted to *The Wizard of Oz*. If there's no place like home, how bad can it be?

I knew I needed to give Kroydon Hills a chance. If Mom loved it as much as her stories told me she did, I needed to know why. But if I didn't love it here, Kansas was always my next move.

When I pull into the parking lot behind Sam's restaurant, Nonna's, I'm hot, hungry, tired, and, if I'm being honest with myself, more than a little scared. Judging by the number of cars, it's a busy Saturday night at Nonna's. Sam talks about this place a lot, the restaurant he named after his grandmother, but this is the first time he's ever asked me to come here. He's brought its namesake, his actual nonna, to my bakery a few times, and I absolutely adore her. But he's never had me come here before.

When Sam called me earlier, he told me to park around back and knock on the kitchen door. He didn't want me to come in through the front entrance of the building. He has an office next to the kitchen, and that's where I'm supposed to go.

Two young guys dressed similarly in khaki pants and stained white button-down shirts are smoking next to a cracked door that's letting the most heavenly and savory smells pass through its opening, ratcheting up my hunger about a thousand percent.

They both watch me like a mosquito they'd like to smack away as I approach them. "Hi."

I wave at the two of them.

They continue to stare, unimpressed. Okay. So maybe I should have changed out of my cotton shorts and Sweet Temptations tank top, but I'd just gotten out of the shower, and it's been freaking hot as Hades outside. "I'm here to see Sam."

Bonehead Waiter One turns to Moron Waiter Two. "Does she actually think the boss is gonna give her the time of day?" His eyes linger a little too long on my tight tank. "I mean, I guess he might. But seriously?"

Moron laughs at Bonehead before letting his eyes travel up my body. "You and the rest of the world, babe."

Just when I'm about to explode from the sheer stupidity displayed in front of me, the door opens fully, and Sam's best friend, Dean, pops his head through the opening. Dean is with Sam at the bakery at least once a week. And he pops in with a few of his own crew too. He likes his coffee with a ton of sugar and loves to sample whatever new recipe I've tried that week while he flirts with my employees.

Sam takes everything seriously.

Dean . . . not so much.

"What the fuck, assholes? Let the lady in." He smacks Bonehead on the back of his head as Moron backs out of reach. "Sorry about that, Amelia." His arm extends out and moves the taller waiter aside. "Ignore these two. Come on in. Sam's been waiting for you." Dean's a little shorter than Sam, but he's just as broad. Maybe not as classically handsome, but there's something magnetic about his personality. It's easy to be drawn into his laughter and stories. I've only seen him get mad once in the two years he's been stopping by my shop, and I was incredibly glad not to be the person on the other end of that phone call.

He reaches out and takes my arm, leading me through the back door and then pulling it shut. "Will they be able to get back in?" I ask, not sure if I truly care.

"Someone will let them in eventually. Come on. Sammy's waiting."

Dean maneuvers me through the industrial kitchen, past a walk-in freezer, and down a hall to Sam's office. He knocks once on the door and waits for Sam to answer before entering and depositing me on the other side. "The dipshit Dalponi brothers were giving her a little bit of trouble when I found her."

Sam's pissed-off eyes snap to mine. "You okay?"

"She's—" Dean starts to answer for me, but gets cut off by Sam.

"I was asking Amelia."

Dean nods. "On that note, I'm gonna go make a few calls."

He turns and leaves the two of us alone, and I waste absolutely no time getting down to business. "Why have I been summoned, Samuel?"

Sam closes his laptop and gives me his full attention. "Full-naming me already, Snow? It usually takes longer than two minutes for me to get on your nerves that badly."

"You're not annoying me, Sam. You're scaring me. And we both know I don't scare easily. Tell me what's going on. Why am I here?" At some point during the course of our forced friendship, Sam became that person I can be completely honest with.

When I left Washington, I promised George I'd never make contact with him again. It was for my own good as much as it was to protect George and his family. But in doing so, I gave up the only people who truly knew me. Yes, I've let Annabelle in more than I thought I would, but that's still not very far. When Sam confronted me about my past, it allowed me to be honest with someone in a way I hadn't been in years.

I'm not sure why I did it, but I can't say I regret it either.

I drop down onto the black leather couch behind me and wait Sam out.

Nothing like sweaty skin sticking to soft leather to remind you just how uncomfortable you are.

When he stands and crosses the room to sit next to me, I know it must be bad. Broad shoulders stretch the crisp black shirt he's wearing. The top two buttons are undone. No tie. His strong chest pulls at the fabric, hinting at the muscles hiding beneath. Muscles I wish I could run my fingers over. Black slacks and leather shoes that cost more than my car finish off his look tonight. And what a look it is.

I'll never tell him this, but I'll miss him most when I have to leave.

Sam lays his arm across the back of the couch as he takes a seat next to me.

I lean my head back against it and close my eyes, soaking in the moment of peace. What's likely to be the calm before the storm. "What's going on? Rip the damn Band-Aid off and just tell me."

"Look at me, Snow." My eyes open and my head turns on command. "Someone's looking for you. I don't know who yet, but someone is. My guy called me today. A PI visited your stepfather in prison. He was asking questions about you. Doesn't sound like the cartel. They wouldn't use a PI. But I'm not ruling anything out yet."

I suck in a breath. I was expecting bad news, but I still manage to be caught off guard. I angle my body toward him and pull my legs up in front of me. "Do you know that I was eighteen when my mother told me my whole life had been a lie? When she finally told me we were in witness protection? I considered running away then. I was so mad at her. I mean, it was just her and me for so long. How could she have lied to me like that? But then I thought about it. Really thought about it. She hadn't been lying to me. She'd been trying to keep me safe. And she did it. For my whole life, all she ever did was keep me safe. I might not have always appreciated it. But then I realized she'd moved across the country, changed her name, and given up everything she'd ever known so I could grow up safe. And how did I repay her? Her body was barely cold when I screwed that all up. And now, that screw-up could cost me my life. I mean, what are the chances my stepfather didn't tell the PI something that could lead him to me?"

Sam's hand comes up and cradles my cheek. His thumb wiping away my tear. "I'm going to kill him someday for what he did to you."

I reach up and grab his wrist, pulling his hand away from my face, and laugh a sad sardonic laugh. "Promises, promises. You're not allowed to hit on me right now, Samuel."

"That's what you tell me every time I try to hit on you, Snow. You're gonna give in one of these days. Don't think I don't know I'm wearing you down." Those cobalt eyes hold truths I'm not ready to accept.

"Believe it or not, killing someone for me is not that sexy."

This is the game we play.

Sam makes a crude comment or a ridiculous attempt at flirting, and I shoot him down. "We'll see."

I close my eyes and watch a movie reel flash across my mind.

A life where I get to stay here.

Where I get to explore this ridiculous chemistry I have with this man.

Where I get to remember what it was like to have a family.

A life lived looking forward instead of over my shoulder.

"How much time do I have?"

"You're not running away, Amelia." He sits up and brings me with him. When he turns me to fully face him, I melt a little while he holds my upper arms in place. "We're all over this. If it gets to that point, I'll tell you. But it's not there."

I nod my head before adding, "Yet. It's not there yet. But it will be." When I turn to stand up, Sam drops his hands from my arms. "Thanks for letting me know."

"You're not leaving Kroydon Hills, Snow. How am I supposed to marry you one day if you leave town?"

Who's he kidding? "You've got plenty of women warming your bed at night. Marry one of them. You'd have your pick."

There's a knock on the door, followed by Dean's voice and, if I'm not mistaken, Sebastian's too.

Sam grabs my hand, but I tug it away. My lips involuntarily tilt up at the corners. "I'm not marrying you, Samuel." I turn and open the door. Yup. I was right. Dean is there with Bash and a pretty brunette behind him. She looks familiar, but I'm not sure why. "Thanks for your help, Sam."

Once I'm through the door, I say goodnight to Bash and his friend and head back to my apartment.

Alone.

When I pull into the parking lot behind my little apartment above my shop, I turn and stare at my go bag, debating. I could just go. Not even get out of the car. Just drive. They'd never be able to track me.

Everything I need is in that bag.

Money. A burner phone. Essentials. A new identity.

Everything I need but nothing I want.

None of this goofy little town I've fallen in love with.

No Belle.

No Sam.

Not liking the sense of dread that thought brings with it, I turn my car off and grab my bag. Nothing is going to change tonight. No need to rush this yet.

SAM

OVER THE NEXT TWO HOURS, I WATCH MY LITTLE BROTHER smile at his new girl, Eleanor Kingston. Bash looks like one of those fucking unicorn emojis with hearts for eyes and rainbows shooting out of its ass. He's mentioned her to me before, and after spending a little time in her presence, I understand why. She's beautiful and funny, and she's ball-busting in a way that reminds me a little of Amelia.

And the way she looks at Bash makes me think this girl is important.

She gets it.

She gets him.

I know he's worried about the arranged engagement Pop has been trying to force on him, so he's trying to not get attached. But he should. Bash has chosen not to be involved in the family business, which means there are certain things he can't be privy to.

He doesn't know he's never going to marry Emma Saba-tini. We just need him to believe it to sell it for her family's sake. Pop and I have been working for years to get something on those slimy fuckers, and unfortunately for Sebastian, this is Pop's in.

Keep your friends close and your enemies closer.

But friends and enemies aren't what we need.

Allies are key.

And sometimes allies have to be gently manipulated into those roles.

You've got to have alliances to sustain success and maintain power in our world. The Beneventis have held the power in Philadelphia for over sixty years, but as most of us modernize and branch out into more legitimate businesses, allies are becoming scarce. We've always had a good relationship to our north with New York, but our relationship with Atlantic City, further south, is lacking. We don't need Atlantic City often. The Port of Philadelphia typically gives us all the access we need. But the international waters off the coast of New Jersey are less monitored and have their benefits occasionally. While Atlantic City may answer to the same commission we all do, they keep to themselves down there as much as possible.

That's where Carlo Sabatini comes in to play. His family came into power ten years ago, but they've been playing the game for closer to thirty. We don't trust him. Never have. Pop has been working on a plan for the last few years to get rid of him.

He thought it would be over in a few months.

He was wrong.

It's been slow moving, and we're all fed up with this shit.

Finding something to hold over Sabatini is proving harder than any of us expected.

I'm on my way to meet with my cyber-specialist now. He's been pulling double duty, working on getting something on the Sabatinis and keeping Amelia off the grid. Mike was a Navy SEAL years ago. And I'm not talking about the average Navy SEAL. He wasn't running normal missions. He was with SEAL Team Six, infiltrating governments and bringing down empires, all with a few swipes of a key.

After a mission gone wrong, he came home with a certain skill set and an aversion to authority that made him the perfect man for the job.

He doesn't work for *The Family*.

He works for me.

He also doesn't like to leave his loft in Old City if he doesn't have to.

When he calls, I go to him.

But he's worth the hassle.

He's the best at what he does, and I trust him. Trust is something I don't give often, but this man has earned his way into the small group of people I trust. Once I've parked my car on the old cobblestone street, I hit the buzzer below his security camera and look up so Mike can see it's me, then wait to be buzzed in.

It may be humid as hell outside, but it's freezing in here. Mike keeps his place at a frigid sixty-five degrees year-round. Says he never wants to be hot again. He got enough of that during his time in the sandpit. He's sitting at a long steel desk lined with expensive computer monitors when I enter. He doesn't look up, instead continuing to type while he watches a screen off to the right.

I lean against a steel pole in the center of the room and cross my arms while I wait for his attention. His place is Spartan. It's an old brick building with exposed beams and one open room making up the massive loft. He has the basics, what he needs and nothing else. The only thing here that appears to be flashy or indulgent is his computer system.

Once Mike finishes typing, he leans back with a flare, a self-satisfied smile settling on his face. "I got it."

"Got what?" I ask, tired, aggravated, and not in the mood for games.

He kicks his feet up on his desk and leans his arms behind his head. "Got *who* is more like it. I got Canada. The Tremblays. I got what we needed for you to protect your girl. They double-crossed their partners south of the border. Well, south of our border. *Really* south of their border. I've got the proof right here." He points to a file on the monitor like it holds the secrets of the world.

When I stand there motionless and glaring, his smile starts to fade. "This is what you wanted, isn't it, man? I thought you needed something on them so you could get them to leave the baker alone." Mike pulls his feet off his desk and sits up. "Did you bring me any of those cupcakes I like?"

I shake my head no. He's right. It's exactly what I wanted. I've been willing to clear the debt Amelia left Washington with, but without any leverage, there was no way to make the offer and guarantee her safety.

And there's nothing in this world I'd put above her safety.

Even if she doesn't know that . . . yet.

She'll be free.

But what will she choose to do with her freedom?

I move next to him and scan the monitors. "Yeah. It's what I wanted. You did well, Mike. Thanks." I point at another file open on a different monitor, then turn back to him. "Have you gotten anywhere with Sabatini yet?"

"No. It's like finding a needle in a flaming fucking haystack full of shit. Nothing that goes on in Atlantic City makes sense. I'm still working on it." He pulls up a few files he's had for a while, but there's nothing new.

"Thanks, man. You got a thumb drive for me? Looks like I need to take a trip to Canada."

AMELIA

THURSDAY MORNING, MY NEW HIRE, LYLA, AND I ARE WORKING in comfortable silence while we restock Sweet Temptation's shelves once the morning rush dies down. I'm a multitasking queen today. Cookies are baking in the oven, cupcakes are cooling on their racks, and the scent of fresh crème brûlée coffee brewing is wafting through the air, mixing beautifully with the sweet smell of the scones Lyla is placing in the bakery case.

And I'm taking inventory. Not the most fun but necessary.

I trained as a pastry chef for two years back in Washington before I left. I never got to finish my training, but I got far enough. Owning a bakery was always my goal. I wanted to be my own boss. To be able to create what I wanted.

I love experimenting with new flavors.

With mixing savory and sweet.

Getting to choose what I want to create and not what I don't has its perks.

I enjoy so many aspects of being my own boss.

Inventory is not one of them.

But if I do it now, during my downtime, I won't need to do it later after the shop closes. This is my version of winning, even though it being the highlight of my day makes me feel much older than twenty-four.

Of course, that highlight gets bumped down a rung when the bells above the door chime and Sam and Dean walk through.

I haven't seen Sam since I left the restaurant Saturday night. He looks good today in a charcoal grey suit with a crisp white shirt unbuttoned at the top. His face is scruffy, and his cobalt eyes are hidden behind dark sunglasses. Sam moves through the shop to stand across from me at the counter and removes his glasses, looking down at me while I kneel behind the shelves. "Hey, Snow. What'cha doing down there?"

Standing up, I wipe my hands on my apron and glance over to see Lyla stumbling over her words as Dean peruses today's coffee options.

I don't blame her.

These two are a sight to behold.

They could probably make a nun blush.

"I was doing inventory." A glance at the clock has me cocking my brow. "You're running a little late today, Sam."

He ignores my comment as a devilish smile creeps across his chiseled face. "Do I smell chocolate chips?" I don't know how he does it.

"I swear you have an uncanny radar for my cookies." I nod my head toward the kitchen. "Come on." Once I let Lyla know I'll be in the back if she needs me, I look over at Dean and point. "You. Don't give her a hard time."

Dean looks at me with a *Who me?* expression plastered across his face and a rumbling chuckle that makes me want to smack him as he smiles at Lyla.

With Sam following me into the kitchen, I adjust my hair and hope I don't look as tired as I feel. "Could you please tell your friend not to bang my new employee? The last one quit after he never called her back."

Sam walks around my commercial kitchen, looking for his cookies, but then he stops and stares at me. "She was a clinger. You didn't want her working here anyway."

"That's for me to decide, Samuel. Not Dean." He studies me, shaking his head before we both laugh.

"Fine. She wasn't the best employee. But there have to be better ways for me to figure that out than them quitting after a one-night stand with your best friend."

I pick up my bag of frosting, ready to continue my multi-tasking badassery and frost some cupcakes when Sam offers me his finger. I know what he wants and pipe a line of decadent chocolate fudge buttercream on the tip of his finger before starting to frost my Death by Chocolate cupcakes.

I watch as he slowly sucks the fudge frosting from his finger and then looks around again. "This is good, Snow, but I know you've got the cookies hiding somewhere."

Damn. I'd love for him to suck that chocolate fudge off my finger.

Shit. I swear my nipples tighten just thinking about it.

No. I refuse to think like that. Sam Beneventi is my friend and needs to stay firmly planted in that zone. The friend zone. The no-sucking-allowed zone.

Unless friend sucking is allowed.

Nope. Not going there.

"Hello, Amelia . . . ?" Sam waves his hand in front of my face, and I become painfully aware that I just spaced out on him.

The timer on the oven goes off, saving me from having to answer whatever question he just asked. I place the cookie sheets on the rolling cooling rack before turning back just in time to stop Sam from grabbing a cookie from the scorching hot sheet pan. I smack his hand away and scold, "Give it a minute. They've got to cool down."

This gorgeous, intimidating man actually pouts like a

child when he doesn't get his way . . . or his cookie. Then he gets serious. It's the look he gives me when he knows I'm not going to like what he has to say, and I'm all too familiar with it. "What's on your mind, Sam?"

"I'm going to be out of town for a few days. If you need anything and you can't get hold of me, I need you to call Dean right away. Okay?"

My heart drops.

I wonder if he's going out of town with one of the women I've seen gracing his arm lately.

Sam's family has money. And even though most of it comes from less than legal streams, they have quite a few legitimate businesses as well. Meaning Sam goes to quite a few high-profile events every month and has had a different gorgeous woman on his arm at each one. He might be a mafia prince, but he's also part of Philadelphia's elite society. He was on Philly's Most Eligible Bachelor list last year, sandwiched between a Kingston and an MMA champion. It's a part of his life I don't ask about because I don't want to know the answers.

I know I can't have him.

But that doesn't mean I want someone else to either.

Call me greedy. I'll own it. I just won't admit it to him.

Instead, I flippantly tell him, "Have fun. I won't need Dean. Pretty sure you know I can take care of myself." Then I hand him a warm cookie and a paper coffee cup filled with milk.

Sam dunks the damn cookie before breaking it in half and shoving the entire thing in his mouth. "Not that kinda trip, Snow. It's work, not play. I should be back by the end of the weekend." He licks melted chocolate from his fingers, and I don't know if it's because he's now done that twice today, but God . . . I want to be that finger. A moan escapes the lips I'm staring at before he adds, "This is the best thing I've ever had in my mouth,"

I swear he licks his fingers slowly.

Seductively.

His eyes locked on mine like he knows what I'm thinking.

I need to stop feeding this man.

"You may have told me that a time or two." I turn my back to him and bag up a few cookies while I give myself a minute to cool down from the heat in the room, not sure if it's coming from the ovens or my imagination.

I hand him the bag and move to push my way through the swinging doors of the kitchen when Sam gently grabs my wrist. "One of these days, I'm going to taste something even sweeter, Amelia."

It only takes the tiniest effort to pull my wrist free.

The attraction is so strong.

Too strong.

But this isn't happening.

Not now.

Not when I'm not sure how long I'm staying in the city. "We'll see about that, Samuel."

The chimes above the door ring, and I hear the familiar laughter of Belle's one-year-old twin girls, Everly and Gracie. These two are never quiet. I leave Sam standing in my kitchen, but not before I hear him quietly agree, "Yeah, Snow. We'll see about that."

His presence looms behind me as we move into the front of the bakery. We're met with Belle fighting to get the twins to sit and Dean holding a cup of coffee out for Sam.

Guess he was waiting for us.

When Dean's phone rings, he tells Sam he'll meet him in the car, and Sam turns to me with an odd expression on his face. He palms my cheek, catching me off guard, and wipes away what I'm guessing is flour with his thumb. "We're going to talk when I get back, Amelia."

He drops his hand and waits for my answer.

I tilt my head, trying to understand what he's saying. "We talk all the time, Sam." This is the strangest exchange we've ever had.

His eyes close briefly, and he nods his head, seemingly annoyed, before he shakes it off. "Be careful. I'll see you next week."

Before I know it, he's through the front door of the shop, and I'm left staring, wondering what the hell that was.

A laughing Everly does her version of a run until she slams into the bakery case full of cupcakes and starts pointing.

"What was that?" Belle moves next to me, bouncing Gracie on her hip.

Good question. What the hell was that?

But instead of saying any of that, I brush it off. "It's just Sam being Sam."

"You cannot be this dense, Amelia. That man wants you."

Gracie reaches her arms out to me, so I take her from Belle and nuzzle my nose in her sweet-smelling curly blonde hair. "Your mommy is crazy, Gracie. Let's go find you a cupcake."

Her drooly little smile melts my heart. "Cookie." She points. "Want cookie."

Everyone wants a damn cookie today.

After we get both girls tucked into the booth while they happily make a mess with their cupcakes, I make sure Lyla has the restocking under control and take a seat with my favorite girls for a few minutes of downtime. Sipping my tea, I smile at Belle. "So what time do you leave tomorrow for California?" She's flying out for her husband's away game and bringing the girls to spend a little time with their Uncle Cooper, who's a Navy SEAL stationed in Coronado.

Belle puts down her decaf coffee.

She's pregnant again and pissy every time she has to order decaf. "Oh, no. You're not changing the subject that easily, missy. What's going on with you and Sam Beneventi? Seriously, Amelia, that man looked at you like he wanted to lick you from head to toe before he left. Spill it." She raises her eyebrows like she's going to intimidate me.

It's not working.

What it is doing is reminding me of his raspy voice telling me he was going to taste something sweeter soon . . .

He couldn't possibly mean . . .

Could he?

Maybe?

"Belles, this was so much easier to do when it was me giving you advice," I admit, frustration creeping through.

Belle claps her hands like the girls do when they see a pretty new cupcake and squeals, "I knew it." She points at me accusingly. "You like him! You like Sam Beneventi." Then her loud voice softens. "Oh my God. I knew it! Declan was wrong. He can suck it."

"Annabelle. What. The. Hell? You and Dec have been talking about Sam and me? Are you kidding me?" I can't believe what I'm hearing.

"Ha ha! You said it. There is a Sam and you. I knew it." She laughs as she wipes the icing off Everly's messy face. Blonde curls dipped in chocolate are sticking to adorably dimpled cheeks.

I blow out my breath, exasperated. "There isn't a Sam and me. Not that way. Not any way. Not yet."

Yet? Where did that come from?

Holy hell. That's the first time I've admitted anything like that out loud. I save myself by adding, "Not ever."

Belle gently kicks me under the table. "But the question is, do you want there to be a Sam and you? Because based on what I just saw . . . what I've seen whenever the two of you are in the same room, he wants an Amelia and Sam."

When I look across the table, unable to force the denial from my lips, Belle's smile grows and she points her finger at me in victory. "I knew it!"

I'm glad one of us did.

SAM

"So, we're agreed. Once the money is transferred, Anastasia Rivell's debt to you is paid in full, and, as far as you're concerned, she will no longer exist." My Uncle Nick and I are sitting in a small restaurant in Victoria, British Columbia. The place is older and off the beaten path. It's been closed for the night, so our meeting is private. Louis and George Tremblay are sitting on the opposite side of the table, eating their steaks as if I'm not waiting for an answer. These two run the Tremblay cartel. The cartel Amelia crossed when she left Washington.

They also fucked up.

And thanks to a well-placed piece of information, I now own them.

"Pay us what's owed, and we want the thumb drive with a guarantee that all other copies are destroyed." Louis is the talker of the two. He's sloppy, in an ill-fitting suit covering his rotund body and has a balding head. I fucking hate sloppy. It's every bad mob stereotype rolled into this one slob. It's hard to look away from his double chins, but the spinach he's had stuck in his teeth all night isn't a better option.

Louis wouldn't know how to shut up if his lips were sewed fucking shut.

Which I'm actually considering at the moment.

It's obvious George is the brains of the two of them.

He's quieter. Taking it all in.

Growing up, my father always told me someone is going to judge you and your power based on their first impression of you, so you better make it a good one.

George knows what he's doing.

He's dressed well in a perfectly tailored suit and Rolex watch.

He's the one I direct my answer toward.

"Do I look fucking stupid to you? I'll give you a thumb drive, but there's no way any remaining copies will be destroyed. I pay off her debt, and we keep your misjudgment to ourselves. And in return, you agree that Anastasia Rivell never existed. That's the offer, gentlemen. Take it or leave it. But know that if my guy doesn't hear from me in . . ." I check my watch, and glance over to my uncle Nick before looking at George, "one hour, he presses a button on his computer that will make life very difficult for you."

Nick clears his throat. "In all fairness, we're being more than reasonable here. I would have counseled my nephew to tell the two of you to go fuck yourselves and not pay off any debt. If you like your pretty little wives alive, you can't have this information sent back to Mexico. If you don't mind them gutted and hung, with your children's bodies dangling next to theirs, do what you want."

Louis jumps up, but George motions for him to sit as my uncle continues. There's a reason that Nick has been Pop's advisor for years, and he's showing it now. "Let's be real. Everyone at this table knows what happens to people who double-cross your business partners, and none of us want that. But Sam still thought the right thing to do was to not come here empty-handed. He wants to clear the debt. I'm betting that's more than you would have offered."

When Louis sputters again, George silences him with a single look before turning my way. "We are sensible men, Sam. If you clear the debt, I give you my word no harm will come to Anastasia. Not from us." He stands, buttoning his jacket and offers me his hand. "I'll have the payment instructions sent over." He looks between Nick and me before adding, "I look forward to doing business with your family soon," and then walks away.

We were supposed to be flying home tonight, but the jet's been grounded due to a mechanical issue they found earlier in the day. The question is was it an actual mechanical issue or did someone fuck with the plane?

So here I am, holed up in an airport hotel.

I wanted to be halfway through our five-hour flight by now.

Nick went down to the bar for a drink, but I wasn't feeling it. Instead, I crack open one of those tiny bottles of whiskey from the minibar and groan when my phone rings. I'm not in the mood to deal with anyone tonight.

That is, until I see it's my father.

You do not make Vito Beneventi wait. "Hey Pop. How's it going?"

"I spoke to the pilot. The jet will be ready for you tomorrow. He believes it was tampered with." Pop is quiet for a moment. "Watch your back, son. We don't know when it was tampered with or by whom. Enemies are everywhere, Sam." Pops is always looking for enemies.

It's the burden of being the boss.

Paranoia keeps you safe.

"Now tell me, Sam. How did the meeting go tonight? Is it settled?"

I might be my father's underboss, but I still had to clear this plan through him before I put it into motion. Anything that could potentially blow back on *The Family* has to be given his approval. His only request was that I take Nick, not Dean, with me.

Nick's a better killer. Pop needed to know I was protected if things went south, and Nick is equally good at calming a situation as he is at ending a person's life. Either way, he was sent to help.

"It's done. They agreed to our terms." I sit down on the edge of the bed and crack my neck as the strain of the day gets to me. "The money is gonna be transferred tomorrow."

Clearing this debt will barely put a dent in my accounts. When my mother died, Bash and I were left with significant trusts. I've never touched mine, allowing it to grow for years while I built my wealth on my own. I've been smart and made good investments. "If the jet was tampered with, I don't think it could have been the Canadians," I tell him, adding, "I don't think they had the time."

"Is she worth this, son?" Pop sounds tired. It's closing in on midnight back home. He's probably sitting in his home office, finishing the last of his work for the day with a glass of wine from his vineyard in Calabria next to him and a cigar in his hand.

But none of that changes that this question was asked and answered last week when I told him what I wanted to do.

What I needed to do.

"My answer hasn't changed, Pop."

"This woman isn't even yours, Sam. I haven't met her. You need to fix that soon if she's important to you. I want to meet the next Beneventi principessa." As if realizing what he said, my father pauses. There hasn't been a Beneventi princess since my mother was alive, but by then, she wasn't a princess. No, she was the Beneventi queen.

As if invading my thoughts, he asks, "Would your mother like this girl?"

All Ma ever wanted was for us to be happy. She was born

into this life. She understood it. She accepted it. But she never stopped pushing for us to have more, whatever that looked like. "Yeah, Pop. I think Ma would have liked her. I think she would have loved her."

Pop sighs. "She was the best of us. Make sure this woman is worth it. When you're an old man looking back on your life, make sure it's without regret, son. Loving your mother . . . it was easy."

"Everything okay, Pop?" It's not like my dad to be this reflective.

"Make sure she's worth it, Sam. And bring her to the house soon. I want to meet her. Give your nonna someone to fuss over."

The call ends, and I momentarily try to picture myself, years from now, looking back on my life. But I can't.

I don't see it.

Can't see it.

What the hell does that mean?

AMELIA

I'VE HAD THIS FEELING ALL DAY.

Like I'm being watched but not.

I know it doesn't make sense, but I can't shake it.

It's unnerving. I didn't notice anyone out of the ordinary in Sweet Temptations today. No one stuck around longer than normal or gave me a creepy vibe in any way. I checked all my security feeds, and nothing was out of place. But I still can't shake it.

It's Saturday night, and I'm in my pajamas, ready to curl up on the couch with the new show on Netflix that Belle and the girls have been talking about. Belle's sister-in-law, Nattie, told me it was a must watch. She warned me that it was steamy, but I could use a little steam in my life.

Gotta get it where I can.

My alarm is set. I know I'm safe. I know I'm paranoid too. But I just don't know what to do about it, which frustrates me beyond belief.

Add to that, for reasons that I don't quite understand, I wish Sam were home.

Knowing he's close calms me, but I'll never admit that to him. I refuse to allow myself to depend on anyone. I refuse to need anyone. This kind of life doesn't leave room for that.

So I soak in the calm where I can.

A few of his crew stopped in today for coffee.

I hate that them being there helps me feel safe, but I have to admit it does.

George would be so disappointed in me. He taught me better.

I'm a stronger woman than this.

As if I produced him from thin air, my phone vibrates with an incoming text from Sam.

Sam: I should be home tomorrow night. I need to see you.
Amelia: Well, hello to you too, Samuel. How's your trip been? I've been fine. Thanks for asking.

I'm not in the mood for his demanding bullshit tonight. But I wouldn't say no if he were home.

Sam: Sorry Snow. It's been a long few days. I was supposed to be flying home tonight, but it got pushed back to tomorrow. You free tomorrow night?
Amelia: It's Sunday. I'm done after the morning rush and Lyla's closing for me. My plans consist of laundry, cleaning, and watching the Kings game.
Sam: Good. I'll be over after I get home.
Amelia: Sir, yes Sir!
Sam: I could get used to that.
Amelia: You wish!
Sam: Goddamn right I do.
Sam: How's your weekend been?

Debating how to answer him, I go with honesty.

Amelia: I've had the strangest feeling all day. Like someone's watching me.

The text bubbles stop and start a few times, but then nothing.

Amelia: Sam??? Hellooooo? Where are you?

He doesn't answer me, so I hit play on the show I was about to watch and get comfy, just in time for the text alert to chime again.

Sam: Sorry. I called Dean. Someone will be outside your apartment all night.
Sam: Don't go anywhere.
Amelia: Are you insane?!? I'm fine Sam. Call Dean back and call off the dogs. I don't need it. It's just a weird feeling.

I knew I shouldn't have said anything.

Sam: I'm not taking any chances.
Amelia: I'm a better shot than any of your men, and my entire building has better security than the White House. Call them off.
Sam: Don't remind me. I should have you come to the range with a few of them. Maybe wear some tight black leather.
Amelia: Sam . . .
Sam: I gotta go. Don't go anywhere tonight. Don't open the door for anyone who's not Dean. I'll come to you as early as I can tomorrow night.
Amelia: You've got to be kidding me.

I wait for a response that never comes.

Amelia: Sam . . . Hello . . .

This man is unequivocally infuriating.

An hour later when I check my security system, sure enough, one of Sam's crew is sitting in a parked car outside my building. I recognize the poor guy who's been tasked with babysitting. He's in the shop once or twice a week. Pretty sure his name's Marco. And I know he has better things to do on his Saturday night than babysitting me. With my mind made up, I brew a cup of coffee, stomp down the steps, and stop in the bakery to grab a few donuts before I knock on his window.

As the window lowers, it exposes the sheepish expression on Marco's face. "You're supposed to be staying inside, Miss Amelia."

I shove the paper Sweet Temptations cup and bag of donuts through the window. "How old are you, Marco?"

"Uh . . . I'm twenty-six." He takes the proffered goods from my hands and peeks inside the bag. "These smell delicious."

"Well, thank you." Then remembering why I came down here, I stomp my foot. "I'm two years younger than you, so cut the 'Miss Amelia' thing, please. And tell your boss I don't need a babysitter." Feeling a smidge better, I turn to storm off when Marco interrupts me.

"Do me a favor, and just stay inside tonight. Okay?"

I turn my head to look at this poor guy stuck watching me for the night and then scan the empty street. "You're not leaving, are you?"

I know his answer before he shakes his head no. "Fraid not, ma'am."

"Ma'am is just as bad as Miss, Marco. Maybe worse." I stomp off before I get nasty with the guy whose night I inadvertently ruined.

Then I hear him call after me, "Make sure you lock up."

Fucker.

The next morning, when Dean stops in for a dozen danish and to flirt with Lyla, I corner him before she can give him her number. "Jesus, Dean. My shop is not your own private Tinder. Find a different place to meet your next conquest." I box up his danish and add a dozen donuts while I'm at it. "Did you let Marco leave yet? The last time I had a chance to check was hours ago. And the poor guy was still out there, and he was still awake."

Dean pulls out one of the white powdered double-stuffed, cream-filled donuts, and shoves the entire thing into his mouth. "Seriously? Eww." I guide him to an open table at the far end of the shop and hand him a napkin. "You guys went way overboard with this."

"When Sam calls me and tells me you're getting the heebie-jeebies, I do what I'm told. Because I gotta tell you, Amelia . . . you're kind of a legend." He finally wipes the powdered sugar from his lips. "Nothing scares you. You're a better shot than most of the guys I work with. If your gut says something's off, listen to it. Sammy's just worried about you. If something happened and he wasn't here, he'd never forgive himself." Dean takes a big gulp of coffee, washing down his donut, kisses me on the cheek, and then turns to leave. "When you see him tonight, try not to shoot him, okay? If Sam dies, I'll have to answer to Nick, and I really don't wanna answer to Nick."

Why do I even bother to argue?

I'm so freaking screwed.

SAM

I'M ABOUT TWO AND A HALF HOURS INTO A FIVE-HOUR FLIGHT the next day when my phone flashes with Bash's name. I swipe to answer but don't get a word out before I hear him.

"Hey, you home?" Bash's voice is hurried.

Pissed.

The days of him being the even-tempered one of the two of us are long gone.

He's been a ticking time bomb lately.

We've gotta get him out of this fake engagement, and we've got to do it now.

I don't know how much longer Pop can keep this going without losing Bash completely.

I look across the aisle to see Nick asleep on the cream leather sofa of my father's private jet and wish I could get that comfortable. I fucking hate flying. Knowing there was something wrong with the plane isn't helping me relax. I'm tired because I slept like shit last night, ready to be home. Now I'm stuck in the air for at least another two and a half hours instead of on the ground getting shit done.

But Bash doesn't need to know any of that. Instead, I tell him, "No. I had business out of town. I won't be back for a few hours. You okay?"

"Do you care if I crash at your place for a few hours? I need some sleep and don't feel like dealing with everybody at mine right now." A door slams shut, and then what I'm guessing is the engine of his Hummer starts.

It's not like him to need to crash at my place.

Not at noon on a Sunday.

Not since he moved out of Pop's. "You've got a key. You okay, Bash?"

"Have you talked to Dad yet today?" he asks, avoiding my question.

The captain comes over the speaker, warning us of turbulence and asking Nick and I to turn off all electronics, just as the flight attendant attempts to wake Nick up to put on his seat belt. "No. Listen, I can't talk right now. Go to my place. Crash for as long as you need. I'll be back in a few hours. We can talk then."

Guess I'm making a pit-stop before I see Amelia.

Four hours later, I'm sitting with Bash and his forced, almost fiancée, Emma Sabatini, in my living room, staring in disbelief. Emma has given me the proverbial keys to the kingdom, keys she didn't know she was holding until now. Which makes me question the validity of what she just told us because, train wreck or not, the woman in front of me has more street smarts than most men I know. She's a knockout and knows how to use those looks to her benefit. Long, dark hair, a tight curvy body, and a sharp wit have served her well. But then why . . . ?

"You're telling me that one of your friends was there when Thomasso Darpino's grandson was shot in Atlantic City? The heir to the New York empire? And this friend has a picture proving it wasn't the Russian your father blamed it on who was holding the gun . . . It was your father?" I'm having a hard time swallowing this.

I look from her to Bash, who hasn't stopped pacing since Emma started talking. "And you knew this? What the fuck,

Sebastian? How could you not think this might be important information?"

"Sam . . ." Bash drags his hand down his face before he sits down next to Emma. "She mentioned it a while ago, that her friend was there the night he died. I didn't really pay attention to the rest."

When Emma smacks Bash and yells at him, "Nice to know what I was good for," I get the picture. Little brother was trying to get a piece of ass and wasn't paying attention to what Emma was saying.

Can't say I blame him.

Bringing these two back around to the issue at hand, I ignore the fact they're about to fight over when they used to be fuck buddies and start working out the logistics of the current situation. "Well at least you fucking remembered now. We can use this. I've got a guy who can get us the images from her phone. I just need you to write down her number."

"I can ask her for the pics. Not a biggie," Emma offers, but that's not an option.

"No. We want as few people involved in this as possible. We need to control any potential blowback." I stand up, trying to assess what needs to be done. First things first, I need to make sure Emma's really on board. "Emma, you do realize I'm going to use this information against your father to get you both out of this engagement."

Her big green eyes look over at Bash, and I think I see a little longing there.

But it's gone as fast as it appeared.

I leave out the part where I'm also going to use this information to destroy her father. She doesn't need to know she'll be his downfall.

"Come on, Sammy. She just gave us the information. Cut her a break." Bash is always looking out for everyone else.

Noble, yes. But stupid.

Emma's answering stare is cold and calculated. "That bastard deserves to die for the things he's done. Do what you want with the information. I don't care. Just get me the hell out of this engagement while you're at it, Sam. I'll figure out how to deal with the rest."

Okay. So maybe she does realize it.

"Done," I tell them both, then hand Emma a piece of paper. "Write her name and number here. I'll let you guys know when we're ready to make our move."

As I slide into my black Bugatti Chiron later that night, I debate whether to let Amelia know I'm coming over. I'm thinking it's better to just show up. I have a feeling, after last night, she may ignore my call or leave her apartment just to spite me. Her feisty spirit is one of my favorite things about her.

Leaving myself a few options, I text Dean to make sure one of our guys is still outside her building and that she's still home.

Once that's confirmed, it's only a short drive there from my place in the city. I find myself smiling as I start to imagine her getting all sorts of feisty about having a body-guard last night. When Snow gets feisty, her milky white skin flushes an incredibly sexy red. I can't say I haven't imagined finding out for myself just how much of her body that fiery flush covers.

Or what other ways I can make her skin hot.

However, when I park my car in front of her building and see the lights off in her apartment, I start to consider the fact that she may have slipped passed her bodyguard tonight.

Goddammit, Snow.

Instead of heading straight for her door, I walk over to Marco's car as he rolls down his window.

"Hey, boss." He tips his head. "You got her for the night? Or you want me to stick around?"

"You been here all day, Marco?"

"Nah. I just came back on an hour or so ago. Pauly was here before me." He nods his head toward Amelia's building. "She's up there. I don't know what the fuck she's doing in the dark, but I've seen her peek through the curtains a few times."

"I need you to stick around. I'm not sure how long I'm gonna be here." I tap the top of his car and turn to head up the stairs.

Snow knows I'm coming. I told her last night.

She also knows I'm here because my girl would have gotten a warning when I purposely tripped the alarm walking up her stairs.

However, she ignores my knock on her door.

She ignores the text that follows the knock on her door too.

Let's see her ignore this . . . I bang on the door one more time, then yell, "Open the damn door, Snow. Or I'm going to put round-the-clock bodyguards on you permanently."

Yup. That gets her moving. I'm greeted by a scene reminiscent of my first night in this apartment when the door cracks open, the chain still in place. "Go away, Samuel. You are not welcome until you call off your dogs."

"No can do, Snow. Let me in. Tell me what's going on. Then maybe I'll call off the dogs. But not a second before I know you're safe." I half expected to be met by the muzzle of a gun, so I'm counting this as a win.

She lets out a groan of frustration before slamming the metal door shut and reopening it seconds later.

When I walk into her dark apartment, it's to see her

storming across the room before she pours herself a glass of wine. "Speak, Sam. And make it fast. I don't like you very much right now."

She's wearing one of those ribbed tank tops she likes with her Sweet Temptations cupcake stretching across her perfect tits. And I get my answer . . . The flush that's worked its way up her neck and face also disappears down the front of her white tank.

"Well? What are you waiting for?" She sips her wine and stares, wanting an answer.

The question is, will she like me more or less once she finds out where I was?

AMELIA

SAM IN A SUIT IS A SEXY SIGHT. BUT SAM IN A PAIR OF FADED blue jeans stretching across strong, thick thighs and a loose-fitting, well-worn Metallica t-shirt with a chunky leather-banded watch wrapped around his wrist is catnip for my already hot and bothered soul. Last night, after I came back inside from yelling at Marco, I binged half of the new series Nattie and Belle had talked about. And oh boy, they weren't kidding. I mean, seriously, it was HOT.

She was hot. He was hot. Hell, both *hes* were hot. And hung.

I probably shouldn't have tried to finish it until after Sam stopped by tonight.

I knew he was coming, but I turned it on anyway.

Anyone who says they can watch two incredibly beautiful people have earth-shattering sex on TV and not get turned on is a liar. A big, fat lying liar. Basically, I'm primed and ready to go, and tall, dark, and sexy just walked through my door, looking like that.

I mean, come on . . .

This is just a cruel and unusual punishment, and I have no one to blame but myself.

The already warm room begins to heat up incrementally as I stand on the opposite side of my kitchen, holding my glass of wine, imagining what it would be like to say *"screw it"* and give in.

To let Sam do all the filthy things to me I've daydreamed about for years.

To not think about tomorrow. Not think about the strings that would be attached.

Not think about whether I'd still be able to run if I needed to.

It's hard to be friends with a man like Sam and not imagine how easy it would be for him to push me up against a wall . . . or spread me out on a counter, licking frosting from every inch of my body.

God, I bet it'd be good. Better than good. I bet—

Sam clears his throat, abruptly ending my fantasy. "You with me, Snow?"

The look on his face is so beautifully sexy and self-assured.

And then there's me . . . Horny.

Damnit. I was mad earlier. I need to channel my inner badass and get back to that.

Annoyed. Angry. Infuriated.

It is not up to him to control my life.

I'm so mad at this smug man, and all it took was for him to walk in my door, looking like that, and I forget. Damnit.

Jesus, how can I forget I've been watching a car sit outside Sweet Temptations all day with an armed guard inside. As if a big fat bucket of cold water is thrown over my head, my thoughts turn on a dime. I push all thoughts of all the incredible things he could do to me out of my mind and quickly remember how angry I've been with him the past few days. "Oh, I'm with you, Samuel. Care to tell me when exactly I became a prisoner in my own home? My own shop?"

"Snow . . ."

Carefully, I place my glass down on my kitchen table before I explode. "Don't you dare 'Snow' me. You're a bully. Do you know that? You're a beautiful bully."

"Beautiful?"

"Do not interrupt me." Of course, he focuses on beautiful. "You push and push until you get your way, and if I don't give in, you do what you want anyway. That's a bully, Sam." I move closer to him and shove my finger against his chest. "It's mean, and I don't like it. I don't like you when you do it. So, you listen here, jackass . . ."

"Jackass?" He manages to laugh at me. And that beautiful, deep sound reminds me that I don't hate him even if I am mad at him. I probably also sound slightly crazy at the moment, but I don't care.

With two hands on the hard planes of his chest, I shove him back. "Don't laugh at me. I'm mad at you." His devilish smile does it for me every single time, but I tamp that feeling down. I've gotten really good at doing that. "Whatever, Sam. I'm a big girl, and I don't need you running my life for me." I realize this comes out more like the whiney complaint of a teenage girl, trying to convince herself of that, rather than the declaration of a strong, independent woman.

Apparently, a little wine and I go soft.

As I step back and pull my hands away, Sam's hands grab either side of my face and pull me back to him. He holds me suspended in a moment I've dreamt of and dreaded in equal measure. With no room left between us, his strong lips brush over mine as he says, "I'm well aware you're a big girl, Snow. I wouldn't be able to do any of the things I've fantasized about doing to you if you weren't."

My lips part on a sigh, and he deepens the kiss with a strong stroke of his tongue.

Powerful. Sexy. Everything I've dreamt kissing Sam would be.

My hands grip the hem of his shirt as we dive deeper.

Tasting.

Teasing.

I lean into him . . . into this as his tongue strokes mine.

He tastes like mint and feels like home.

Home, safety, security.

These things most people take for granted feel like such foreign concepts to me. So much so that I refuse to accept them. Not yet, when they're a carrot dangling at the end of a string. So close, yet always out of reach. I refuse to put myself through that. Refuse to allow myself to fall in love. To build a life, then have it ripped away when I have to leave.

And I *will* have to leave. I always do.

Sam likes to call me Snow, like the fairy-tale princess.

But my life is far from a fairy tale.

Even a prince can't change that.

Needing to break the kiss, I step back, pushing away from him and immediately feel the loss. With shaking fingers pressed against my lips, I apologize, "Sam, I can't. I . . ."

He drags his thumb along his bottom lip as his lust-filled blue eyes set my body on fire. "I'm not sorry, Snow. I've been wanting to do that for years. But we need to talk first."

And just like that, his sexy smirk transforms back into alpha-dog dominance with ease. He forgets that I don't like to be dominated though. "You're right. We do." I move into the living room, turn off the television, and turn on a light. "I am fully capable of taking care of myself. I was okay before I met you. And I'll be okay after I leave Philadelphia. I don't need you to protect me. I told you I didn't need a bodyguard, Sam, and I meant it. Seriously. You just had to go and get your guys to babysit me around the clock like a child."

Sam stalks into the room after me. "You're fucking right, I did. You said you had an eerie feeling. Like someone was watching you. You aren't crazy, Amelia. You don't overreact. You know to trust your gut. And I know to trust you. You tell me something feels off, and I'm sending someone to make sure nothing happens to you."

"But Sam—"

He interrupts me, "No. No buts. I was in another fucking country. I couldn't be here, so I was damn well making sure someone was. For all I knew, what I was dealing with was blowing back over here." His eyes soften as his voice lowers. "I had business to take care of in Canada."

The hairs on the back of my neck stand at attention, and I pray I'm wrong. "Canada?" My voice cuts like a hot knife through cold butter. "What were you doing there?"

"I need you to understand . . ." Sam starts, and my stomach drops.

"Sam," I grasp for the words, desperate to know but scared to ask. "What happened in Canada?" The last words come out on a whisper.

He reaches out for me, but I back away. "I was meeting with the Tremblay cartel."

"Sam." I drop down on the couch behind me. "Why? What happened?" I always knew there was a chance I'd be found. I've expected it. Been waiting for it. But a small part of me held onto hope that it wouldn't happen.

That I'd get to keep the makeshift family I've been lucky enough to find here.

That I wouldn't have to be alone again.

Sam sits down next to me, but this time, it's not comforting. "I've had one of my guys working on getting me something on the Canadian cartel for a while now. He finally got it. It was the leverage I needed to confront them. I paid off your debt and agreed to keep the information I have about them to myself in exchange for your safety. If anything happens to you, the leverage gets turned over to their partners in Mexico who wouldn't just kill the Canadian kingpins for the betrayal. They'd kill their families. They'd brutalize them and then kill everyone they loved. Their wives. Their kids. Everyone."

Oh my God.

The room starts closing in.

I can't breathe.

As if a boa constrictor were tightening around me, my lungs can't take in oxygen, and my heart can't pump. My entire body starts shaking. I think I'm having a heart attack. Somewhere on the edges of my sanity, I'm aware it's a panic attack. But I feel like I'm dying.

"Amelia."

What? I hear Sam's voice, but it sounds like it's underwater.

"Snow, look at me." His deep baritone registers in my brain, but I can't manage the simple task he demands until he wraps me in his arms and holds me to him. "Stay with me. Breathe with me. You've got to breathe." He takes one of my hands and moves it to cover his heart. "Feel that." Then he places my other hand over my own heart. "Feel us. Stay with me. You're safe. I promise you on my life, you're safe. I made sure you'll always be safe." Sam's lips press against my forehead and linger.

Everything starts to slow down, and the vice around me begins to loosen as his words take hold.

I'm safe.

I've been dreaming of those words for longer than I can remember.

So why am I so angry?

"Sam." My voice is hoarse as the first tear tracks down my cheek. "Please tell me you didn't handle my life without talking to me about it first."

I wait for an answer that isn't coming. "Please tell me you respect me enough to talk to me before you make decisions that could cost me my life." Rising from the couch, I look down at this man I want the impossible from. Because the one thing Sam has never done is lie to me. He won't start now. "Sam, tell me you didn't. That you know me well enough to know I could never forgive you for doing this." Another tear falls. "I trusted you."

"Snow, I didn't . . ."

"Don't you dare," I wipe the tears from my eyes. "I can't look at you right now. You need to leave. "

"Sn—" I glare at the use of my nickname. "Amelia, listen to me." His voice is demanding, but I refuse to bend.

"Get. Out." My words leave me more broken than I already am.

With those two words, I turn around and walk slowly into my bedroom, slamming the door behind me. I sit down on the edge of my bed and wait.

I listen for his next move.

There are no footsteps on the creaky wooden floors. No movement.

But then I hear it. "This isn't over, Amelia. I'll do anything to make sure you're safe. I guaranteed that yesterday. You're safe. I protect what's mine. And you, Snow, are mine. So, this isn't over." The words aren't said in anger.

There's a conviction in his voice I recognize.

It petrifies me.

I can't be his.

I refuse to be his.

I refuse to be anyone's.

It hurts too much.

SAM

I LEFT AMELIA'S APARTMENT AND LET MARCO KNOW HE WAS not to move tonight. I'll pull him when I send Dean into Sweet Temptations for coffee in the morning. By the end of the day, Mike will have eyes surrounding the perimeter of the building, and that will have to do. I should have fucking done that before.

I don't want to make her feel unsafe, but I need her to actually be safe.

I know my girl can take care of herself.

But that doesn't change the fact that it's my fucking job to take care of her.

Instead of going back to my place, I take a detour to Crucible, an MMA gym on the outskirts of Kroydon Hills not far from Pop's house that a friend of mine owns. Cade St. James and I went to school together before he joined the Marines. He put in a few years before something happened over there. He doesn't talk about it, but his sister said he lost some friends. As soon as his enlistment was up, he came home bigger and angrier than when he left.

Cade bought this gym as soon as he got home. He'd trained for years here before he left, and within a few years of being back, the Savage Saint, as he's known, was dominating the fighting world. He's retired now, spending most of his time training up-and-coming fighters. His sister, Immogen, helps him manage the gym.

He gave me a key to the building a while back, so I could

train after they close to the public. I'm usually in here before the sun comes up or long after it sets. And after my argument with Amelia, I need to work off some of this energy.

A few of us have keys, but I wasn't expecting anyone else to be here this late on a Sunday night. Once I grab my gym bag out of my trunk and head inside the dark building, I look to see who else is here. The only section of the massive warehouse illuminated is the area with a few heavy bags hanging around the perimeter and a regulation-sized octagon in the center.

Becket Kingston is alone, beating the hell out of a bag when I drop my things on the floor and catch his attention. "King," I yell.

"Prince," he responds. Something we've done since we were teenagers. Becks, Cade, and I all went to high school together. We got into more trouble than anyone will ever know. The fucker always told me he was born a king, while I was a lowly prince in waiting. Cade was our saint, but not because he was our conscience. Just the opposite. If Becks and I weren't sure about something, Cade was the one to push it past the limit. His last name may be St. James, but he's always been more sinner than saint.

I kick off my shoes, throw my t-shirt on my bag, and grab my hand wraps while Becks grips the bag and watches. "You been here long? Wasn't there a Kings game today?" Becks's family owns the local pro football team.

He shrugs. "You know your kid brother is trying to nail my little sister?" Only fucking Becket would say that about his own sister with a smile and then hit the bag as hard as he can.

"Lenny? Yeah. They were at my restaurant a few weeks ago. I like her. Pretty sure he's looking for more than an easy lay. Sebastian's got a good head on his shoulders. I wouldn't worry about him." I meet him at the bag and hold it steady as he starts to jab.

"Wasn't worried. She'll kick his ass if he fucks up." Another jab.

If this were anyone else, I might have a problem with his words, but it's not. "So what are you doing here this late?"

"Fucking women. We're supposed to be mind readers. Yet they can't manage to tell us a single thing." That's all he needs to say as he continues his assault on the bag. "What about you? Shouldn't you be out shooting someone?"

Becks has a fucked-up sense of humor. Always has.

"Nah. That's tomorrow. Tonight, I'm with you. Fucking women."

"You two pussies seriously come to my gym at ten o'clock on a Sunday to bitch about fucking women?"

The two of us turn and watch Cade St. James walk in from the back of the building where the offices are housed, holding a pink teddy bear in one hand and wearing what looks like plaid pajama pants with a white undershirt and bare feet.

Becks attempts to hold back a laugh but fails. "Couldn't sleep without your teddy, Saint? I'll bet those cage girls would love to know that the Savage Saint needs his teddy to get a good night's sleep."

As Cade stalks our way, Becks jokingly hides behind me. "Save me, Sam. He's gonna kill me, and I'm too pretty to die."

I shove him away. "Serves you right, Becks. Seriously, do you ever shut the fuck up?"

Cade smacks the back of Becks's head. "Douche. Brynlee left it here earlier. I got her to sleep without it, but she keeps waking up. Immogen's home now, so I figured I'd run over and grab it." He looks between the two of us. "You haven't lived until you have a two-year-old going on a sleep strike."

He leans against the octagon in the center of this room and closes his eyes. "It's fucking exhausting."

Becks and I join him. "Gen isn't playing at Kingdom tonight?" Cade's sister's band, Sinners & Saints, is the house band at Becks's brother Sawyer's bar in the city.

"Nah. She got home a few minutes ago. She keeps telling me she needs to look for her own place, but I swear, I don't know how I'm gonna do it when she moves out."

"Women suck. They just want so much from you," Becks laments.

I shake my head. "Or they won't take anything from you."

"Guys, I'm talking about my sister. At least the two of you are getting laid."

Yeah. That's not happening tonight either.

The next morning, I skip my normal stop at Sweet Temptations in an attempt to give Amelia some space and go straight to Pop's house to catch him up on the trip and the new information we're working on about the Sabatinis. As I pull through the front gates, the Bluetooth in the car alerts me to an incoming call from Dean.

I left him a message earlier with instructions on how I wanted Sweet Temptations handled today. "What do you have for me?"

"Yo, Sammy. Got your message from earlier. Sorry, I was a little preoccupied."

"Just tell me it wasn't the new girl at Sweet Temptations, and we're good." There's no answer from the other end. "Oh, come on, man. Just leave Amelia's shopgirls alone. Christ, she already wants to kill me."

Dean coughs. "It wasn't Lyla. Anyway, I've already talked

to Marco. All was quiet overnight. I'll be at the shop to check in soon and then fill you in later."

"Thanks, man. I appreciate it. See you at the restaurant." She might not want to see me, but she's not getting rid of me that easily.

With that settled, I walk up the front steps of my father's compound and step through the massive arching doors of the house. The heavenly scent of the imported Italian coffee Nonna insists on drinking draws me into the kitchen like a kid following the Pied Piper. I'm greeted by the additional smell of freshly baked banana bread and Nonna as I enter.

"Mi principino," she claps her hands, then reaches out for me until I bend over in front of all four feet, eleven inches of her and let her grab my face.

No one knows exactly how old Nonna is because she refuses to tell us. Her long white hair is neatly pulled up in the same style she's worn for years. A gold cross that belonged to my grandfather before he died rests on a thick chain around her neck that she never removes. A summery red cotton dress with long sleeves is covered by one of her many aprons, and a smile revealing the history of our family in its depths spreads across her face when she forces me to taste her banana bread.

I take a bite from the piece in her hand, then kiss her cheek. "Sei bellisima, Nonna."

"I want you to bring your principessa over soon, Samuel. I have a new recipe for her to try. But you must go for now. Your father is in his office, and he is grumpy this morning." She takes a piece of banana bread from the counter and wraps it in a white linen napkin. "Take this with you. He's always happier after he eats."

She's not wrong.

She's also met Amelia and loves to torture me about

bringing her around. I've brought Nonna to Amelia's shop but haven't brought Amelia to Pop's house.

Not yet.

You don't bring girls who are friends home to meet the family.

You bring *the girl* home. The one who'll be your family.

I won't do that until she's ready.

I bend down and kiss Nonna again before moving down the hall to my father's office. His door is open as he reads over something in a folder in front of him. "Mornin', Pop." I knock on the door as I enter the room and drop into one of the chairs across from him.

The lines on his face seem deeper today. "Do you ever just sit? Do you always have to throw yourself into the furniture, Samuel?"

Guess Nonna was right. Not in a good mood this morning.

I nudge the banana bread across the desk toward him.

He peeks under the folded cloth and pushes it to the side. "How did the meeting with the Tremblays go?"

Guess there's no foreplay happening today. "It went as well as can be expected, Pop. They might be saying Louis and George are equals. But they're not. Louis is reckless. He's careless. George is calculated. He sees the bigger picture. George is in charge. He accepted my offer. It's done. The money has been moved. The evidence is safe and enough to keep them in line. The alternative isn't an option. Nobody wants to see their kids gutted and hung."

Pop stops what he was doing and leans back in his chair, blowing out a long breath. "There is nothing on this planet I wouldn't conquer for you and your brother. Nothing I wouldn't do to keep you safe. Let's hope they feel the same . . . and that she's worth it." His eyes level me from across the desk as he sips his coffee, then breaks off a piece of the bread.

"Awfully deep for first thing on a Monday morning, Pops." I reach across and attempt to break off my own piece of bread only to have it pulled away from me.

"What's the update on the Sabatini front? You said you had news."

I spend the next hour going over the information Bash and Emma gave me yesterday and walking him through what we're going to do next. Pop isn't much of a tech guy, so I brief him on the main points of it all. "Give me a few more days, and I should know what kind of time frame we're looking at."

"Good. We need this over. I owe it to your brother. And you."

AMELIA

I HATE THAT IT'S BEEN WEEKS AND I'M STILL LOOKING FOR SAM every time the bells above the door of Sweet Temptations alert me to new customers. It's never him. Not anymore. Not since I threw him out of my home and my life.

I wasn't wrong.

He had no business taking risks with my life without discussing it with me first.

I'm not an object to be managed.

But still, I miss him.

I miss his physical presence in my shop and in my life. Dean and a few of their guys stop in often, so Sam is never far from my mind. Especially on days like today, when Dean orders an extra coffee to go, along with a box of cookies.

I know exactly who that coffee is going to.

Whose lips will be touching that damn cup and eating my cookies.

It's probably a good thing I haven't seen him, though, because I'd want to simultaneously strangle him and throw myself into his arms, which leaves me wondering exactly what that says about me.

At the very least, I think I may need to reevaluate my feelings for Sam Beneventi.

Goddamn him for crawling into my heart when I thought I had that door slammed tight and triple-locked it.

I don't know how many times I've considered grabbing my go bag and leaving.

How many times I've stood there, ready to say goodbye to Kroydon Hills and all the people in it. Just driving away.

But I can't. Not yet. I don't feel finished here yet.

If he'd at least tried to apologize, I could rationalize forgiving him. But I haven't heard so much as a peep from the jackass. I stare at my phone, willing it to ring. I consider sending him a text, growing more annoyed with myself by the minute.

I'm literally and metaphorically saved by the bell when the bells over the front door of the shop chime. Belle and Nattie walk in, each holding the hand of a tiny little girl. They're bundled up like little pink snowmen to ward off the frigid chill from the arctic freeze that's blown into Philly this week.

Who knew it could get this cold this early in the fall?

I adore my friends and love these little girls, but their nosey selves are not who I was hoping to see right now.

Lyla has class, so it's just me in the shop today. I paste a smile on my face and move to my freshly brewed, French roast decaf that Belles has been craving for the past few weeks, her adorable little baby bump already on full display.

"God, I love you, Amelia. It might not be full-caff, but at least your decaf tastes like coffee. Not the watered-down crap Declan brings home."

Gracie points a mitten-covered hand at the pink and white kitty cat cupcakes lining the shelves and squeals, "Crap!" She runs over to her mirror image, Evie, and both girls break into a fit of baby girl giggles that brings a smile to my face.

Belles looks over at Nattie with an exasperated look on her face.

"Oh, no. Don't look at me. This one's all you." Nat crosses her arms over her chest and does a lousy job of holding back her smile. "Hey, Amelia. Could I get two pumpkin spice coffees to go, please? I've got to get going. I'm meeting Murphy for a study group."

I stop mid-turn, and make sure I just heard Nattie right. "I'm sorry, did you just say Aiden Murphy is going to willingly drink a pumpkin spice coffee?"

Nattie shrugs. "He'll never admit it. But if I show up at the library without one, he'll drink all of mine. And I don't share my coffee with anyone. Not even Brady, and I share all sorts of things with Brady." Nattie lives with her boyfriend, Brady, their roommate Murphy, and Sam's brother, Sebastian.

"Enough," Belles cuts Nattie off. "It's bad enough the girls are saying C-R-A-P, I don't need them repeating anything in front of your brother when we get home about what you and Brady share."

I hand both coffees to Nattie while Belles tells me to add them to her tab before kissing her sister-in-law on the cheek. "Good luck. Study hard."

"I always do." She blows a kiss back as she dances through the door.

I let Gracie and Evie each pick a cupcake while Belle pulls their puffy little coats off. "Ok. Now that Nattie's gone to study, let's get these girls fed so you can tell me why you look like someone ran over your cat."

When I ignore her comment and pull out chocolate milks for the girls, she laughs. "Amelia, you might be fooling everyone else, but not me. You've been miserable the last few weeks, and I haven't seen Sam Beneventi in here once in all that time. Dean, yes. Sam, no. I'm not stupid. I know something's going on, and there's not another soul in the shop besides us, so you're going to sit down right now and tell me what's up."

I hate when she's right.

Well, in truth, I don't hate when she's right.

I just hate that she's noticed.

I haven't exactly been miserable. But I haven't been happy. Scared . . . yes. Sad that I lost a friend . . . yes. Okay, maybe I was miserable. Shit. I guess I let my emotions show more than I realized. Time to fix that. "I don't have a cat. But that sounds like a perfect Christmas present for my favorite little girls. Thanks for the idea." I wink at the twins whose cherubic faces are already covered in pink frosting, their white-blonde pigtails sticking to their cheeks.

Definitely enthusiastic about their cupcakes.

"No pets, Amelia. We've already got Goober. One dog and three, almost four, kids counting Tommy. Tommy, who by the way, is officially a teenager, with all sorts of new things to work through. Nope. That's already more than enough for us. Now, sit down and talk to me. I feel like we've barely seen each other this entire month." She blows on her steaming coffee before lifting the mug to her lips. "Spill it, sister."

Giving in, I hunker down across from her in my favorite emerald-green, crushed-velvet armchair and get comfy. When I decorated the shop, I went with a Central Perk vibe. The furniture is an eclectic mismatched assortment carefully created after weeks of sorting through secondhand shops scattered throughout the Delaware Valley. I love it. "Fine. What do you want to know?"

"What's going on with you lately? You refused my last three dinner invites. You've skipped the last two Kroydon University home games and the last Kings home game. That's not like you. You love football. I, on the other hand, just love the football player. I'm worried about you." Belles drags her finger through the cream cheese icing on her red velvet cupcake and then points it at me. "And don't bother trying to deny it. Don't bullshit a bullshitter, Amelia. This screams guy problems. And unless you're hiding another guy in your life, I think this is all Sam Beneventi's doing. He may be Kroydon Hills's resident badass, but I'm not afraid to go toe to toe with him if he hurt you."

I'm not sure when it happened, but this woman snuck past all my armor.

Damnit. First Sam, and now Belles.

I wasn't supposed to be letting people in.

I wasn't supposed to get attached.

Just then a smiling Evie claps her frosting-covered hands together, sending pink sugar all over the table. Belles attempts to clean her daughter up, but then she turns back around, a look of horror on her face. "Oh my God, Amelia. Are you crying?"

"No," I sniff, then wipe my eyes. Damn it. "I'm not crying. I just got some frosting in my eyes."

"Amelia..." Belle's tone softens.

"I swear to God, Belle. I'm not ready to talk about this yet. But when I am, you'll be the first person I call. Maybe even before Sam."

"Swear?" She lifts her pinky in the air and leaves it hanging there.

I look at her, half expecting to be taken back in time to see someone else sitting in front of me. I haven't pinky-swore to anything since I was a preteen back in Washington. Instead of linking pinkies, I cover her hand with mine. "Yes, Belle. I promise. I've got to figure a few things out on my own. Once I do, I'll fill you in on everything."

Evie claps her now clean hands together, and Gracie smacks her frosting covered hands down over ours.

I think two of my three best friends are toddlers.

What does that say about me?

It says I need to figure my shit out. Because they can't help me, and their mother only wants everyone to find the kind of love she did.

She has no idea just how dangerous that can be.

SAM

"ARE YOU FUCKING KIDDING ME?" I SLAM THE FRONT DOOR OF my father's house shut behind me as I walk in, hearing my words bounce dramatically off the vaulted ceiling. Lowering my voice, I try to calmly ask, "What do you fucking mean you can't fucking find her, Dean? She's a twenty-one-year-old waitress at Sabatini's casino. According to Emma, she still fucking works there. FIND HER." We've been working around-the-clock to gather the information we need against Sabatini.

Even with Mike working his magic, we still need to get Emma's friend Maria on board with our plan. She told us she'd do what she needed to. But she's been unreliable. I'd hoped we wouldn't need her. But I was wrong.

Mike was able to get the pictures from her phone, but Pop wants more.

He wants concrete evidence.

This means Maria has to fall in line and be kept safe.

A dead Maria will fuck up my world right now.

"Her apartment's been cleared out. Not a fucking trace of her, man." A door slams in the background, and I cringe.

"FIND HER." I control the urge to throw my phone across the room only because Nonna is staring at me, concern shining in her eyes.

Frail arms lace through mine as she guides me into the kitchen. "Sit," I'm instructed with a nudge toward one of six stools surrounding the butcher block island. "Your father is in with the doctor." Her pale blue eyes hold mine, whispering secrets that aren't registering yet. "He'll be out in a minute. Let me get you something to eat." Nonna grabs a bowl from the cabinet and picks up the ladle next to the stove. "I made minestrone soup. It's been simmering all afternoon."

"Nonna, I'm not hungry." My grandmother still believes she can fix all our problems with a bowl of soup and a piece of bread.

She pushes the hot bowl in front of me and rests her small hand on my arm. "Eat, my boy. You need your strength."

The creak of a door is followed by two voices I immediately recognize. One belongs to Pop. The other to *The Family's* physician, Doc.

"I'll check back in with you next week," Doc tells Pop.

The two of them stop in the kitchen, my father's eyes hardening when they land on me. "Thanks for coming, Doc."

Nonna moves to usher Doc out while I'm joined by my father at the counter. "Didn't realize you were stopping by this early, Samuel."

"Why was Doc here, Pops? Is somebody hurt?"

Pop glances around the room, no doubt looking for Nonna. "Come on. Let's take this into my office. These walls have ears."

Once the door closes behind us, he sits down at his desk and picks up a cigar resting next to his keyboard. "Your mother used to hate when I'd smoke these things." He lifts it to his nose and sniffs. "Guess I should have listened."

"You wanna tell me what's going on?" My stomach drops as my father avoids my eyes.

He places the stogie back down on his desk, then steeples his fingers and blows out a long breath. "Doc was checking in on me, Sam. He's been doing it for the past few months." He absentmindedly straightens the picture of Mom on his desk before continuing, "Have I taught you everything you need to know about sitting in this chair, Sam?"

"Pop . . ." I stop him, my brain swimming with what he's telling me.

"My job as your father, not just as your boss, is to render myself useless by the time I die. To have imparted all the knowledge and ability a man needs to not just survive, but also to thrive in this world. In our world. Have I done that?" He subtly shakes his head. "It's cancer. Aggressive fucking cancer." He opens the top drawer of his desk, pulls out a key, and then hands it to me. "That key unlocks the safe behind my wedding picture, Sam."

The weight of this single key is more than I want to own right now.

A thumb drive gets pushed my way. "And that has all the information you'll need. Accounts and that kind of shit." Pop starts coughing, and my mind begins to focus. To piece together everything he's not saying.

"Keep your circle small—Uncle Nick, Dean, and Bash— when you can. No one else. Don't give your trust away. It's your most precious commodity." He clears his throat. "Iron fist, son. They need to fear you."

I nod. "Yeah, Pop. I remember. I learned from the best." Thirty fucking years old, and my voice just cracked at the thought of losing my father.

"The crown is heavy, Sam. You need to be strong to wear it. Never forget that."

"You're gonna be fine, Pop. The crown's yours. I don't want it yet." I lean forward, my elbows on my knees, feeling like that little boy who'd just been told his mother died.

"Fairy tales are for women. You need to be ready. Now tell me about the girl. Do we have her yet?"

"They're looking for her now." I pull my phone from my pocket, but there are no new messages from Dean.

Pop brings his fist down on his desk. "Well, go fucking find her. I need this done." Angry eyes meet mine when I don't get up fast enough. "Get it done."

Five fucking hours later, I've had my fill of crying women. We found Maria. She's terrified Sabatini will kill her. She changed her mind. She tried to say she didn't want any part of going against him until Dean pointed out she should be more scared of me and what we'd do to her if she didn't help us.

She cried harder but cooperated.

My first call was to Bash. I forgot he had a game today. Once he finally called me back, I was able to tell him the forced marriage was over, and he was free. He's going to meet Pop and me for lunch tomorrow. He couldn't get off the phone fast enough when he realized that meant he could go get his girl.

Eleanor Kingston better be ready because Bash is coming for her tonight.

Pop was my next stop. I filled him in on everything and gave him copies of it all. We've got him. Sabatini's a dead man walking. He just doesn't know it yet.

Hours later, I'm finally home with a glass of bourbon in my hand when my phone rings with Mike's name flashing across it. "Mike?"

"Sam, man. We need to talk."

I run my fingers through my hair. This fucking day is never gonna end. "We're talking now, Mike."

"Meet me at my place. Come tonight, Sam. It's about Amelia."

"Is she alright?" Christ. I can't do this.

I've given her the space she wanted.

I've waited for her to come to me.

And now she's in trouble.

Fuck.

"Sam . . ."

"I'll be there in ten minutes." I'm already grabbing for my coat and keys before the call ends.

Mike's watching for me and buzzes the door open before I even bang on it. He's in the same spot he's always in, in front of his wall of technology, but this time is different. Looking over the monitors, I recognize the people and dossiers up on the screens. These people are Kingstons.

They own the Philadelphia Kings football team.

It's Eleanor's family, including Eleanor.

"What the fuck, Mike? What do the Kingstons have to do with Amelia? Is she okay? Is she safe? Did the Tremblays fuck us?" The thought of this woman hurt affects me in ways I can't even comprehend.

Way too fucking calm, Mike asks, "What do you know about the Kingstons, Sam?"

"Did you make me drive over here for a goddamn history lesson? They're the fucking Kingstons. Everyone in Philly knows them. Bash is dating Eleanor. I've known Becket since high school. Max Kingston is an uptight dick. And the one married to old man Kingston while he was fucking someone else was hot as hell. What do I need to know about them? And what does this have to do with Amelia?" How the hell could the Kingstons hurt Amelia?

Mike spins in his seat, then grabs two bottles of beer from the mini fridge under his desk. He tosses one my way and cracks the lid open on his, then points his bottle at me. "You might want to have a drink, man. Things are about to get all sorts of fucked in here."

Holy Hell.

Mike wasn't kidding.

"Let me make sure I've got this straight. Amelia's mom had an affair with old man Kingston before she went into witness protection. She got pregnant with Amelia. She saw someone from Sabatini's old crew murder a Russian and testified against him. Then she moved across the country and changed her name. Kingston never even knew Amelia existed until Mom called him right before she died?"

"No. She wrote a letter. But by the time he got it, she was dead and so was the information on Anastasia Rivell. The Kingstons have been looking for her for years, but she's good at covering her tracks." Mike smirks and then turns back to his monitors. "But something changed. They brought in a new guy to help. I think you know him."

A picture of my Uncle Dino comes up on a monitor. Dino is my mother's brother. He refused to be part of *The Family* years ago, and Mom's parents cut him off.

I've seen him a few times over the years but didn't realize he worked behind the scenes for the Philadelphia Kings football team until a few years ago. It was the day I met Amelia, after the shooting at Belle's house.

He came with Declan.

He's the fixer for the team.

"Yeah. He's my uncle. So he's searching for Amelia?" This is fucking insane.

Mike starts pulling information up on the screen directly in front of him. "Yeah. He's been tracking her. He's covering his tracks as best he can, but he's not as good as me. He doesn't have her yet. But it looks like he's close."

"What the hell do they want with Amelia?"

"Man . . ." Mike looks at me like I'm an idiot. "She's their sister."

Fuck.

SAM

MIKE FILLED ME IN ON EVERYTHING HE'S FOUND ABOUT Amelia and the Kingstons. It's all there. She's their sister. Older than Lenny and Hudson, but younger than Sawyer. She's got a family out there that's looking for her. They want her, and they have the means to protect her. Not that she'll need them for that when she has me. But if they claim her as one of their own publicly, it will be big news. Not just in Philadelphia, but everywhere. The Kingstons are a powerful family. Old money. Big name. The papers will run wild with this. They only just stopped talking about old man Kingston dying in bed while he was cheating on his wife, a wife who was pregnant with his eighth kid and who herself was younger than at least four of his other kids. I might have taken care of the Tremblays for her, but I don't know how she'll feel about living her life in the public eye.

Once we call it a night, I barely make it to my car before I'm calling Amelia. I need to see her. To tell her before someone else has the chance to blow her world up. Her drowsy voice answers after the third ring.

"What the hell, Sam? Do you know what time it is? I've got to be up in like . . . I don't know . . ." I hear her hit something and then move the phone. "Sam, I've got to be up in three hours. I haven't heard from you in a month. What do you want?" Her voice is raspy. Sleepy. So fucking sexy.

"Snow, I need to see you . . ."

My next words are cut off when we get disconnected.

I call back, thinking we lost the connection. Her sexy, sleepy voice lets me know I'm wrong. "Take a hint, Sam. I don't want to talk to you. It's the middle of the night. Sunday mornings are huge for me. I have to get up at the ass crack of dawn. I'm sleeping. And you haven't bothered to call me in a month. You haven't apologized. You don't get to call me now and tell me you have to see me. If you want to see me, call me tomorrow." She waits a beat, then adds, "After the shop closes. Good night, Samuel."

I manage to get her name out, praying she doesn't hang up on me again, "I'm not sorry, Snow. That's why I didn't apologize. I need you safe. I need you safe and happy in my city. I want you safe and happy in my bed, where I can feel you breathe. Where I can worship you. I want you to be mine, Amelia. But for that to happen, I need you safe first. I need you breathing. I need you to live a long and happy fucking life. I'd do it again. I'd do anything if it meant I got to keep you safe." My eyes close, and I lean my head back against the leather seat that's still cold from the frigid night air.

There's a quick intake of breath on the other end of the phone.

Amelia doesn't answer right away, but she doesn't hang up either. Then her quiet voice tentatively asks, "Do you promise to at least talk to me about it first next time?"

Holy shit.

"I promise to try, Snow. Can I come over?" Will I lose my man card if I admit I may have held my breath waiting for her answer?

"No, Sam. Not tonight. I have to go back to sleep now. But I'll make an extra batch of cookies tomorrow with your name on them, and we can talk after the shop closes. That was a whole lot of information you just unloaded, and I'm too tired to sift through it right now." She yawns, and I want to be there with her now.

"Let me come over tonight, Snow. We don't have to talk. We don't have to do anything but sleep. Let me see you." When she doesn't answer me, I add, "Jesus. I've never begged anyone for anything before. But I'll get down on my knees and beg for just one single moment in time if I have to. Only for you. Only ever for you."

The movement of blankets rustles through the phone before I hear the sound of her breathing change. "The door's unlocked. I'm going back to bed." There's a pause before she adds, "No talking, Sam."

"Just sleeping, Snow." Thank you, Lord.

It takes me less than fifteen minutes to get to Amelia's and about thirty seconds to get from my car to her front door. Taking the metal stairs two at a time, I can't believe she left it unlocked for me. Once it's shut, I lock all three locks and the chain. She left the light over the stove on, and I wonder if she did that for me or if that's what she usually does.

Is this strong woman scared of what's hiding in the dark?

Did I make it worse?

I quietly make my way back to her bedroom, and I'm rewarded with the sight of her sleeping peacefully in her bed. She's tucked in under a silver blanket, her dark hair a stark contrast to her pale sheets.

God, I missed her.

I kick off my shoes and throw my coat over the chair resting in the corner of the room. I'm debating whether to take off my pants and shirt when her voice cuts through the silence.

"Don't even think about getting into this bed with your suit on, Sam Beneventi. You've probably been in those clothes all

day. God only knows where they've been and what's on them."
She rolls over to face me and gives me a small smile. Her eyes
stay closed, but she lifts the blanket in invitation. "No talking
tonight, Sam. We can talk tomorrow. Tonight, we sleep."

I strip down to my boxer briefs, my eyes never leaving the
sleeping princess in front of me. The light of the full moon is
filtering through her blinds, illuminating her pale, flawless
skin and giving her a luminescent glow.

This woman has no idea what she means to me.

That's my fault.

That gets fixed tomorrow.

Tonight, I settle for sliding into bed next to her.

She rolls over. No longer facing me.

I don't hesitate, wrapping my arms around her and
pulling her back against my chest. I haven't seen her, haven't
touched her, for a month. Why the fuck did I listen to her
when she told me to go away? Nobody tells me what to do,
but this tiny slip of a woman has the ability to destroy me.
After I take a moment to bury my face in her hair, I whisper
in her ear, "Never again, Snow."

"Hmmm," she mummers sleepily.

"Sleep tonight, talk tomorrow." I tighten my arms around
her and wait for her breathing to even out, then kiss her head
and close my eyes.

Tomorrow.

SAM

I HEAR THE ALARM ON AMELIA'S PHONE CHIME AFTER WHAT feels like five minutes of sleep but in actuality is more like a few hours.

Once she's reached over to her nightstand and turned it off, she rolls back over, dropping her head on my chest. "I've got to get in the shower and go to work. Stay as long as you want, but Sam . . ." She lifts her head and looks at me. "We've got to talk tonight."

The tips of my fingers run through her soft hair, then wrap around the back of her neck. Pulling her face to mine, I brush my lips over hers, forcing myself not to deepen the kiss. "I'm meeting Pop and Bash for lunch, but the rest of my day is wide open. Want to have dinner with me tonight? Come to my place. Let me cook for you for a change."

"Sam . . ." She pulls back and climbs out of bed. I'm expecting her to say no. But this woman always surprises me. "Can you even cook? Or are you going to have Nonna cook it for you?" She bends over, her thick hair tickling my chest, and places a chaste kiss on my cheek. "I'll see you tonight. But plan to spend the dinner talking."

"What are we going to spend our time doing after dinner?" I may have a few ideas, but this ball needs to be left in her court.

"That depends." A beautiful smile graces her face before she walks away, and I'm left watching her delicious ass encased in tiny little panties vanish behind the bathroom door, before the shower turns on.

I close my eyes, knowing without a doubt, that woman is mine.

When I finally wake up, after sleeping in later than I have in years, I run my hand over cold sheets and breathe in the scent lingering on Snow's pillow.

Sugar and spice.

I need to find out if that's what her skin tastes like.

Once I'm dressed, I grab my coat and move into the kitchen where I stop when I see a white paper folded in half, sitting next to a stainless-steel mint green Sweet Temptations tumbler and a blueberry muffin. I pick up the paper, my hand brushing the hot tumbler.

Sam,

I'm not sure what happened last night to make you call, but I'm glad you did.

I missed you. I heard everything you said. Thank you for respecting me enough to not push harder. We'll talk tonight.

XO - Snow

Back at my place, I have just enough time to shower, shave, and throw on clothes before I have to be at Pop's restaurant Saprorito. He owns a few different places in the city. But this is his favorite. It also doesn't open to the public until four o'clock, so when I walk through the door, it's just Pop, his driver, and a few members of the staff getting ready for the shift.

He rises from his favorite booth in the back corner and reaches his arms out to me. One thick arm wraps around my shoulder as he squeezes. "You did well, Samuel. Today we speak of only good things with your brother."

"You're gonna have to tell him at some point, Pop." I leave off the part that Bash deserves to know the truth. We've kept him in the dark enough these past few years. He's gonna be pissed today when Pop tells him what's actually been going on this whole time.

Happy that it's over but mad as hell we kept him out of the loop.

That was a business decision.

He doesn't deserve to be left out of this.

This isn't *Family* business. This is just family.

Pop pours us wine from the family's vineyard in Calabria, and we start going over what happens after lunch today. Pop's meeting with Sabatini this afternoon. He wants Uncle Nick and me with him for the meeting. We go over how it will be handled one more time before Bash drags his ass through the door with a strange expression on his face.

Pensive.

He pulls a chair over to sit at the end of the booth.

As Pop fills him in on what was going on behind the scenes while he was under the impression he was being forced to marry Emma Sabatini, I watch Bash for his reaction.

It's not a good one.

He struggles to speak before finally settling on one question. "You used me?" His face morphs from relief to anger as that fact sets in. "Are you fucking kidding me?" Bash stands, towering over us and pushing back from the table, his chair tipping back as he stumbles to face me. "And you knew? You knew it was a sham?"

"Sebastian," my father orders Bash's attention back to him with that one word. "Your brother had his orders. You chose not to be a part of the business. These are the consequences of your actions as much as the consequences of ours. If you're angry, be angry with me. Sam didn't know at first and fought me every step of the way until I told him what my plan was and what part he needed to play in it."

"Bash—" I've never seen him this angry before.

My father cuts me off, "Sebastian, this is over as far as the three of us are concerned. I'll deal with the Sabatinis tonight. That is as much as you need to know. Now, sit back down and enjoy the food. I want to hear about med school and the draft. Sam tells me that you're considering playing professional football."

Pop changes the subject, letting us know that the business part of today's conversation is over. Pop begins talking about Sebastian's future. He's always planned on going to medical school. But that was before he knew he had options that didn't include Emma.

That could include Lenny.

Now he's free to do what he wants.

My phone vibrates in my pocket with an incoming text.

Snow: Just got done at the shop. What time are you thinking tonight?
Sam: I've got a meeting to go to after this. How does 8pm sound for dinner?
Snow: That works for me. Gives me time for a nap.

Once the meal is over and Saporito readies to open its doors, my father's driver approaches and whispers something in his ear. Pop nods his head. "Go. Be with your wife.

Let me know if she has a boy or a girl. Sam can drive me home."

I glance up from my phone. "Yeah. I got ya, Pops."

The three of us stand from the table and grab our coats.

Ready to move on to the next steps of the day.

One more meeting to get through, then dinner.

I turn to Bash. "Guess that's my cue to drive him home. I thought I'd get promoted after pulling this off. Not demoted to driver."

Pop pulls his coat on, and pops his collar. "Shut up and turn the damn car on. It's fucking freezing out. Did you see they're calling for snow this week? In fucking November? Goddamn weather is crazier than it's ever been." He pushes through the door, coughing as the cold air hits his lungs and reminding me of what we didn't discuss today.

Bash and I follow him through the door before I turn to my little brother, knowing he gets today to be happy but soon I'll have to burst his bubble and tell him what's going on with Pop's health. "We'll talk this week, Bash. Go home and celebrate because it's over. Try not to be too pissed that it happened. You got what you wanted. You got your freedom. You got your girl. And you get to choose what you want to do now. I'd say I've secured the title of brother of the fucking year."

The look he gives me tells me I may have pushed it too far. Conceding I add, "You may have helped . . . a little."

Bash's phone rings, and a picture of his roommate Murphy flashes across the screen. "Tell the dumbass to buy his own orange juice," I chide. Murph's a good kid. He's been Bash's friend for a good decade now, but I stand by the fact that their codependence isn't normal.

I laugh to myself. Then I turn around in time to hear Pop groan again about the cold weather. "I'm turning it on, Pop."

I hit the remote starter on my key fob to get the car and the heater started.

The world explodes around me.

AMELIA

I MAY HAVE SPENT A LITTLE EXTRA TIME IN THE SHOWER tonight, but in all fairness, I haven't had a reason to be quite so thorough with a razor in a really, really long time. As in years.

Not weeks.

Not months.

Years.

When Sam called last night and demanded to see me, I had no problem hanging up on him. I will never be that woman. You don't get to not speak to me for a month after you throw my life into possible chaos and then dictate to me what I have to do. Tired, half-asleep Amelia was having no part of that. But when he called me back and attempted in his own way to explain why he did what he did, I got it. Albeit reluctantly. But I got it.

Even I can be reasonable when presented with a different side of a story.

It's easy to look at this from my point of view.

He made decisions about my life without giving me a say. That will never be okay. But he did it coming from a place of caring. He did it while trying to protect me. He didn't apologize for what he did because he didn't want to lie to me and say he was sorry when he wasn't. Even tired, I get that. At least, I think I do. After we talk tonight, I'm hoping I'll still feel good about this decision because giving in last night was so damn easy. Inviting him into my bed and spending a few hours wrapped in Sam's strong arms was everything I never knew I needed.

I don't want to fall into this life because it feels easy to let someone else do the work.

When I'm ready to move forward, I want to take a running jump into my future, a future Sam may have given me by dealing with the one thing I've spent years running away from. But I don't know if I'm there yet. If I'm actually ready or if I just want to be ready.

There's a big difference between the two.

I drop my towel and walk into my bedroom to get dressed. Rummaging through my dresser drawer, I look for a bra and panty set I bought a few months ago but have since relegated to the back of the drawer. It's the kind of set you put on when you want to feel a little extra confident about yourself. Or when you think someone might see them. You don't put this on for comfort.

Once I've slipped into the black lace set, I put on my favorite dark-wash, skinny jeans, the ones that make me look like I actually have an ass. I grab a cute, lacy camisole from a hanger and rip the tags off. Yup. Never worn this before either. Man, I really need to get a life.

I finish off the look with my favorite long black-and-white striped cardigan.

Sexy, but not too revealing.

Hopefully, I don't look like I'm trying too hard.

Shit. I hear the damn phone ringing but can't find it in my room. By the time I find it hiding under the pile of my dirty work clothes I kicked in the corner, I've missed the call from Belles. Yeah. I'll call her back tomorrow when I have a clue what I want to tell her about the past twenty-four hours.

Just as I slip it into my pocket, it rings again.

It's Belles, again.

Sliding my finger across the screen, I expect to hear her

usual happy voice. What I don't expect is for Belle to be crying hysterically and for Declan's voice to be the one that greets me.

"Amelia. Are you home?" Dec's voice comes out strong, but there's an underlying tone of fear there.

"Dec, what's going on? Is Belle alright? Are the kids okay?" Oh my God. Is she losing the baby? Before I can let my thoughts wander off that cliff, Declan interrupts me.

"Amelia. We're on our way to your place. We'll be there in a minute."

"Declan. You're scaring me." I grab my keys and coat and run down the stairs. "What's going on?"

"I'm turning the corner now, Amelia. I see you. Hold on." The Infinity QX SUV comes to a screeching halt directly in front of me. Declan's window slides down, and I have a clear view of Belles, who's sitting in the passenger seat, crying. Declan looks at me, then nods to the back seat. "Get in."

Not needing to be told twice, I throw myself in the car and count to five. "Can someone please tell me what the hell is going on? Guys, I'm scared to death right now. Please tell me everyone's okay."

Belles turns her head around to look at me as Declan drives. "Amelia . . . Bash and Sam were out to lunch with their dad, and something happened. We don't have all the details yet, but there was an explosion."

"What?" I'm not fully comprehending what she's trying to tell me. "What kind of explosion? What happened? Are they alright?" I scooch forward and grab Annabelle's hand.

"Buckle your seat belt, Amelia." Declan's voice leaves no room for argument. I sit back and lock the belt in place as he takes a corner on what feels like two wheels. "All three of them were brought in to Kroydon Hills Hospital. That's all we know. Nattie and Brady are already there. But they haven't been able to get any information yet."

My world tilts on its axis, and my breath catches in my throat.

No.

This is not happening.

They're going to be fine.

They're *all* going to be fine.

Sam is going to be fine.

When we enter the hospital, we're directed to the emergency room where a nurse makes the mistake of telling Annabelle Sinclair that she can't give her any information because she's not family.

"I don't give a flying fuck whether you're supposed to tell me what's going on or not. I am his family." Belle pushes through the waiting room doors behind the desk without looking back to see that she's being followed by the pissed-off nurse. Declan reaches out, and without even seeing his hand next to her, Belle slips her fingers through his and squeezes. Everyone in the waiting room turns to see where the ruckus is coming from. But it's the sight of Bash, standing in the middle of the room, that sends Belle running. She throws her arms around his banged-up body as he stands there, surrounded by our friends.

His friends.

He gently rubs her back and kisses the top of her head. "Belles, I'm okay. I've got a little burn on my arm and a bump on my head. It's not even a concussion. I'm fine. They even cleared me to play in next week's game."

She sniffs loudly and wipes her face with her sleeve, then points her finger at him. "Don't scare me like that again. You are not allowed to get hurt. Got it?"

"Got it."

I glance around the room, surprised to see the faces I don't know outnumbering the ones I do. The Kroydon University crew are all here. I recognize the woman standing by Bash's side as Lenny Kingston. There are a few men scattered about that I've seen in my shop with Sam or Dean over the years. My heart sinks as I scan the room but don't find Sam anywhere.

I move around Belle and Dec and wait for Sebastian to look up. "Bash . . . ? They said Sam was with you." I shift from foot to foot, chewing on my thumbnail, scared to find out the answer to my question. The one I can barely bring myself to even ask. "Is he okay? Is he here?"

"He's in surgery. That's all I know." Bash's pale face falls.

Feeling like my legs are going to give out beneath me, I drop down in the seat directly behind Annabelle. "What happened?" I look around, but no one heard me. Finally, repeating myself, I force myself to ask louder, "What happened?"

"I don't know. One minute, we were walking to our cars, and I was on the phone with Murphy. The next minute, I was thrown ten feet backward through a glass window, and an ambulance was bringing me here." He turns to face Dean, who looks as shaken as I feel. "Is someone with Nonna? Does she know what's happening?"

Whatever Dean's answer is, I can't make it out. Belle sits down next to me and pulls my hand into her lap. I lean my head against her shoulder, as we sit there silently, taking everything in. Trying to block everyone else out isn't working. It's the strangest thing, but every time I look at one of the people surrounding Lenny and Bash, they look away.

Not Nattie and Brady.

Not Bash's roommates.

But the people I don't know.

Wait . . . I take it back.

I do know some of them. They must be Lenny's family. I recognize Max Kingston. He's the GM of the Philadelphia Kings. The football team Lenny's family owns. The team

Declan Sinclair plays for and his father coaches. I've seen him and his brother Becket and sister Scarlet before at the games. They all work for the Kings. They've all made appearances in Coach's box. I guess the rest of them are their siblings. I remember reading somewhere there was a ton of them. "Belles," I whisper. "What's the deal with the Kingstons? Why are they staring?"

She leans her head against mine. "They've probably just never seen me quite so loud before. They'll get over it."

Nattie Sinclair sits down on my other side as our other friends take the seats against our backs. "I think you scared the Kingstons, Belles. They keep looking over here."

"Whatever." She blows them off and rubs her baby bump. Then she takes my hand and puts it on her belly and pushes down.

Something small and strong pushes back. "Belles." I look at her in wonderment. "Was that a foot?"

Her green eyes twinkle. "Not sure yet. But I think so."

After a little while, Bash is pulled into a separate room by a doctor, and I want so badly to go back there with him. It's a reminder that I'm not Sam's family. I'm not anyone's family. Instead, I'm forced to sit tight. I don't know if they're talking about Sam or their dad.

Jesus, this sucks.

A few minutes later, Bash and Lenny return to the waiting room, and he tries to send everyone home. After a bit of pushback, the Kingstons take Lenny with them, but the rest of us surround Bash.

Dean sits down next to me and squeezes my shoulder. "Sam's gonna be okay, you know?" he whispers in my ear. "He's gotta be okay."

I look up at the usually silly Dean and force a smile. "He has to be."

The exchange is quiet.

It's just for us.

But I see Sebastian watching us as an older woman with floral scrubs and a pair of light pink Crocs comes over to speak with our group. "Mr. Beneventi, your brother's been moved to a private room. He's sleeping, but you can go in now." She looks around at the crowd surrounding Bash, then adds, "He can have two visitors at a time, but that's it. I'll be at the desk. Let me know when you're ready to go back."

"Thank you," Bash answers politely before turning to the rest of us. "Guys, I appreciate you all coming, but you should go home too. I'm gonna spend the night here."

Oh. Hell. No.

I jump to my feet and move next to Bash, ready to put up a fight if I need to. "I'm staying with you." When I turn around to say goodbye to Belles, her smile is enormous and kinda creepy, like Jack Nicholson's in *The Shining*. With a finger pointed at her, I add, "I don't want to hear a word about it from you."

I ignore the rest of the group as I walk across the room to the nurse but still manage to hear Belle tell them, "I know nothing."

Little liar.

AMELIA

WE'RE LED BACK TO SAM'S PRIVATE ROOM. IT'S DARK. THE only light is coming from the machines monitoring his heart rate and oxygen. He's asleep, tucked into a starchy looking white blanket. His handsome face is covered in cuts and bruises. The stitches above his eye are red and angry, and white gauze peaks out from the top of his hospital gown.

Readying myself for a long night, I throw my jacket down on the couch and sit on the edge of his bed, picking up his hand in mine. Then, leaning down with my face next to his, I swallow down my fear. "You don't get to tell me everything you told me last night and then get hurt like this, Sam."

A throat clears behind me. "Can I ask what's going on between you and my brother?" I completely forgot Sebastian was in the room. Shit. Way to not give him a minute with his brother, Amelia.

Trying to hide my discomfort, I move back to the couch and pull my legs up in front of me. "Nothing is going on. We're just friends."

"Friends?" His voice clearly indicates he doesn't believe me, but I don't have the energy left to care.

My eyes are drawn back to Sam. "Yes, Sebastian. Friends. Your brother has been a better friend to me than I deserve." I wad my jacket up to use as a pillow and shove it behind my head. "It shocked the hell out of me too."

Bash sits down in a horribly squeaky, vinyl recliner. "Guess we might as well get comfortable."

"Why?" Sam's raspy voice interrupts the two of us.

Bash jumps up before I can and moves next to the bed. "Hey, you're awake."

"Leave it to the smart ones to always state the obvious," Sam says, barely above a whisper.

I pour him a cup of water from a nearby pitcher and add a straw before holding it up to his lips. "Don't try to sit up yet. Just take little sips."

The infuriating man refuses to listen to me, tries to sit up, and then winces in pain. Sebastian moves to the other side of the bed. "Wait, you stubborn ass. Let me adjust the bed. It'll be easier for you." He grabs the remote and pushes a button to raise the back of Sam's bed.

"Could you two stop fussing over me? I'm okay," Sam groans, trying to take the plastic cup from my hand but wincing at the small movement.

"Really convincing, Sam." I pull the cup away from him and move the straw back to his lips. "Let us help." I stop talking before the tremble I feel in my voice is audible. Then I quietly add, "We were worried about you."

"Sam—" Bash starts but is cut off by Sam.

"Where's Dad?"

"He's still in surgery. We haven't gotten any news yet. Dean and a few of the others are still in the waiting room."

"The house. Who's at the house with Nonna?" Sam asks.

"Uncle Nick has it under control," Bash tells him, and I begin to feel like an outsider who shouldn't be here.

Maybe this is a family matter.

Maybe I should have stayed in the waiting room.

A disgusted noise leaves Sam's throat. "Nick doesn't have shit under control. Get Dean in here. I need to talk to him."

Just when I start to think seriously about excusing myself, Sam reaches for my hand. "I need you to go home. Don't go to your home. I need you to go to my father's home. It's the safest place for you right now."

"No." I sit back down on the couch and cross my arms. Then, with my mind made up, I add, "I'm staying. Don't bother arguing. You won't win, Sam."

"Amelia, don't argue with me. Haven't I kept you safe? I promised you I would, and I've kept my promise." There's an urgency in Sam's voice. "Now, listen to me and go to the house. Go. Tell Nonna that Bash will be there soon."

Bash turns to me, a shocked expression on his face. "You know Nonna?" His eyes bounce between Sam and me. "She knows Nonna? What the hell's going on, Sam?"

"I don't know, little brother. But there's a whole lot going on that you can't know. Now go. Get Dean—" Sam is cut off by a knock on the door.

A surgeon in navy blue scrubs comes in. "Mr. Beneventi's family?"

"That's us, Doc," Sam tells him, and Bash and I move to stand on either side of the bed. Instinctively, I reach for Sam's hand.

The surgeon pulls his surgical cap off his head, his tired eyes failing to hide his exhaustion. "Your father was unconscious when he arrived at the hospital. He'd suffered trauma to his head, chest, and abdomen from the explosion. He took shrapnel to his head and chest. We did everything we could but were unable to stop the bleeding from his liver. I'm sorry to tell you that your father didn't make it through surgery."

Sam's fingers tighten around mine.

The surgeon continues, "If there's anything you need, please let the nurse know. If you need any questions answered, she has my contact info. Again, I'm sorry for your loss." He slips quietly out of the room, having just changed Sam and Bash's lives forever.

"Bash . . . Bash." Sam grabs Sebastian's hand and pulls him in closer. Sebastian looks dazed, but Sam's gotten his attention. "Sebastian. Go get Dean. Get him now. Bring Sal back with you too."

No sooner has the door shut behind Bash than Sam's stern voice cuts through the thick air. "Don't argue with me. You need to go to the house. Sal will drive you. I'll be there as soon as I can get out of here."

I sit back down on the bed next to him and resist the urge to cup his face in my hands. Instead, I shove them under my legs. "You have to stay here where they can watch you, Sam. You just lost your father. Don't make me lose you."

"Snow . . ."

It's the tone of his voice that does me in. The one word says everything I need to hear. "I'll go to the house if you promise me that you'll stay here. Let them take care of you."

He tries to reach up with his hand, but the IV gets in the way. Instead, I lift his hand to my lips, kiss his raw knuckles, and then press them to my cheek.

"I can't take care of everything else if I'm worried about you, Amelia. Go to the house. Stay with Nonna. Bash will be home soon, and he can tell her what's going on. But you can keep her company, and I'll know you're safe."

I carefully lay down and tuck myself into his side. "Can we go back to last night? Just hit rewind? Maybe take back the last month of wasted time?"

Sam kisses my head, and we stay like that until Dean and Bash walk through the door.

Once Bash comes back into the room with Dean following behind, I can tell it's time for me to leave. I begrudgingly stand from the bed and grab my coat just as Dean throws an arm over my shoulder. "You doin' okay, Amelia? You need anything?"

I squeeze him back and muster my strength. "No. I'm fine. Just make sure this one stays here for me." Motioning to Sam, I add, "Free cookies for a week if you manage to keep him here."

Sam groans, and Bash's mouth might as well hit the floor, it hangs open so wide. "What? Are the three of you like a throuple or something?"

I wouldn't have believed it if I wasn't hearing it myself, but Sam actually growls like an animal at Bash's suggestion. Dean laughs like it's the funniest thing he's ever heard, and I smack the back of Bash's head the way Belle always does. "Get your mind out of the gutter, Sebastian. Not everything is about sex."

"But it could be, Snow White." Dean slides his hand down my back but gets stopped by Sam.

"Get your hands off her, shithead. You don't get to call her that." If looks could kill, Dean would be incinerated before Sam continues, "Where's Sal? He needs to take her directly to the house and make sure Uncle Nick has everything set before he leaves." The unspoken words float through the otherwise quiet room.

Is the house secured?

Was the car bomb the only act of violence set to happen today?

"I gotcha, Sam. Sal is waiting outside the door. He knows what to do."

And just like that. Sam is in business mode. I lean down and kiss a cut on his cheek, whispering, "Stay here. Let them take care of you. I stay safe, you stay safe. Got it?"

His free hand slides up to my cheek and pulls my lips

down to his. "Soon, Snow. Go with Sal. Stay at the house. I'll be there soon."

I vaguely hear Bash mutter, "Just friends, my ass," before I'm escorted out of the hospital and back to the Beneventi compound.

The drive to Sam's dad's house is made in silence and takes less than ten minutes. Kroydon Hills really is that small of a town, on the outskirts of Philadelphia. It's one of the reasons I picked this place to start my new life. The city was close enough for blending in, but the town was tiny enough that I thought I'd be able to protect myself more. Be more aware of everyone around me.

And what do I do with my desire to stay safe?

I fall for the son of a mob boss.

A now dead mob boss.

Is now the time? Is it time to run . . . before things get worse?

We drive down Main Street.

Past Sweet Temptations and Hart & Soul Academy of Dance.

We drive past Belle and Declan's neighborhood.

We drive past my friends' homes, past our businesses, and into Sam's father's compound.

Is this my future?

Old oak trees line either side of the long driveway. Men are stationed on either side of the closed black wrought iron gate. Sal rolls down his window as we pull to a stop. "Sam sent me. I've got Amelia with me."

The guard lifts a phone to his face as he turns away from us momentarily. Then he nods his head toward Sal and opens the gate.

Sal slowly drives us toward the huge house looming in the distance. "Listen, Amelia, you need to understand that everyone's going to be on edge tonight."

Annoyed, I glare at the older man inching slowly down the driveway. "How often do you come into my shop, Sal? Once a week? More?"

He pulls the car to a stop and opens his door, letting the cold air whip in. "What's your point?"

I get out of the car and shut my door with a little extra emphasis. "In all the time you've spent in my shop, have I ever given you the impression that I need to be handled? Do I look like a stupid woman? I may not have known Sam and Bash's father to be mourning him the way everyone here is, but I know Sam and Bash. I don't want to be here, but this is where Sam needs me right now. So I'm going to go inside that house, find a bedroom, and stay put. Don't worry about me. I know everyone has other things to deal with tonight, and trust me, I don't want to get in the way."

I storm up to the front door feeling slightly better, thanks to my dramatic exit, until I try to open the massive arching door.

It's locked.

I should just go home.

Back to my apartment.

Better yet, back to the hospital . . . to sleep in the chair in Sam's room.

But that's not an option. Instead, I wait for Sal to walk up the steps and stand by my side. He pulls his phone out to send a text before the front door opens with Marco standing on the other side. "Hi, Miss Amelia. Do you have anything you need me to take for you?"

I breathe in deeply, trying to keep my calm. "What did I say about the 'Miss Amelia' thing, Marco? Please. Just call me

Amelia. And no, thank you. I was ordered here without anything from my apartment. So just point me in the direction of a guest room, and I'll get out of everyone's hair."

Marco and Sal have a silent conversation before I'm instructed to follow Marco up the stairs. He walks me down a long hallway before opening the last door. "I was told you were to sleep in here . . ." Marco pauses, then forces himself to say, "Amelia," without adding the "Miss" to it.

When I step through the door, I'm struck by the fact that this is most likely Sam's room. Or at least, it was Sam's room when he was younger. A picture of a tween-age Sam and a smiling woman I'm guessing is his mother sits on his dresser. I know he doesn't live here now, but this room has been lived in. The furniture is a beautiful but worn rich wood. A king-sized bed covered in a black and grey comforter sits off to the right with a sitting area and a fireplace off to the left. Wow. He was a kid, and his room was the size of my apartment. I turn to thank Marco, but he hasn't set foot in the room and instead is staying on the other side of the door.

"Thank you, Marco. Has anyone checked on Nonna?"

He shoves his hands in his pockets and looks anywhere but at me. "Nonna's sleeping. She knows something's going on but doesn't know what. I'm supposed to make sure you know to make yourself comfortable. Don't feel like you're stuck in this room. You have the run of the house. Just stay away from the office. Nick just left, but he should be back tomorrow. I'll be downstairs all night if you need anything." He looks around the room one more time, then shuts the door.

With all my adrenaline slowly seeping out of my body, I curl up on the bed, disappointed that Sam's scent doesn't linger on the pillows, and text Lyla that I won't be at the shop tomorrow.

Once that's done, I lie in bed, thinking about the events of the weekend and wonder how I went from being so angry with Sam Friday night to sleeping in his childhood bed on Sunday.

And how I'm ever going to sleep without him again.

AMELIA

WHEN YOU'RE USED TO LIVING ALONE, TRYING TO SLEEP IN A noisy house, and worse, an unfamiliar place, is unnerving. Kroydon Hills is a surprisingly sleepy suburb of the city. My street isn't busy at night, so I'm used to a certain set of noises.

What I'm not used to is people moving around all night long. I can't ignore the hushed voices talking at two a.m. or the not-so-hushed ones drifting up the stairs sometime around four-thirty. I spent hours counting the rotations of the ceiling fan, willing myself unsuccessfully to fall asleep. When that failed miserably, I started counting the different masculine voices floating through the halls.

Uttering words like "retribution," "retaliation," and "act of war."

Then there was a new voice added to the mix this morning. A feminine voice.

I guess Nonna is up.

What I didn't hear was Bash coming in.

I guess Sam didn't have a problem letting him stay at the hospital.

When I finally give in and get out of bed, I'm tired and cranky. I don't exactly smell amazing, and one look in the mirror tells me I look like I haven't slept in days. I'm tempted to say screw it and leave. Just go home. Shower in my own shower with my own shampoo and be baking cookies in Sweet Temptations before the morning rush is over. But I promised Sam I'd stay.

Damn it.

Taking a quick peek around the bathroom, I find shampoo and conditioner. It's the good stuff too. No wonder this man's hair always looks amazing. Inhaling deeply, I close my eyes and let Sam's scent relax me. Fresh and crisp and all man.

A hot shower and an old tube of toothpaste have me feeling brave enough to search through the walk-in closet for something I can wear that might be a little more comfortable than the clothes I picked so carefully for my date last night. No need for my boobs to be on display for Nonna today. Luckily for me, tucked in the far corner of the closet is an old plastic bin full of clothes I'm guessing high-school Sam owned.

Jackpot. There's an old faded Kroydon Prep hoodie and sweats.

Guess this will have to do today.

When I slip it over my head, I relax in the soft material and try to picture a teenage Sam wearing it, but I can't.

There's no surprise to be had when I make my way through this giant maze of a house to find every chef's dream of a kitchen and come across Nonna taking a batch of biscotti out of the oven. I thought that's what I smelled, but I wasn't sure.

She places the hot tray down on her eight-burner Viking range, and I think I may weep with how much I want that in my kitchen one day. Nonna reaches her arms out for me, gripping my shoulders tightly until I lean over and let her kiss my cheeks. "Principessa. Sit. I have fresh biscotti."

She doesn't ask me any questions about why I'm here.

Why I'm in Sam's old clothes.

Or even where Sam is.

I don't think she's oblivious. Just the opposite.

I think she's aware something is very wrong and is waiting to be filled in.

She doesn't need to ask. She already knows.

We sit, chatting about baking, something we both love. And cooking, something I'm not very good at but Nonna is convinced she can help me with.

I guess with a kitchen like this at your disposal, why not?

Lifting the cookie to my lips, I take a small bite and let the taste explode in my mouth. It's exquisite. Crispy on the outside, but it somehow melts in your mouth. A touch of almond and something I can't quite place coming together perfectly.

"Of course, it is, principessa. These are not recipes that can be found in books. Bring me to your kitchen one day. Let me see you work. Let this old woman feel useful again. I may even share a recipe or two." Nonna fills our coffee cups, then sits back down next to me at the table.

Our quiet morning is interrupted when Bash's bulldog, Butkus, comes trotting into the kitchen, letting us know Sebastian is home. He marches over to Nonna on stubby little legs and starts whining until she gets up and finds him his puppy treats she's got hidden away in the pantry. Once Butkus is happy, she offers Bash a contented smile. "Prupetta. Come. Come. There are biscotti for everyone."

An awkward laugh bubbles up in my throat. "He looks more like a string bean than a meatball, Nonna," I raise my eyes to Sebastian's and find a surprised smile. I don't think he expected me to understand Italian. After a moment, that silly smile disappears from his face. Knowing what needs to happen next, I excuse myself to call Lyla, wanting to give Bash and his grandmother some privacy.

He doesn't need an audience for the news he has to share.

No one should ever have to bury their child. No matter their age.

I usually love having a few hours with nothing to do. It doesn't happen often when you run your own business. Work doesn't stop just because I'm not baking, and when it does, there's always something. Laundry. A football game. Dinner at Belle's house or a girls' night out. But today, while I sit in this room, feeling slightly claustrophobic simply because I know I'm not supposed to leave, I'm not enjoying it.

I've tried to get lost in my favorite fantasy world for the last few hours, but it isn't working. I've read the same chapter about the werewolf rejecting his mate at least three times, and other than him being an asshole, I couldn't tell you anything else about it.

Staring at the book open on my phone, I contemplate toggling over to my contact list and calling Dean. I haven't seen Sebastian since this morning, and I need someone to tell me what's going on or I swear to God, I'm stealing someone's keys and driving myself to the hospital. But then, just when I've reached my limit and am about to abandon this ship, I hear voices downstairs.

Specifically, I hear one very distinct voice telling someone he doesn't need help.

He might not need it now, but he's going to in a minute when I kill him.

So much for keeping up his end of the bargain.

My legs carry me down the stairs so quickly, my feet don't feel the carpet beneath my toes. When I get to the bottom step, I'm met by a tired-looking Marco.

"Ma'am," he stutters. Hesitance evident in his weary eyes.

"Don't even think about it, Marco. Where is he?" I'm ready to bulldoze through this man if that's what it takes to find Sam.

When I move to pass him, he moves with me, effectively blocking my path. "Miss Amelia, I can't let you . . ."

Yeah, I don't think so. "Marco. I like you. You're a sweet guy. But if you don't move the hell out of my way, I'm going to scream at the top of my lungs. And we both know if I scream, Sam will be here immediately." I raise my brows. "What do you think he'll do then?"

The color drains from his face.

"Now," I smile sweetly, "move." I push past him, not waiting for his answer and follow the sound of Sam's voice down the hall before bumping into Nonna.

I can tell from the look on her face she's not thrilled with Sam's choices at the moment either. But unlike me, she's allowed to leave and is heading to church.

After contemplating whether to stow away in the back of her car, I continue down the hall, forcing myself to slow down and peek inside the office rather than slamming the door open like I want to.

"Come in, Snow. I know you're there." Sam's voice is still scratchy from the anesthesia, and I'm betting, lack of sleep.

When I walk through the door, Sam and Dean both stare at me.

Dean is standing on the other side of the room, still wearing the same rumpled suit from yesterday. His honey-brown hair is sticking up, and dark circles are heavy under his eyes. Doesn't look like anyone got any sleep last night.

Sam is seated behind the massive wooden desk in sweat-pants and a t-shirt. His complexion is dull, and the cuts and stitches are a stark contrast to his pale skin.

I walk slowly into the room, taking my time and trying to control my words.

My mother used to tell me to choose my words and use my words.

It's worth a try.

I cross the room and lean against the desk, facing this beautiful, stupid man and allow my voice to betray my emotions for one brief moment. "What happened to 'I stay safe, you stay safe'?" The words come out on a whisper while my hands move gently through his hair and trace his face.

"Snow . . ." Sam's hand reaches out for me, but I smack it away.

"Are you fucking stupid, Samuel?" Guess I chose my words.

"I—" he starts to answer.

"I don't want to hear anything you have to say," I cut him off. "You were supposed to stay in the goddamn hospital. What were you thinking?" I push off the desk and move out of reach. "You said you'd stay safe. This isn't safe, genius. Did a doctor say it was safe for you to leave the hospital?"

When Sam doesn't answer, I push harder. "Well, did he? Because I'm guessing not."

He leans his head back against the chair and closes his eyes. "Are you going to let me speak?"

With my arms crossed over my chest, I stare at him without opening my mouth.

Inside, I'm calling him a dumbass.

But I'm trying with all my might to let him speak before I explode.

His eyes open, looking at me through heavy lids.

Then this frustrating man smiles, and I lose any semblance of control.

"Sam . . ." I scream, unable to help myself.

"Stop yelling, Snow. My head fucking hurts, and there's too much going on. It's safer here."

"Safer, my ass." This man infuriates me!

The door, which I hadn't realized had been shut after Dean snuck out of the room, cracks open, and Bash walks in behind me. I throw my hands in the air. "Maybe you can talk some sense into him," I grate out before storming out and slamming the door closed.

Dean is standing at the island in the kitchen with a plastic bag from the pharmacy that's two doors down from my shop in front of him.

I march over and try to grab the bag before it's pulled out of reach. "You okay, Amelia?"

"Did you have to let him check himself out?" My voice softens.

Defeated.

Dean laughs, a half-assed laugh. "Have you ever been able to tell Sam what to do? Because I haven't, and I've known him all my life." Satisfied with his answer, he hands me the bag. "All his meds are in there. I think he's supposed to take a few of them now. I could be wrong though." He leans over and kisses me on the cheek. "Don't kill him, okay? I'll be back."

With a glass of water in one hand and his bag of medication in the other, I walk back into Sam's office in time to hear him telling Bash, "I signed myself out. Dean has a nurse coming to the house who's going to stay with us for a few days, just until I'm up and moving. I can't be in that fucking hospital. Not when there's so much to do here."

"You're a stubborn pain in the ass. You know that, right?" Bash's voice does a lousy job of hiding his annoyance. "You willing to sleep in Dad's room? It's the only bedroom on this floor other than Nonna's. And I don't think you can walk up the stairs tonight."

"Stop worrying about me, little brother. I'm paying a nurse to do that."

He's doing what? "Oh, yeah? Where is this nurse? I don't see anyone here, Sam." I place the water in front of him and a bag of prescriptions on the desk. "Give me a minute to go through these. Dean didn't have a clue what you should be taking and when." My eyes focus on the stitches above his eye. "Did you eat anything? It looks like you need to eat with some of these pills. Nonna mentioned earlier she has minestrone soup in the fridge."

Sam's fingers circle my wrist, stopping me. "Where is Nonna? How is she handling everything?"

"Well—" Bash starts to answer, but I cut him off as I pull my hand free.

"She's at church, praying for your stupid ass. When she told me she was going, I tried to talk her into staying home. I told her your father wouldn't want her going out right now to pray for him."

When I turn, it's to see Bash staring at me in shock. "How well do you know Nonna?"

"Wanna know what she told me?" I ask Sam, completely ignoring Bash's question. "She told me she wasn't going to church to pray for him. She was going to pray for the two of *you*. I don't know what exactly she's praying for, but I hope it's for God to bless you with some common fucking sense." When Sam smiles at my tirade, I spin on my heels and stomp out of the room before I kill him myself.

SAM

Amelia storms out of the office after telling me off, leaving me to watch that heart-shaped ass of hers. All I can think is that I'm going to make that woman my wife as soon as I can get this fucking situation under control.

With the surgery I had last night and the swirling pit of shit my life is in right now, I shouldn't be sporting a dick that's as hard as steel, but sure as fuck, I am. Watching that beautiful flaming red crawl up her creamy white skin has me wanting to bend her over this desk and smack her ass hard enough to see my handprint there while I'm fucking her. It's not until Sebastian speaks that I'm pulled back from the spell Snow just cast over me.

"Damn. When did Amelia become the type to yell? And how did I get lumped into that outburst?" Bash is staring at the open door, his mouth hanging wide open in shock.

Not sure how to answer that, I sort through my pills and swallow a handful. "There's so much you don't know, Bash."

"About that . . ." Bash closes the door and sits down across from me. "I had breakfast with Lenny's family yesterday," a muscle ticks in his jaw as he adds, "before we met for lunch." He leaves off before the explosion that killed Pop. "Have you ever talked to Amelia about her childhood?"

Well, fuck.

Maybe Bash knows more than I thought. "We're not talking about this, Sebastian."

"We have to, Sam. I told Max—"

"Stop. Don't finish your sentence. Before I talk to you about this, I need to talk to Amelia." Over the course of the last twenty-four fucking hours, I managed to forget that I needed to tell Amelia that she has an entire family who's actively looking for her. "She doesn't know anything. And my plate's a little full. Give me a few days, man. I can't do this with you now. Not today. Not because of Max Fucking Kingston."

Bash leans forward in the chair and picks up the framed picture of Mom that's sat on this desk for years. He studies it for a minute, then looks at me. "They're together now. Mom and Pop." He places it back down in its spot and stands up. "Do what you gotta do but know that they've involved Uncle Dino. I'll hold them off for as long as I can."

"Thanks, little brother. Listen, I need you here this week. We don't know who set that bomb. We don't know if it was meant for me or if there's more planned. Let me figure out what the fuck's going on before you go home. Okay?" I know this isn't what he wants to hear, but he knows it's the right thing. It's not just to keep him safe. It'll keep everyone around him safe too.

That's Bash's MO.

He's the protector.

He'd never willingly put anyone else at risk.

"I gotcha, man. I'm here till the funeral. Then I'm going back to my life. This . . . This isn't my life. It's yours." He reaches for the door, but I stop him.

"Bash." He doesn't turn. Doesn't look at me. "We'll talk to Sabatini at the funeral. You've got to give me till then. Just a few more days."

Sebastian nods his head and walks out of the office.

I owe it to him to get this handled.

To keep him safe.

I go to grab my cell phone from my pocket but then

remember it blew the fuck up with my car. Eyeing the landline Pop always kept on his desk, I wonder briefly how long it's been since I've picked one of these up. Muscle memory has me dialing Uncle Nick's number. I hear the phone ringing in my ear but also ringing in the hall right before Nick walks through the office door. "Tell me what you've got."

He slams the door shut behind him, throws his coat on the back of the couch across the room, and sits down in front of me. "Our people reached out to the Commission. New York says this wasn't sanctioned. We've had ears to the street since last night. Nobody's talking. Nobody's taking credit. None of these cocksuckers know a fucking thing." Uncle Nick has been Pop's consigliere my entire life, a position I plan to keep him in.

I want Dean to take over as underboss.

He needs to be me.

But I've got to get this shit dealt with first.

"I don't give a fuck who you have to torture. Call in every fucking favor. Turn over every fucking stone. Get me a name. Find this motherfucker. And bring him to me alive. I want to look him in the eye before I kill him myself."

When Dean enters the room, he throws a new cell phone down on my desk. "I dropped some clothes in your room upstairs too."

"Thanks, man. Now get Mike on the phone. Let's see if he's found anything."

Mike answers on the first ring. "Listen, I'm searching everything I can find. But it takes time, Sam, and the blast knocked out the cameras around the restaurant. I've put everything else on hold, and I'm only working on this. I should have something soon." The sound of Mike's fingers flying across a keyboard is the only noise heard in the room.

"There can't be a 'should' with this one, Mike. I need this

information, and I need it now. Call me when you've got something for me." I hang up the phone, no closer to an answer than I was this morning.

When someone knocks on the door later that afternoon, the three of us yell in sync for them to go away before the door creaks open and Amelia enters with a tray of food.

My girl walks into this room full of killers with her back straight and head held high.

She cowers to no man. "Sorry to interrupt. But Sam needs to take his medicine, and he hasn't eaten anything all day." She places the tray down on the credenza under the window, then hands me a fresh glass of water. "Your nurse is here." She eyes Dean with one brow raised as he reaches for a sandwich.

Dean pulls his hand back and mutters, "Sorry."

Snow continues, "He's asking questions I don't have answers to."

Nick stands. "I think we're good for now, Sam. What do you guys think?"

"I'm good. I know what I've got to do," Dean adds.

"Okay. Meet back here tomorrow morning." I tell them.

Uncle Nick sizes up Amelia. "Any chance one of those sandwiches is for me?"

She smiles at him, her brown eyes sparkling. "Take whatever you want. We made plenty."

"Got any cookies?" Dean asks, licking his lips like a fucking dog.

She nods. "Yeah. There are chocolate chip cookies in the kitchen."

"Hey. Don't give him my cookies." I pull on the pocket of her hoodie. "I don't share."

She takes a step back from me. "And I don't make cookies for men who should still be in the hospital."

Uncle Nick whistles, surprised by the way she just spoke to me.

Probably impressed.

The fucker.

Amelia glances his way, then softens her tone. "Whatever." She plants her hands on her hips and glares, and my cock jumps to attention. "I made them for you anyway. I think you can manage to share. Besides, the guys who have been here since yesterday have been eating them all afternoon. I made enough to stock the bakery for days. So there'll be plenty left for you, Sam."

She baked for my men.

Jesus. I glance over to the guys. "You good?"

They both agree and go on the hunt for cookies. My fucking cookies.

Dean shuts the door behind him, and I slump a little in my chair, allowing my muscles to relax for the first time today. The move is small. Insignificant. But Snow notices.

Stepping back into me, she turns and sits on the edge of the desk. "Sam. You've got to stop. You shouldn't even be home, and you're pushing yourself way too hard."

How have I been so oblivious that I haven't noticed before now? She's wearing my old clothes. I run both hands slowly up the outside of her thighs. Knowing I've never touched her like this before, I enjoy the sudden intake of her breath. No hiding that reaction. "Where'd you find these?" A slow smile appears on her face. "I like seeing you in my clothes."

She doesn't push me off like I'm expecting her to. Instead, her hands rest on mine. "They were in the back of your closet in a bin. I don't have any clothes here, Sam. I'm going to need to go home."

My gut instinct is to tell her no, but I hold that in check. "Amelia. Please don't make me be a dick." Well, I tried.

She laughs at me. "A wise man once asked me if anyone could make Sam Beneventi do something he didn't want to do." She leans in closer to my ear. Her warm breath, a caress against my skin. "I've got a business to run, Sam. The world isn't stopping because of all this." Amelia motions to the room around us. "I have to go home."

I move my hands to the desk and stand up, forcing her to lift her head to meet my eyes. My hands move to either side of her face and hold her there. "I need you here. With me. Please, Snow."

The words are out before I have time to think about them.

I've never needed anyone before.

Not like this.

"You've got me, Sam. But I have a shop to run. Send someone with me if you have to, but I'm going to work tomorrow." Her fingers wrap around my wrists and hold my hands in place. "But I'll stay here tonight, and I'll come back once I'm done if that's what you need."

Jesus. This woman.

My mouth crashes down on hers.

There's nothing tentative or sweet about this kiss.

It's life and death.

It's fire and ice.

It's everything that's ever been between us in one fucking kiss.

Amelia wraps her arms around my back, her hands resting on the staples from my incision, and the sudden pain is a white heat shooting through my body. When I step back on a painful hiss, she realizes what happened, and I swear she looks like she wants to cry.

"Oh my God, Sam. I'm so sorry. I didn't think." Her eyes well up, and our moment is over.

"Soon, Snow."

She turns away from me and starts going through the medicine bottles on my desk. Once she's got what she was looking for, she hands me a few pills and a new glass of water.

When I glare at her fussing over me, this feisty woman rolls her eyes. "Fine. I'll stop for now. Besides, Nonna's been asking to see you." Amelia steps away, opens the door, and stands like a sentry, waiting for me to follow her. "Sam," She turns back to face me, determination shining in her eyes. "I'll stay. I'll stay tonight and come back tomorrow night after the shop closes. But I'm going to Sweet Temptations, one way or another. Please don't make it more difficult than it has to be. Let me go, and I'll come back."

AMELIA

THE HOUSE HAS ITS OWN HEARTBEAT.

The mood changes.

The energy changes.

People come and go. Escorted in and out by Sam's men. Never alone.

Some I recognize. Others I don't.

Some bring food. Some bring flowers. Most come under the guise of paying their respects to Nonna. But all of them want a piece of Sam. The poor nurse Dean hired looked petrified all afternoon. He tried a few times to get Sam to rest, but the stubborn man wouldn't listen.

I don't know how Sam's lasted all day, but he has. He's survived through a meeting with his priest and endured a meeting with the funeral home director. Then, he sat through an afternoon of closed-door meetings with his men, his uncle, and Dean.

It's never-ending.

Daniel, the nurse, stayed with me in the kitchen most of the afternoon before quitting sometime around eight when Sam refused to listen to his orders to rest.

Bash and I are sitting at the kitchen table, each with a bottle of beer and a bowl of Nonna's soup in front of us. A loaf of fresh bread just out of the oven is sliced and sitting between us when Dean comes back for the evening. Judging by his lack of stubble and damp hair, he's showered and changed into a different Armani suit. He moves behind Bash, grabs a piece of the bread, and dips it in Bash's soup like a child with a devilish expression on his face.

Bash throws an elbow and catches Dean in the gut, causing him to double over, gasping for breath. I slide my bowl and beer away from the two overgrown children and wonder if this is what having siblings, or hell, even cousins, must be like. They remind me of the Sinclairs.

I strain to see down the hallway when I hear the now-familiar squeak of the office door opening, trying to get a peek at the latest visitor before he's escorted out of the house.

Dean straightens and moves toward the office, but I jump in front of him, "Oh no, you don't." I place a palm on his chest. "Listen to me. The nurse quit. Sam hasn't stopped once today. Can it wait? Because he needs to rest."

Sebastian chokes on his beer, and Dean smirks, then covers my hand with his. "Oh yeah, Amelia . . . ? You gonna play nurse now?"

"Get your fucking hands off her."

Oops.

Sam's voice sounds lethal, causing Dean to drop his hand immediately, taking two steps back.

"We were just kidding, Sammy." He looks at Bash and me as if we can help him now.

Sebastian stands with our bowls and deposits them in the sink before striding across the kitchen to stand between Sam and Dean. "Dean, you got anything that can't wait till tomorrow, man?"

Dean eyes Bash warily. "Nah. I was checking in. Wanted to see if you guys needed anything. I'm meeting with a few of the men later tonight to see what they've got for us."

Bash nods then turns to Sam. "You good if we tell everyone to get out now? Anyone who's not staying the night?"

"Yeah." Sam looks from Bash to me. "You ready to go to bed?"

"Yup." I start cleaning up dinner. "Want me to bring anything upstairs for you to eat?" The look he gives me leaves no room for guessing what he'd like to eat tonight, but I picked Daniel's brain as delicately as I could manage earlier and was given strict instructions that specifically included no exertion for the next five days.

Bash glares at Dean. "Night, Dean."

Dean leaves, muttering something about baby doctors growing balls, and the three of us laugh once the front door shuts.

"Fucking asshole." Sam coughs. "Don't make me laugh. It hurts."

Bash moves to put one of Sam's arms over his shoulder, but Sam pulls away.

"Sammy, you fired the nurse. You look like you're seconds from falling over. You had major fucking surgery yesterday and have ten fucking staples in your back. Let me help you." Bash says his piece much more nicely than I did earlier.

When he looks at me instead of answering his brother, I add, "If you want me in your bed tonight, let him help you."

Sebastian looks between Sam and me. "Friends share beds?"

I start to answer, but Sam beats me to it. "Don't act like you and Murphy haven't slept in the same bed."

"Amelia's hotter than Murphy." Bash points at me and then at the bag of pills and medical supplies Daniel left earlier.

"Aww. I really feel the love, Sebastian," I mock, then grab the bag. "Now, let's get the world's worst patient upstairs."

Sam's eyes dance between Bash and me as he shakes his head. "You know, people were here, pledging their loyalty and respect to me all day, right?"

I force Sam's other arm over my shoulder, then answer. "I don't see any of them volunteering to give you a sponge bath, Sam. So unless you want me to call Dean back to help with that, listen to your brother."

My threat worked.

Well, it kinda worked.

Sam let Bash help him up the stairs. He could have slept in his father's room on the first floor, but he refused. So instead, I got to watch this man with staples in his back take the steps one at a time, trying to not lean on Bash as much as possible.

Why are men so stubborn?

I really don't think it's only this one.

Apparently, Dean had stopped by Sam's apartment earlier today and packed him a bag. I didn't actually give him a sponge bath, but I did have to clean and redress his incision. Nursing is not for me. Staples in skin are not for the faint of heart.

Ha. Faint of heart.

That's not something I've ever considered as a description for myself before.

But it fits tonight.

Once Bash turns in for the night, and I've got Sam comfortable and a little doped up on pain pills, I hop in the shower, knowing I have to be at the shop in five hours to get everything going for the day. I stole one of Sam's t-shirts from his bag to slip into after my shower. The worn cotton sits softly on my bare skin. And I do mean bare. It's not like I even have an extra pair of panties with me.

This certainly isn't how I imagined this weekend going.

I sort of expected to end up panty-less at some point, but not like this.

When I walk back into the bedroom, Sam is asleep on top of the blanket in black boxer briefs, and I'm taken aback all over again at the burns covering so much of his body. The strength it must have taken to do what he did today is unimaginable to me.

I pad over to the bed and pull the blanket up over him before turning off the light and getting in myself. Once the alarm on my phone is set, and I've sent a quick text confirming with Marco that he'll be driving me to Sweet Temptations in a few hours, I settle in next to Sam, lying on my side to face him but making sure not to touch him.

Sam's cobalt blue eyes open, and his hand slides up my hip. "We need to talk, Snow." His tired voice pulls at my heart.

I move my head next to his shoulder. Not on it but close enough to be engulfed by his body heat. "Not tonight. Sleep, Sam. Your body needs to heal, and it needs sleep for that. We can talk tomorrow when I get back."

Sam turns his head and kisses my hair. "Tomorrow."

As I lie here next to this man, talking about what we did wrong doesn't seem all that important anymore.

He's alive.

He's next to me.

And I'm pretty sure he's mine.

AMELIA

MARCO BROUGHT ME HOME THIS MORNING WITH JUST ENOUGH time to run upstairs and change before I had to be in the shop and baking. It's a Tuesday, so I made the mistake of assuming it would be a slow day because it's usually our slowest day of the week.

You know what they say about assuming...

Today was the absolute opposite of slow.

Lyla and I were slammed from the second we opened the door and throughout the entire morning. Thank goodness, I had Lyla working. When she leaves for her class around noon, I contemplate closing the shop for the day. Maybe just cut the hours back a little this week. I have a new person starting next week to help with the baking. I advertised for the position at the culinary institute and got a few great candidates, but none of them came close to Brooklynn. She's a senior, and she's amazing. With a little extra effort, I was able to help her get this approved for internship credits. She's going to lighten my load.

At least I hope she is.

I wish she was starting this week.

Or even better—last week.

When Annabelle stops by in the afternoon, she's without the twins. "Hey, where are my favorite girls?"

"I left them at home with Lexi today. I'm a little nervous. It's the first time I've left her alone with the girls since we hired her." She absentmindedly rubs her baby bump as she stares at the coffee brewing behind me. "Got any fresh decaf?"

"Nope. But I'll make some for you if you've got a minute." I start the process before she even answers, knowing what she's going to say.

"How are Bash and Sam doing? Have you seen them?" Belles looks around the shop, her eyes scanning the few random customers taking up the tables. Then she leans in, whispering, "Isn't that a Kingston over there?"

I look over to the far corner Belles is rolling her eyes toward in her attempt at being nonchalant.

Newsflash, it's not working.

"Yeah. I think that's one of the brothers who was at the hospital the other night. He looks younger than Lenny." I'd noticed him earlier when he came in. The kid doesn't look much older than eighteen.

Belles leans her arms against the counter. "So, how are Sam and Bash? Nattie said Bash is staying at his dad's house."

I pass the steaming cup of decaf across the counter and decide to pour myself one too. Well, maybe a full-caff. I need the boost. "Let's see. How are Sam and Bash?" I think about that for a hot minute before answering. "They're annoying. Sam checked himself out of the hospital against doctor's orders. Then he fired the nurse Dean hired for him. Bash is a little bit of help but seems to take Sam's side instead of listening to reason. The two of them are driving me nuts."

I blow on my cup and watch Belle stare in disbelief across my counter.

"What?" What the heck did I say?

"Umm . . . I didn't realize things had progressed?" There's a question mark on the end of that sentence, emphasizing her disbelief.

"I guess you could say that. I stayed at the compound

Sunday night, then again last night." I point my cup toward Marco. "That's my driver slash bodyguard for the day."

Belle's smile grows as she leans in closer. "Are you going back tonight?"

I mimic her stance. "Why are we whispering? This is my shop."

"I don't know. It seemed like it should be whispered." When I start to laugh at her, she chews her bottom lip. "Whatever. Are you?" Her annoyed eyes go wide with excitement. "Oh my God. Where did you sleep, Amelia? I mean the poor guy just had surgery. You better be delicate with all that sexy man."

I throw my rag across the counter at her. "Shut up. There is none of that happening. He's pushing himself way too hard already. I'm not even thinking about that. I doubt he is either."

She gasps in horror. "Oh, honey. He is. I know he just lost his dad, and he's gone through hell in the last few days, but I guarantee he's still thinking about it. You're gorgeous. You're sexy. You always smell like coffee and cookies. And Sam Beneventi is crushing on you. He's definitely thinking about it."

"Crushing on me? Seriously, Belles? What are we, ten?"

Belle's phone rings, and I swear to God, I don't know how she finds anything in that Mary Poppins bag of hers. "Crap. It's Lexi." She looks back up at me. "I gotta go. Call me if you need anything."

I watch her leave and scan the shop, noticing that it's cleared out. "Looks like it's just you and me, Marco. I think I'm going to close early. Do you want to wait down here while I go upstairs and grab some clothes to bring with me back to the compound?"

"No, ma'am. I go where you go." He gathers his things and

his trash, then goes above and beyond and helps me close up the shop.

When I walk through the front door of the compound, I'm met by the delicious smell of garlic and onions as well as the deep timbre of Sam's voice yelling.

"Fucking find him. He's not invisible. He didn't fucking disappear into thin air. Find. Him."

As I walk further into the house, I see a few of Sam's men walking by. Nonna is in the kitchen, in front of the stove. "Hi, Nonna. I brought you white chocolate macadamia nut cookies." I place the pink box on the counter and kiss her offered cheek. "Is Sam in the office?"

"Yes. He's so much like his father, that boy. You may want to take some cookies in with you. He's barely eaten today." She pulls one out of the box, then pushes the rest my way.

A moment later, when I knock on the office door, I'm expecting Sam to be alone. Not for Bash and a woman I don't know to be standing inside. As I step across the threshold, Bash takes the beautiful brunette by the hand and pulls her toward the door. "Hey, Amelia. See you later."

He ushers the gorgeous woman out of the room while she stares at me like I'm a freakish circus act. "Aren't you going to introduce me, Sebastian?"

"No," is all the answer he gives her before shutting the door behind him.

I drink Sam in, sitting in the same spot where he sat the entire day before. The sweats from yesterday are long gone. In their place is Sam's usual custom-cut black suit, a white dress shirt with the sleeves rolled up his forearms with muscles straining against his skin. If it weren't for the stitches above his eye, or the scrapes and burns I've seen covering his body, I wouldn't know he'd been through hell. "Hey." I place the cookies in front of him and sit down in the oversized leather chair on the opposite side of the desk from this beautiful killer.

I'm not sure what triggers that thought.

Not sure why I have it now.

It's not even meant in a judging way.

Who am I to judge him when I spent my life training for the same thing?

Sam peeks inside the pink box, his lips turning down in disappointment. "What are these?"

"White chocolate macadamia nut. Try them. They're good." I watch him pick the cookie up, like a bug he wants to squish, before smelling it, then finally taking a bite. His eyes relax and watch me watching him. "Like what you see, Snow?"

"Not yet, Sam. How do you feel? And don't bother lying to me. Have you taken a break? Have you taken your meds? Have you eaten anything besides that cookie?" Those blue eyes confirm my suspicions. "Come on." I rise from the chair and put my hand out. "Stand up."

"I'm not finished yet." His voice is cold and void of emotion. Sam, the new boss, is talking to me now.

But if anything is ever going to work between the two of us, he won't be doing that again.

"Listen, you may be the boss to everyone else in this house, but none of those people are looking out for you. They want to make you happy or make you proud or do what they're told. I'm looking out for your well-being, dumbass. You shouldn't be home yet. If you fall over, you're no good to anyone. So, stand up, and come upstairs with me. Let's take a nap."

When he looks at me as if I'm asking for the world, I add, "An hour. Give me an hour. Give your body an hour." My heart beats faster as I wait for his answer, knowing I don't talk to Sam like this. Well . . . not normally. However, nothing about the past few days has been normal.

I lower my voice. "One hour, Sam. Please." Then I add, "I'm tired. And I'd really like you to lie down with me."

Sam's eyes soften as he rises. "One hour, Snow."

He won't do it for himself.

But he'll do it for me.

SAM

I FUCKING HATE WEAKNESS.

Hate it.

From a young age, I was taught to never show weakness.

Weakness is an excuse. And I don't make excuses.

My entire body hurts today. Pretty sure I ran off adrenaline yesterday.

Today the pain has set in, no matter how much I try to will it away.

Today I feel weak. Mentally drained and physically failing.

We're no closer today to finding who set the bomb that killed my father. Dean and Nick think it was the Sabatinis. They believe the old man knows we're up to something. That this was a preemptive strike. They've got no evidence. My gut says they're wrong. Old man Sabatini isn't that fucking smart. I'm missing something. Someone. I just can't figure out what.

Truthfully, I'm glad Amelia wants to lie down, though I'll never tell her that.

She takes my hand, thinking she's forcing me to follow as we pass by Marco, who's talking with one of the guys. "Boss, you need anything else from me?"

I look over at the tempting vixen in front of me. "Do you have anywhere else to be today?"

She shakes her head no, then raises her eyes suggestively.

"Just bed." Her devious smile conjures all sorts of filthy thoughts.

"No, Marco. Go home. But you're on Amelia for the rest of the week. She'll text you later with her schedule for tomorrow." Snow drops my hand and stomps up the stairs, no doubt pissed off that she has a bodyguard again. I take a step closer to him. "Listen to me very carefully. Your entire job this week is to make sure she stays safe. Keep checking in like you did today. Let me know what's going on. It's gonna piss her off, but so long as she's safe, I don't care."

When he looks like he's about to argue, I grab the front of his shirt and pull him toward me. "If one single hair on her head gets hurt, I will kill you. It will be slow. It will be painful. And by the time I'm done with you, you'll be praying for death. Begging for it. Got it?"

"Yeah, boss. I got it." I drop my hold, and he straightens his shirt. "Nobody gets near Amelia."

"Good. Now go home. Get some sleep. She's probably going to want to go to the shop before the sun fucking rises again tomorrow." I turn and walk up the stairs, careful not to let him see how much the movement takes out of me.

These men need to think I'm unbreakable.

Indestructible.

When Dean originally placed Marco on Snow, I couldn't figure out why. He's on the young side. He's lean and lanky with a baby face. A fucking pushover. Not intimidating at all. Nothing like his father, who can make a man piss his pants without even touching him. Marco always comes across as mellow. What I didn't know was that he's a perfect shot. He might even be able to give Amelia a run for her money. And that's saying something.

Dean told me he's the best shot we've got in the entire organization, said he was a sharpshooter in the Rangers.

Until I know who killed my father and what they're after, I'm not taking any chances.

Not with Sebastian.

Not with Nonna.

And not with Amelia.

Not on my watch. Not ever again.

When I open the door of my old bedroom, there's no Snow to be found. The blinds have been drawn, leaving the barest hint of the late afternoon sun to leak through. The men have been talking all day about how cold it is outside.

Frigid.

Everyone's talking about snow. It doesn't often happen this early around here. Not this early in November.

The sound of the shower running draws my attention toward the bathroom. The door is open. Well, it's cracked open. It's open enough that I can see in. Jesus Christ, it's like her entire goal in life is to torture me. The glass shower doors are fogged over, but I can see Amelia, whose eyes have locked with mine while she washes the shampoo out of her hair. The sweet-smelling white bubbles sluice down her shoulders and over the most perfect breasts I've ever seen.

Breasts I need to touch.

Need to taste.

Now.

As I step through the door, I hear her. "Uh-uh, Sam. You can't shower until tomorrow. Doctor's orders, remember?" She turns her tight body away from me as the spray of the shower dances over the curves of her back.

"Amelia." The word comes out sharper than I intended, but only a saint could resist the vision in front of me.

And I'm no saint, that's for damn sure.

The water shuts off, and the door cracks open, letting out a billow of steam. "Could you hand me that towel, please?"

This temptress. "You're playing with fire, Snow."

She wraps the towel around herself, securing it just above her chest, and steps out of the shower. "Fire and ice, Sam. That's a good analogy for us." She grabs a second towel and starts drying her hair.

"How do you figure?" That's about as much as she's getting out of me right now. Pretty sure all my blood has rushed to my cock.

When she flips her long dark hair back over and pierces me with those eyes, I know I'm a goner. "Are you trying to say we're opposites, Amelia?"

"No. Not exactly." She walks into the bedroom and slips my old t-shirt over her head, giving me another brief glimpse of that skin I want to slide my tongue over. "We're so similar, you and me. Most of the time, we're ice. We don't give. We don't bend. We can be brutal. Unforgiving. We're cold." She drops the towel at her feet once the shirt is in place and spins back toward me. "Until we're not. Until we're hot. Until we're raging with anger or fear or love. Until we're so hot, we force the things around us to bend to our will. Until we consume them." She sits down on the bed and pulls her knees up in front of her, watching me. "We each play off the other's emotions. I think we always have."

Standing in front of her, I wonder how I ever thought staying away was going to work. How could that ever be a good thing? Why was waiting my plan?

Reaching for her, I move her damp hair off her shoulders and cup her face in my hands.

Her lashes kiss her cheeks as her dark eyes close, and she hums out her approval. "Lie down with me, Sam." Reaching over, she pulls the blanket back and tucks her feet underneath. "Come here and lie down with me, please."

Not able to deny this woman anything, I strip down to my boxers and climb into bed, refusing to show any pain. If I don't acknowledge it, it doesn't exist.

After a minute of getting comfortable, I pull her toward me. "We still need to talk, Snow."

She lightly traces the lines of my face, careful not to touch my stitches. "I know we do. But none of it seems important now." Amelia rolls over and scoots back so we're spooning.

I wrap an arm around her waist and close my eyes. "Some of it is. There are things you need to know."

After yawning loudly, she wraps herself around the arm that's anchoring her to me.

"After we sleep, Sam. You need to rest, and I'm too tired to think." Her voice drops to a whisper. "Sleep now. Talk later."

When I crack my eyes open, I'm guessing it's hours later, and a few things hit me all at once. There's no more sun peeking through the blinds. Something about sleeping with Snow keeps the demons at bay. She may have slipped a shirt on, but she skipped panties. The feel of her warm naked skin resting against me is more than even a good man could resist. And I never was a good man.

I slip my fingers down her bare thigh and trail them up her creamy skin. She backs up the tiniest bit, seeking out my touch, and something primal inside of me roars to move faster.

To take.

To claim.

To never give back.

But this woman is worth so much more than that.

I trace my way along the small thatch of hair at the apex of her thighs.

Exploring. Playing. Teasing.

When her hips begin moving, I bury my face in the crook of her neck and slowly start to lick. To suck. To bite.

To make her want until she's writhing beneath me.

I don't stop until she leans her head back toward me and pants, "Sam." She doesn't stop grinding against me. Doesn't tell me no. But the tone of her voice says she's going to try.

I dip my finger in her juices and run it up the length of her pussy, careful not to give her what she wants. Not yet. Sealing my lips over hers, I push my tongue into her hot mouth. Tasting. Tangling. Wanting more. "Jesus, Snow." One finger slips inside, and she cries out in pleasure.

Her hips move in rhythm with my finger, and I add a second, then a third. "You're supposed to be taking it easy." She moans, "Oh . . ." Her lips search for mine, her hand reaching back and around my head, holding me to her before pulling back. "You're not supposed . . . Oh . . ." her other hand grips my wrist, "to have any strenuous activity."

The words are there, but the protest is hollow, and there's no way I'm stopping now.

I take my hand away, and she cries out at the loss before I push her shirt up over her head and bend her leg. "Stay right there, Amelia. Don't move." I shove my boxer briefs down, just enough, and drag my cock along her hot, wet pussy. "Do you want me to stop, baby?"

"God, no. Don't ever stop. Just let me do the work, okay?" With her head turned, those cherry-red lips seal over mine. Her back is against my chest, and she angles her ass beautifully, taking my cock in her hand and rubbing it along her wet pussy.

"You're playing with fire again, Snow." I'm not a man used to being teased.

Her response is to seek out my lips as she places me at her entrance and inches down.

So fucking slow.

So fucking wet.

Lying on our sides, her ass snug against my lap, she tears her mouth away from mine and buries her face in the arm I've got wrapped around her. "Patience, Sam. I haven't waited this long to be in a rush now." She circles her hips and cries out before doing it again.

And then again.

She rides me slowly.

So fucking sexy.

All fucking mine.

My hand ghosts over her hip and up her taut stomach until I finally get my first handful of the tits I've dreamt about for years. Amelia moans as I roll her nipple, tugging it, so I do it again. Harder. And I'm rewarded when her pussy flutters around me, and a loud, beautiful moan I decide I need to hear every single fucking day for the rest of my life escapes her lips. "Yeah, baby. Take what you need. Take it all."

My mouth goes back to that delicious spot on her neck, sucking until she loses control, and her hips buck harder.

"Sam. I'm so close." She arches her back, one hand reaching behind my head and holding me to her while the other covers mine, forcing me to squeeze her breast harder. "Come, Sam. Come with me. I can't hold out any longer. I'm right there."

My free hand grips her hip, and I pull her down hard onto my cock as her walls tighten around me. Fucking perfection.

She comes with my name on her lips.

I follow her over the cliff, knowing I'll never let her go.

AMELIA

Sam's lips press down on my shoulder and linger there. "Jesus, Snow. Why did we wait so long to do that?"

I roll over onto my back to face him and burst into tears. Covering my face with my hands, I try to stop them from coming, to hold them back. But it's no use.

"Amelia . . . Did I hurt you? What's wrong? What's going on?"

The complete confusion on his beautiful face as I pull my hands back makes me cry harder. "No," I sniff, trying to gain control over my emotions. "You didn't hurt me. You would never hurt me, Sam. Everyone else maybe, but never you." I try wiping the tears away, but they come faster. "It's just . . . How am I supposed to leave? I never wanted to cross this line because I knew, once I did, I'd never come back. I'd never be able to leave you."

"What the fuck, Snow? You're planning on running away? You're going to leave Philadelphia?" The hurt in his tone is like taking a hammer to the chest.

It hurts my heart.

"When were you planning on leaving? Tonight? Tomorrow?" He sits up, anger lacing his tone. "You leaving me or the city?"

I can't look at him.

Not now.

Not as the tears fall harder.

I swallow, trying to get myself under control. "I was

thinking about it. After the Canada thing last month. Of course, I thought about it, Sam. But I didn't do it."

There's a silence before Sam grabs my face. "Is there a 'not yet' at the end of that sentence? Were you really going to do that to me? To us? Before we ever had a chance?"

I grab his shirt off the floor and throw it over my head. Then I stand up, needing to put space between us. "I didn't know . . ." How do I explain this? "Sam . . ." I plead. "I didn't know you felt this way. I didn't know you felt the same way I did."

"Are you fucking kidding me, Amelia? How could you not know? How many ways do I have to show you how I feel? Doesn't everyone say you need to show it, not just say it? Do you really need me to say it?" Sam gets out of bed slowly, burned and bruised, literally being held together by staples. He pulls his boxers back up, then moves around the bed until we're toe to toe. Taking my hand in his, he places it over his heart the way he did last month. "Do you feel that? That's yours. My heart is yours."

He waits for a beat, staring down at my tear-stained face. "You're the only person who will ever have it." He looks at me, unsure, then drops our hands before stepping back. "And you're planning on leaving?"

How do I make him understand? "No, Sam. I wasn't exactly planning. But there's a part of me that's always ready to leave, always prepared to run. Because that's my life." He doesn't look convinced, but I push on, desperate for him to believe me. "So, yes, the thought crossed my mind. I was scared. If I'm a target, then I'm putting anyone near me in the crossfire. I would never want to do that to the people I love." The words are out of my mouth before I think better of it.

Before I realize what I just said.

Sam looks like I slapped him across the face. "Right. Because if someone's gunning for you, someone else can end up dead." He moves across the room and pulls a pair of sweats out of his drawer.

Shit. I hadn't thought about the guilt he's working through over his father's death.

I was too caught up in my own concerns to even consider that.

"Sam . . . It's not your fault." Damnit.

He walks out of the room, slamming the door behind him so hard it bounces off the frame. Deafeningly yelling, "Everyone who doesn't live here, get the fuck out of my house. If you're on duty, go stay in the guardhouse."

I move to the door and watch him pound down the stairs, praying that he doesn't tear open his back the way that I just tore us to shreds.

Sometime around midnight, I work up the courage to go hunting for Sam. Tiptoeing down the stairs and through the hall, I don't see anyone. It's quiet. Eerily so. Sebastian's door is closed. Nonna's door is closed. There's no one sitting in the living room and no one talking in the kitchen.

No sign of life.

The house's heartbeat that's been rapidly pulsing for the last few days has stopped.

It's sleeping.

With butterflies dancing a jig in my stomach, I raise my hand to knock on Sam's office door but hear him tell me to come in before I get the chance.

When I peek my head in through the door, it's to find a wall of monitors sitting on Sam's desk, hiding his face.

That's new.

"What do you want, Amelia?" The look he gives me

freezes me in place. "I thought you'd be asleep in bed by now. Or gone."

"That's not fair, Sam." I softly shut the door behind me and cross the room, working up my nerve for what I've got to say next. "I need you to listen to me." When his glare grows, I add, "Hear me out. Please. This isn't easy for me. I've never really had friends before you and Annabelle. Not in a really long time, and never as an adult. I've never been in a real relationship. I've never been in love, Sam." When he looks away, there's no doubt I'm losing him before I ever had the chance to have him.

Moving around the desk, I stand next to his chair and lean against the desk, facing him.

Close, but not close enough.

"Do you want to know the first time I knew, like really honest to God knew, that I loved you, Sam?" When he doesn't answer, I push on. "It was a year ago. Well, a little over a year. It was the twins' christening. You were wearing this navy blue suit, more royal blue than navy, actually. It almost matched the color of your eyes. You had on this crisp white shirt and a silver tie, and you were holding Gracie. She was babbling and cooing, and you were smiling at her. The next thing I knew, she puked all over your shirt, and you . . . You didn't get mad. You laughed. Then you snuggled her closer to you. You ran your hand over her head and patted her back and told her you were going to go find her momma."

"Snow . . ." His voice finally softens.

"I remember watching you and thinking 'man, he's going to be an amazing father one day.' But when I pictured it . . . when I thought about you with a baby, it was our baby." I manage to hold back the tears that want to flow again. "Then I remembered I don't have a future here. At least, that's what I thought then. You changed that. You gave me a future here.

But Sam, you've got to remember I spent years running away. Years thinking someone was going to catch up to me. It's hard to change that mindset, and I'm not quite there yet. It's hard for me to believe I'll get to stay."

I slide over just a little bit so that I'm sitting between his legs. "Here's the thing, Sam," I reach out and take his hand, laying it over my heart. "I want to be sure I can stay here. My head knows you said I'm safe. But I've spent most of my life not believing that. I need my heart to catch up to my head. Because my heart is so freaking scared it finally found the one thing it's always needed, only to turn around and lose it."

Sam's hand wraps around my waist and pulls me toward him. "You're not losing me, Snow. This is a fight. Fire and ice, right? We're going to fight." He tugs me down on his lap. "We're going to fight. Hell, we've been fighting since the day we met. It's our foreplay. And we've had two years of it."

I laugh and bury my face in his shoulder. "You're not mad at me?"

"I'm not thrilled with the fact you're still thinking about leaving. But we'll work through it. I plan on giving you so many reasons to stay. I'll give you reasons every day." His hand slides up my thigh, giving me all sorts of ideas about what kinds of reasoning he's planning. "Plus, there are things I need to tell you, things you need to know. I tried to tell you earlier. I tried to tell you last night."

"Seriously. Hasn't this been enough of a heart-to-heart for today? I don't know how much more I can handle, Sam. I have to be awake in four hours."

He holds my face in his hands, and his fingers wrap around the back of my head. "You might want to close the shop tomorrow, Snow. This may take a while."

SAM

"You're gonna have to repeat that. Because I'm pretty sure you just told me that my father is Bash's girlfriend's dad. Actually, it would be *was*, right? He's dead, so it's *was*, not is. He *was* a Kingston. Hell, he was *the* Kingston." I watch her, waiting to see actual smoke coming out of her ears before her head explodes, but it never comes. Although her big brown eyes make her look like one of those anime chicks as she stares at me in disbelief.

I wrap my arm around her shoulders, wondering if I should have waited to drop this bomb but knowing it would have been worse if I had. "Snow, I need you to sit down."

"How am I supposed to sit down, Sam?" Her voice raises an octave. "I can't sit down. I can't sit still."

Dear God, I think dogs would have a hard time listening to the high-pitched squeak that's coming out of her mouth right now.

"Do you know how often I thought about my dad when I was growing up?" She wiggles out of my hold and blinks up at me like a doll. "I'll tell you. All. The. Time. I thought about him all the time. I wondered if he'd be handsome. If he'd be kind. If he was secretly a superhero who knew where we were but was too busy saving the world to save us. I used to daydream he would rescue us once he was done. I grew up knowing my mother was scared of everything. I never knew why. I just knew she was. I always thought my dad would come and make it all better. Take care of her. Make her safe.

And maybe, just maybe, if he did that, I'd get to have a normal life and real friends."

John Kingston is lucky he's dead, or I'd put a bullet in his brain for the hurt I hear in her voice.

When I reach for her, she backs away and wraps her arms protectively around herself. "I don't know much about John Kingston, but what I do know, I don't like. I know when he died, he was on his fourth, maybe his fifth wife, and he died cheating on her, right? With a girl who was barely twenty. It was still all over the papers when I moved to Philly."

"The papers? Who reads the papers?" I laugh, trying to lighten the mood, but the look she shoots my way definitely says I failed. "Take a breath, Snow. It was his fourth wife. The wife was at least twenty-one, so I think the chick he cheated with was at least the same age. Now take a deep breath. I know that him being dead means you'll never get the father you dreamed about. It doesn't really sound like you were going to get that out of John Kingston anyway. But if you want, you could get a family. I've met Lenny, and she's great. I know Becket, and he's a bit of an ass, but we've been friends for a long time, and I can tell you he's a good guy."

Amelia moves in front of me and drops her head to my chest. "Oh my God, Sam. How many of them are there?"

That's a good question. "A lot. Seven or eight, I think. It's a lot to take in, Snow. You don't need to decide what to do with it tonight. But keep in mind, I found out the night before the bomb. And from what Bash told me, they found out who you are the next morning." I lift her face, tilting her chin up. "I don't know how long they're going to hold off on contacting you. But it sounds like they've been looking for you for a long time."

"What if I'm not ready?" The quiver in her voice has me wanting to destroy the Kingstons.

"Bash said they'll wait until after the funeral. That gives

you at least two days to decide what you want, Snow." My lips press against her forehead, lingering. "Why don't we go to bed? You might feel different about all this tomorrow morning."

Once the lights in the office are off, I guide her back up to my bedroom.

The door closes behind us, and as if on autopilot, she slips out of her leggings and sits down on the bed. "What if I don't want a family, Sam? What if I just want us? You and me. What if I don't know how to be a part of a huge family? What if I can't even handle us?"

"You know, this thing between us might feel new, but we've been dancing around it for years, Snow. And you wanna know what's good about that?" I sit down on the opposite side of the bed and pull her to me, then cover us both with the blanket.

"Even if we both suck at relationships. Even if neither of us has really done this before . . . it doesn't matter. Because the foundation we've built can withstand fighting. Hell, I fucking love watching you get pissed off. You're so incredibly sexy when you're mad, when the fire flames your cheeks. We're going to fight. We're going to yell. But at the end of the day, you're mine, Amelia. You are the strongest woman I've ever met. You impress me at every turn. I'll never let anyone hurt you, including the Kingstons. Take some time. Think it over. Don't rush this decision." I run my fingers through her soft hair and close my eyes. "I'll be right here next to you."

"Sam." She curls into me. "We've talked about a lot of stuff tonight."

I stare down at the beauty in my bed and push a lock of hair from her face. "We have. You doing okay?"

Her hand reaches up and caresses my cheek while her teeth worry her pillowy bottom lip. "I'm going to screw this up, Sam. I know I am. But I won't run. I promise you, I won't run. I wish I could say I won't want to, or I won't think about it, but I can't. I can only tell you I won't do it."

"Fire and ice, right, Snow?" I run my thumb along her lip, tugging it free, and then lean down and suck it between mine.

She lets out the sweetest, softest moan I've ever heard as she wraps her hands around my neck. "Sam," she whispers against my lips. "We didn't use a condom earlier."

I pull back and try to read her face but can't. "Shit, you're right. I'm sorry, Snow. I wasn't thinking." I've never done that before. Never not worn a condom. Never been so in the moment I didn't even think about it.

"I'm clean. But I'm not on the pill." Her hands go to my boxers, and it fucking kills me to stop her.

"I'm clean too. But I don't have condoms here." I lean back and smile. "You know what that means?" The pout on her pretty lips tells me what she's thinking. "Oh baby, there are other things we can do. Now climb up here and sit on my face."

"Sam." She smiles and purses her lips. "You can't be serious."

"No exertion, right? Isn't that what you said earlier?" A flaming red blush creeps up her cheeks. "Now, take off that shirt and get that pretty pussy up here. I'm hungry."

I've dreamed of tasting Amelia for two fucking years, and for a minute, I think she's going to fight me. I think she's going to act shy or even scared. But this woman loves proving me wrong. A sexy smile curves her pretty lips as she lifts my t-shirt from her body, then licks her way up my torso and chest and finally, positions her knees on either side of my face.

"Hands on the headboard, Snow. Don't let go." Spreading her open, I feast. My tongue runs up the length of her pussy and around her clit, as her body shakes, letting me know just how sensitive she is.

I'm not ready for this to be over before it starts, so I slide back down and dart my tongue inside this gorgeous woman, her taste finally exploding on my tongue.

A taste I've been dying to know for years.

Her legs start to shake, and I devour her. Ravenous for more, I add my fingers as she starts riding my face.

I'm pretty sure I could die a happy man right now.

Running my teeth over her clit causes her to cry out. "I'm gonna come, Sam. Oh, God! Don't stop!"

I double down my efforts and bend my fingers just right, hitting the spot that makes her explode on my face. Grabbing her ass, I pull her down harder and keep working her until she can't take it anymore.

Amelia slides down my body so she's leaning on my rock-hard dick and searches for my lips. "Sam, I need you."

Her tongue slides into my mouth, tasting herself while her hands push my boxers down. "Just tell me when you're ready, and you can pull out." She kisses me again. Needier. "I want you. Need you. Now."

I'll never deny her anything.

Grabbing her face with my hands, I hold her to me as her soaking wet pussy slides down my cock, making us both moan at the all-consuming perfection. "I'll never get enough, Amelia."

She throws her head back, arching her chest so those magnificent breasts are positioned perfectly for me. I latch onto her pink nipple with my mouth and palm her other full breast, loving the feel. Massaging. My thumb brushes over her nipple until she cries out.

Snow rocks her hips at a frantic pace.

Chasing what she wants.

Giving me everything she has.

Her velvety heat is better than anything I've ever experienced.

Being inside her bare. Skin on skin. Nothing between us.

Jesus, it's everything.

Moving my hand down her beautiful body, I circle her clit with my finger until she starts to shake and her body begins milking mine. My muscles tighten as a haze of need and want claims me.

"Mine," my entire being screams.

This woman is mine.

She only waits a few seconds before crawling down my body and dropping her head between my legs, her lips covering my cock as I come in her mouth.

Her hand pumps me harder. Faster. Until I'm spent.

Only after grabbing a t-shirt from the floor so I can clean us off, does Snow curl up next to me with her head on my chest, both of us sated.

Both of us knowing there's no going back to the way things used to be.

"Amelia . . ."

Her fingers stop tracing my tattoo as those beautiful eyes look up at me.

"Don't leave, okay? Don't leave me. Don't give up on us. I've loved you for a long time, and I'm not letting you go. Ever." I push a long, loose black curl away from her face.

"Then you better hold tight, Sam. I've wanted this for a long time too, even if I didn't want to admit it. But those words scare me. I love you so much that the idea of you getting hurt because of my past scares me more than anything ever has." Fear shines in those expressive eyes.

"We both know what we're getting into. I'm not a saint. My world's never going to be completely safe. But I'll keep you safe. Always." I run my lips over her forehead.

She lays her head back down and closes her eyes. "I won't run, Sam."

"I'll keep you safe and with me, principessa."

Her eyes open again, confused. "What does that mean exactly? Nonna has been calling me that all week. I mean, I know it means princess. But it seems like there's a deeper meaning I'm missing."

"You know they call Bash and me the Beneventi princes, right?" She bats her eyelashes at me, smiling. "It means you're my princess. It's a term my family and *The Family* both hold in high regard. You're the first Beneventi principessa since my mother. It means you'll be my queen one day and rule the city by my side." She tilts her head, showing no emotion on her face. "You still not running?"

Snow takes my hand in hers and places it on her heart like I've done to her. "My heart is yours, Sam. And I may not be part of your family, or *The Family*, but I'm pretty sure you're already the next Beneventi king."

"I guess I am." I may have been trained to wear this crown my entire life, but it doesn't lessen the weight of it.

But somehow, knowing this woman will be by my side, it feels just a bit lighter tonight.

SAM

THE FOLLOWING DAY, I STAND UNDER THE PIPING HOT SPRAY OF the shower and let it beat down on my sore muscles. I've never enjoyed hot showers more than I have this week. Those first few days of not being allowed to get my staples wet have made me appreciate this more than I knew possible.

It might also be the first time I've had more than five minutes to myself in days. I've never been so constantly surrounded by people, all looking for answers I don't have yet, but I'm damn sure gonna get.

Amelia left an hour ago. She agreed to not go in at three a.m. but was out of bed and out of the house by six this morning. Waking up with her in my arms, where she belongs, has me thinking thoughts most men would be running from and wondering what she'd do if she knew.

Would she want to live here? Fuck . . . Do *I* even want to live here? I know I don't want to leave Nonna in this house alone. A week ago, I was in a penthouse in the city, and now I'm in a compound in Kroydon Hills.

I can see why Pop moved us here. It's easier to secure this house than my penthouse. I'll need to talk to Amelia and see what she's thinking.

I already hear that whip snapping in the back of my mind, and I'll be damned if it doesn't make me smile.

She's the only person I'll ever bow down to.

I come down the stairs expecting to see Dean, who's

picking me up soon for a few meetings today. Instead, I'm greeted by a quiet house. Nonna's coffee is brewing in the kitchen, but she's not in here. When I step back into the hall, I see my father's bedroom door open and move quickly to see who's inside.

I'm met with the sight of Nonna sitting on his bed, one of Pop's shirts clutched in her hands as silent sobs wrack her small body.

The floor creaks as I step inside the room, causing her to look up and quickly wipe her face. "Ignore this old woman. I didn't want you to see me like this, Samuel."

"Nonna." I sit down next to her and wrap my arm around her. "Are you okay? I'm sorry I've spent so much of this week behind closed doors."

"I'll be fine. You have enough on your plate. Please don't worry about me." She wraps her hand around mine, bringing it to her lips and kissing my knuckles. "Be careful, Sam. This life will take everything from you if you let it." She studies my face before standing from the bed, still holding Pop's shirt. Her hand lifts to cup my cheek. "Don't let it."

She holds the shirt close to her chest. "I love you, piccolo principe. I know you will make your parents proud. But remember, do not start a war if you can't finish it. I heard your grandfather say that many times through the years. He had his battles, but he always won." Her blue eyes glisten. "Win, Sam. Kill them all. Make them pay."

I'm trying, Nonna.

Later in the day, as Dean drives the two of us over to Mike's loft in the city, we decide to make a detour to Sweet Temptations. I haven't set foot in here in the month since Snow and I had our argument over how I handled the Tremblays.

When we walk in, she's standing in front of the counter with a sleepy-looking Gracie resting on her hip. Annabelle Sinclair stands next to her while Evie sucks on one of those weird cups with a pink lid.

Amelia's eyes light up when she sees us walk in, giving me all the permission I need to move across the room and kiss her cheek before turning to look at Annabelle and Evie. "Hey, ballerina. Little ladies."

Evie hides behind her mother's leg. She's Bash's goddaughter, and Declan Sinclair is going to be screwed when these girls grow up. They're beautiful like their mother. But this one in particular is going to be serious trouble.

"Hey, Sam. How are you feeling?" Belle asks sympathetically.

"Good. Thanks." I watch Dean talking to Lyla while she gets our coffees.

"Do you need anything for tomorrow?" Belle asks, referring to the funeral.

I shake my head, no, then think better of it. "Actually, would you mind giving Amelia a ride, so she doesn't have to go by herself?" I wrap my arm around Amelia's waist, knowing she'll be annoyed by this but not wanting her to be alone tomorrow. She can't ride with Bash and me. There are too many unknowns and too many other things at play besides the funeral.

Amelia hip-checks me with the hip not holding a one-year-old and rolls her eyes. "I can drive myself, Sam."

Dean moves down the counter with two coffees in one hand and a pink box in the other. "Hello, ladies." He hands me a coffee. "You ready to go, Sam? We gotta get moving."

I look down at Amelia and tilt her chin up to brush my lips over hers. "See you tonight, Snow."

As Dean and I walk through the door, Annabelle's words trail after me. "Bye, Sam."

And so does a little girl's voice, mimicking, "Bye, Sam."

Then Belle whistles, followed by, "Damn, girl. That was hot."

The door shuts behind us before I can hear more.

Dean and I slide into his car and head to Mike's loft.

"So it's finally like that, huh?" Dean glances my way as he makes his way through the streets of Kroydon Hills, heading into Philly.

"Like what?" I ask. "Are we teenagers, Dean? You've never kissed a woman before?"

The fucker laughs. Hard. "Well, I've never kissed Amelia before. And you've never kissed her in front of me before. So, I'd say that was new, asshole. Not that we haven't all known you wanted to be kissing the cookie queen for fucking years." When I glare at him, he adds, "I mean, come on. You were pretty obvious about it."

"If you don't wanna die, you'll never put you and kissing Amelia in the same fucking sentence again."

"Calm down, man. I'm the only one who'd ever dare to bust your balls over that woman. Fuck. I'm the only one who'd bust your balls over anything. You need me to keep you grounded. You don't need another yes-man. You're the man now. The boss. The Don. The guys are going to be lining up to wipe your ass. But I'll always be real."

Dean and I were born six months apart. His mom was my mom's best friend. She happened to marry Pop's cousin, making Dean and me family. And the shithead's right. I need to know he'll always tell it like it is. Give it to me straight and not just say what I want to hear.

When we pull up in front of Mike's loft, Dean throws the car in park and grabs the Sweet Temptations box.

"What's in there?" I ask, eyeing the pink box as I slam the car door behind me.

Dean looks a little embarrassed as he tells me, "Cupcakes for Mike. Not gonna lie. This dude scares me. I feel like he could wipe away my entire existence with a few keystrokes. Hit the delete button, and bam, I don't exist anymore."

"Jesus Christ," I mutter as I push the buzzer and look into the security camera, waiting for the door to click open.

When we get to the top of the metal stairs, it's to see Mike standing in his kitchen, steaming coffee mug in hand. "Pass the box this way, Dean, and I won't erase you."

I laugh. But Dean doesn't look as amused. "Guess you heard that?"

"Don't piss me off, and you've got nothing to worry about, man. I only deconstruct and destroy bad guys and their governments. Think of me as Robin Hood. Now pass me the box. Are there cupcakes in there?"

Dean pushes the box across the counter. "Lyla said these were fresh."

"Lyla?" Mike asks.

"Snow's counter girl," I tell him.

"Oh, right. Hot little blonde Dean wants to nail." Dean chokes, and Mike laughs, then points to his wall of monitors. One of them is tuned to the front of Sweet Temptations. "I'm worse than Big Brother, Dean."

Dean glares at Mike. "You know I kill people, right?"

"Yeah, man. But I'm better at it." Mike stares back.

"You two think you could have your pissing contest later?" I look between the two of them before settling on Mike. "You said you had something for me."

Mike licks the chocolate fudge off the top of his cupcake and moves over to his keyboard to bring up a screen with some type of report displayed. Then he turns back to us and breaks his cupcake in half. "This is the report that the Transportation Safety Board of Canada wrote up after the issue with the jet last month. It was completed yesterday. It hasn't been released yet, but . . . I have my ways."

He takes a bite of the cupcake, and I want to rip it from his throat. "Get to the fucking point, Mike."

"The problem is they can't pinpoint when the engine was tampered with. Was it done in Philly and not done properly, so the jet didn't crash on the way over? Or was it done while you were in Canada?"

Dean looks from Mike to me, adding, "You were only supposed to be there for a few hours, and the pilot never left the plane. They'd have really had to have had their shit together to have done that while you were in your meeting."

"It's possible though?" I ask Mike.

"Not just possible, Sam. That's what happened." He hits a few more keys, bringing up a new image. "The pilot told your father there was no way he missed it in Philly. That it couldn't have happened here. Your dad thought he was covering his tracks. Thought your pilot missed it."

"Yeah. Pops had this guy on his payroll for years. He always took good care of him because it's not easy to find a pilot willing and capable of going over everything himself. Fewer hands in the mix mean less chance of missing something. Pops put all three of this guy's kids through UPenn, and we really don't use the jet that often."

"Well, your guy deserves a bonus. He caught it as soon as he could have." Mike pulls up another image, then points at the screen. "See that?"

When I stare blankly at him, he starts explaining what I'm looking at, but he might as well be speaking another language. "Mike." When he finally takes a breath, I add, "Dumb it down for those of us who have no clue what you're saying."

"It was tampered with in Canada. If the pilot didn't catch it, you'd all be dead."

Less than an hour later, I'm sitting behind my desk in my office at the restaurant. It feels good to be back. I haven't enjoyed doing business at the house. If Snow and I stay there, that's going to change. Business needs to happen here, not where we live.

Dean and Nick are standing across from me, arguing, and I've had enough.

"Jesus Christ, Dean. Just because the jet was tampered with in Canada doesn't mean it was the Canadians who did it." Nick turns to me. "I've been your father's advisor longer than either of the two of you shit-stains have been alive. You need to listen to me, Sam. This was Sabatini. The jet. The bomb. This has Sabatini written all over it."

"Listen up, old man. You may have been the advisor, but you can step aside now," Dean mocks, over this conversation already. These two have never gotten along.

Nick pulls his gun from inside of his jacket, and Dean takes a step forward.

Daring him to use it.

I stand, ready to kill both of these assholes. "Knock it the fuck off. Am I babysitting or talking to my top men right now? Put the fucking gun away. Nobody is getting killed in my office. Not today. Not yet." I wait until my uncle returns the gun to its holster and straightens his jacket before continuing, "Nick, I know you think it was Sabatini. But unless you have proof, we're not acting on it. I don't think it was him. One of the first things you taught me was to trust my gut. And my gut says he's too stupid to pull this off. If it was local, maybe. But he doesn't have the pull he needs for the international shit."

When Nick starts to sputter, I cut him off. "Listen to me. I'm handling Sabatini tomorrow after the funeral. He's being dealt with the way I planned. I want the two of you to work together to get me everything you can find on the Tremblays. My gut tells me this was them. And from what Mike is telling me, it sounds like I'm right." Once I sit back down, I add, "But I can't retaliate based on my gut. Get me something firm. Get me something we can act on."

Nick pounds the wall. "Your father would never . . ."

I round my desk and shove him against the wall with my forearm at his throat. "I'm not my father. We're not doing this his way. We're doing this *my* fucking way. If you've got a problem with that, tell me now." Rage drips from my every word.

This week has been the worst week of my life, but it could have been worse.

My men could have questioned my ability to do this job.

My ability to take this position.

But they didn't. They trusted me. And I'm sure as fuck not going to bend to my uncle.

"Well?" I get further in his face and push harder against his neck. "Do we have a problem?"

It takes a minute before Nick answers, "No problem, Sam," as he gasps for breath.

"Good." I step back and cross my arms over my chest. "Now get out. Go get me the information I need to finish this."

SAM

THAT NIGHT AFTER DINNER, AMELIA, BASH, AND I ARE SITTING in the kitchen, going over the plan for tomorrow when Bash's phone vibrates with an incoming text right before he walks out of the room, grumbling, "Fuck" as he goes.

"Well, that doesn't sound good." Snow refills her wine glass, but I pull it away before she can take a sip. "Sam," she scolds. "You're not supposed to have alcohol with your medication."

She's so fucking sexy when she's bossy. After a hearty gulp, I push it back in front of her. "A little won't hurt, Snow."

She cocks her head and smiles condescendingly. Suddenly, a feminine voice I'm not in the mood to hear speaks, bringing an end to the first few moments of peace I've had all day.

"I don't care, Bash. I need to hear it from Sam. Where is he?"

Emma Sabatini pushes her way into the kitchen, followed by Sebastian. She has on a hot pink hoodie with the hood pulled up, hiding half her mascara-stained face. This can't be good.

"What the hell happened to you?" I ask, not sure I actually want to know the answer.

Emma drops the hood down, revealing the beginning of a nasty bruise forming on her cheek. She shoves her hands in her pockets and stares at the woman sitting next to me. For once, I understand Emma's reticence.

We're taught to not trust outsiders.

Amelia looks between the three of us before she turns to me. "I'm going to go upstairs and make sure I have everything I need for tomorrow." She finishes her glass of wine and grins wryly at me.

This woman is getting her ass spanked tonight.

My hand grabs hers as she turns away. "I'll be up in a few minutes."

Emma watches Amelia leave the room before speaking, "Tell me this farce is over tomorrow, Sam. Tell me everything we did worked, and you're still planning on ending it tomorrow."

When I stare at her without answering, she continues, "Because if you don't end this, I will. And I'm way too pretty for jail, Sam." Emma grabs the bottle of red wine off the table and takes a swig. "He's controlled me long enough. I'm done."

"Emma." Bash holds a bag of frozen peas to her face before she replaces his hand with hers.

"I did everything you guys asked. I gave you everything. Now get me out of this. He hit me because I said I didn't want to sit with Bash tomorrow at the church. I didn't want to ride with you guys. He said I had to. How dare I ask him why. It's not like the engagement was announced, so I don't see why I have to be up there with you. I'm over this. I'm done putting on a show."

Bash wraps an arm around her shoulder. "Is this the first time he's hit you?"

She squirms out of his hold, offended by his coddling. That's not Emma Sabatini's style. "No. It's not the first time, but I swear to God, it's gonna be the last."

"Emma," I recapture her focus. "This will be over tomorrow. I give you my word."

A lone tear spills over her cheek. "He's evil, Sam."

"So am I."

When I walk into my bedroom after leaving Bash to deal with Emma, it's to find Amelia in those damn cheeky panties and another one of my t-shirts, packing a bag. "What are you doing?" I step behind her and move the hair away from her neck so I can taste the soft skin behind her ear.

"I'm packing, Sam. I need to go home so I can get ready for the funeral tomorrow." She balls up one of my t-shirts and throws it in her bag. "I can't stay here forever. This isn't my home."

"Hell, Snow, it's not even my home. It hasn't been for ten years. But having you here with me makes it feel like it could be. You can't leave." I spin her around in my arms and cup her face.

Her hands grip the tie hanging loosely around my neck. "We sort of fell into all this just this week, Sam. Your dad died. You were hurt, and I was here. The adrenaline was running high, and our emotions were running even higher. But that can't be an excuse. I don't want to do this with you because it's convenient."

"That's bullshit, and you know it. None of this was an excuse. It wasn't fucking convenient. We were on our way to this the day before the bomb. We were on our way to this for years, Amelia. We were on our way to this the first goddamn night we met, and I promised to keep you safe. I don't make anyone promises. But you were different from day fucking one. You're mine, no matter what your name is. No matter where you live. You're mine, Snow. And as soon as you let me, I'm going to put a ring on your finger and give you a last name you'll never need to outrun."

She sucks in a sharp breath. "Sam . . ."

"You don't want to live here, no problem. We'll find a different place to live. I don't care as long as you're there with me. There are so many things in my life I'm not going to be able to share with you. But my heart, my home . . . they're yours. They're only yours. Unconditionally."

She tugs my tie, pulling me closer, her warm breath skimming over my lips. "You say the prettiest things, Sam Beneventi." Her head tips back, her black hair spilling over her shoulders. "I love you, Sam. This wasn't me running away. We just need to figure out what we're doing. And we don't need to do that tonight. I wasn't trying to pressure you into anything. I just know that tomorrow is a big day, and you're going to have your hands full. I don't want you worrying about me too. But I'll go home in the morning, then catch a ride with Belle and Declan to the church. I've already arranged it with Marco. He's bringing me home early tomorrow so I can get the shop set up before I go to the church." She leans up on her tiptoes and kisses my bottom lip.

"Say it again," I demand.

"I love you, Sam." Her declaration washes over me like holy water cleansing my soul. "I've loved you for a long time." Amelia loosens the hold she has on my tie and pulls it off my neck. Next, her fingers begin working on the buttons of my shirt.

"I've loved the way you protected me, even though I could do it myself." One button undone.

"I hated seeing you on dates with other women." Another button pops.

"I hated knowing they were on your arm and in your bed when I wanted you to be mine." Two more buttons, gone.

"You were always mine too, Sam. I just didn't know I'd get to keep you." She pulls my shirt from my pants and forcefully shoves it off my shoulders. Her lips tease mine quickly before she licks an electrifying trail down to my chest.

Jesus Christ. This woman has no fucking idea what she does to me.

After unbuckling my belt without taking her eyes from mine, her fingers teasingly skim the button of my pants before she asks, "What do you want, Sam?" Her teeth glide over my nipple, and my cock strains at the sensation.

"I want you on your knees, Snow. Show me I'm yours."

My girl drops to her knees with a wicked smile on her beautiful face, and then she reverently frees my dick from its confines. Once I step out of my pants and boxers, she gently pushes me back until I sit on the bed. She licks her lips and slowly runs her velvety warm tongue from base to tip, licking the pearl of precum with the tip of her tongue. Her nails run lightly up my thighs, sending shivers through my body. Finally, with one hand cupping my balls, she swallows the head of my cock, and I can die a happy man.

Those big brown eyes look up at me through her dark lashes, and my fairytale princess transforms into a seductive goddess before my eyes. She hums around my dick as she works her way down to the base and takes me into the back of her throat.

The pressure.

The warmth.

The wetness.

Her tongue. Her suction. Her throat.

I was born to be a king, but I've never felt like one until now.

Snow's nails dig into my ass as she grips and swallows me down.

My hands tug on her hair, knowing I'm not going to last long. "Snow, I'm gonna come."

Her pouty lips pop off my cock. "Not yet, you aren't. Lean back, Sam."

In one swift move, she shimmies out of her panties and

slips the grey shirt over her head. Her legs move to straddle my lap as she grips my dick and pumps it once, then again before lowering herself over me.

"I still don't have condoms."

She wraps her arms around my neck and covers my mouth with hers. "I don't care, Sam. I need you." Her tongue pushes its way inside my mouth as her hips start to rock against me. "You feel so good." Nimble fingers slide through my hair, grazing my scalp, and sending a tremor down my spine.

The sensations are too much.

Too good.

I need her to get there soon.

Grabbing her ass in both my hands, I rise and flip her over, laying her down on the bed with her legs draped over the edge while I stand at the foot of it.

"Sam . . . your back."

"Is fine." I rub my cock along the most flawless fucking pussy I've ever been inside and watch her squirm on the bed before I slam home. "But I may never get over it if you don't come before I do, Snow." Sliding my hands up her smooth skin, I wrap my fingers around her tiny waist and pull her against my cock as I pound into her over and over until she's screaming my name.

"Give me one more, Snow," I tell her as my thumb circles her clit.

She shakes her head. "I can't. Oh my God, Sam. It's too much."

It is too much.

But it'll never be enough.

Pulling out slowly, I inch my way back inside her gorgeous cunt, soaking it all up. Every moan. Every shiver of her body. Every fucking sensation. My fingers squeeze the flawless white skin of her soft breast, my thumb teasing her nipple. Tugging. Pinching. Working her up slowly, only to stop when I think she's close and then do the same to the other.

"I can't. Oh my God, I can't, Sam."

Bringing my other hand up to her throat, I squeeze.

Not hard. Just enough that her beautiful eyes sparkle behind hooded lids and her breath is staggered. "Yes, you can, Snow. Give it to me now."

Those red lips part, forming the perfect O. Her entire body shakes with aftershocks as I stroke inside her one more time before pulling out, and hot threads of come coat her stomach.

She drags her index finger down her body before lifting it to her lips and sucking. "That was the hottest thing I've ever experienced."

I lean down and run my tongue around her rosy nipple. "It's only the beginning."

AMELIA

WE RARELY GOT SNOW WHEN I LIVED IN WASHINGTON.

Rain, yes. A ton of rain.

But snow, no.

They've been calling for it all week. Thundersnow, the weatherman said this morning on the news. We could see a foot of it by the time this storm is over tomorrow. When Marco picked me up this morning from Sam's father's house, the powdery white snow looked beautiful as it fell from the sky. Peaceful. Pure. Now, a few hours later, I curse myself for wearing black heels instead of snow boots as I get behind the wheel of my car. The funeral is being held at The Cathedral Basilica of Saints Peter and Paul, and I told Belle and Declan I'd meet them there. They wanted to pick me up, but I stopped into the shop this morning and have been running late ever since. We're all meeting in front of the church, and when I finally see them, it looks like I'm the last to arrive.

Everyone's here. Belle and Declan. All of Bash's room-mates. Even Declan and Nattie's brother, Cooper, flew in from California to be here. These are the people who've taught me that family isn't blood. Sure, some of these people are related, but all of them consider each other family. Everyone but me.

Apparently, I'm not the only outsider joining the tight-knit group of Sinclairs and their extended family today though. Because Eleanor Kingston and her little brother—the one who stopped into my shop twice this week, I'm guessing so he could get a glimpse into who I am—are both standing next to Nattie and Brady when I finally make my way over to them at the bottom of the stairs. I have no idea if the brother found what he was looking for, but he's looking at me now like he's busted. My thoughts are sidetracked when Cooper Sinclair, Nattie's twin brother who must have gotten leave from the Navy SEALs, blocks my view when he picks me up in a big bear hug. "Cooper, put me down!"

Annabelle smacks the back of his head. "Don't hurt my friend, Coop."

"Put her down before you drop her, Coop," Declan tells him in a way only an older brother could.

When he gingerly places me back on my feet and holds my arms to steady me, I hear Sebastian's best friend, Murphy, laugh. "I'd back away now, Coop. Sam looks pissed." The ginger giant is looking over my shoulder.

Sure enough, when I look up the cathedral stairs and see Bash and Sam standing there at the top, Sam looks furious. I'm not sure if his anger is directed at Cooper or me, but regardless, he's not happy. Their uncle Nick rests a hand on each of their shoulders, and the two men turn and enter the church, leaving me feeling empty and useless and wishing so badly I could be by his side today.

Belle must sense my frustration because she slips her fingers through mine and holds my hand like I imagine a sister would. "You doing okay, Amelia?"

My eyes dance over Eleanor, who's standing with her brother, and I wonder briefly if I could find a friendship like this with her. Does she love Sebastian? Will we be connected because of these brothers? Or if I choose to, will we be connected because we share the same blood?

Knowing I'm not going to find the answer out here in the snow, I squeeze Belle's hand back. "Yeah. I'll be okay. It's freezing. Are you ready to go inside?"

Declan moves next to his pregnant wife and wraps an arm protectively around her waist. "Be careful on the steps, Belles. They look slippery."

She kisses his cheek and turns back to me. "You ready?"

"Now or never."

We end up waiting in line to pay our respects for what feels like forever. The line wraps around the church and moves so slowly, I have plenty of time to watch the girl from the other night who's standing with Sam and Bash. She's pretty. Her dark hair hangs down past her shoulders. Her makeup is done perfectly, hiding any hint of the bruise that was forming on her cheek last night. She has no problem talking to either brother, and I've watched her touch both of them without care. Not intimately, but there's a comfort there between the three of them that I'm guessing comes from years of knowing each other and living in the same world. It leaves me a little jealous.

Although I hate to admit it.

I hear Murphy ask Brady why Train Wreck is up there with Sam and Bash.

She looks more like a broken Barbie than a train wreck to me.

As we move along the line, the church continues to fill, and I can't help but wonder how many of these people actually knew Sam's dad. How many knew him as a friend. As a family member. Not as a mob boss.

How many people will be able to say that about Sam one day?

Me. Bash. Dean.

Will anyone else be able to say they truly knew him?

Just as that thought begins to upset me, I see the girl next to Sam rest her hand on his forearm and smile. It's small and borders on intimate.

I immediately want to claw her eyes out.

I know it's irrational. I just don't really care.

When we finally make it to the front of the line, I kneel at the closed coffin and say a prayer before rising to face Sam, Bash, and broken Barbie. Sam must recognize the annoyance on my face because he smiles a knowing smile and reaches for me. But the point in not coming with him today was to keep our distance, so I bypass him, *accidentally* step on broken Barbie's high-heeled foot, and let Bash wrap me up in a big hug.

"Feeling feisty today, Amelia?" Bash whispers in my ear. "Don't shoot her. It's not worth it."

"Ha ha. Very funny. You okay, Sebastian?"

He doesn't answer right away. Instead, looking over my head—I'm guessing at Eleanor behind me. "Not yet. But I will be. Sam will be too." He moves on to Cooper, who's behind me in line, and I move on to hug Nonna.

She doesn't let go of me right away. "Are you coming back to the house after the service today, principessa?"

"I'm not sure, Nonna. Sam has a lot on his plate. And I don't want to complicate things."

"Don't let him push you away. He needs you more now than ever before, and he is a man who doesn't know how to need anyone."

I walk away as Cooper moves over to hug Nonna, letting that thought ruminate in my head. When I moved to Kroydon Hills, I thought I didn't need anyone.

I was wrong.

Having people in my life I could depend on . . . people who could depend on me, made life better. And I don't want to ever go back.

As I take my seat in the pew next to Belles, I let my eyes track Eleanor and her brother . . . my brother . . . Wow, that's trippy.

I have brothers and sisters.

Holy shit.

I have a whole family, and they've been looking for me.

I lean in and whisper to Belles, "What's Eleanor's brother's name?"

Of course, Belles has no clue and starts a whisper down the line, asking Nattie, "Nat, what's Lenny's brother's name?"

Nat shrugs her shoulders.

"Jace," a male voice says from behind me.

Well, shit.

All three of us turn to look at Jace and Lenny as they sit in the pew behind us.

I guess it's Jace.

SAM

Catholic funerals aren't for the dead.

Catholic funerals are for the living.

All the pomp and circumstance of the ceremony, the mass, the service at the grave. That's all for those who've been left behind. I don't believe Pop is in that box. His body might be there, but his soul is somewhere else, on a different plane.

Maybe Heaven, if it does exist.

If he made it past the gates.

I have to believe no matter where he is, he's with Mom.

That's what I tell myself as I watch them lower his coffin into the ground while the priest canonizes a man who committed more sins in a day than most Catholics do in a lifetime.

A few inches of heavy white snow coat the ground around us, but a large black tent is keeping it off those of us under it. Nonna is sitting to my left, Bash on her other side with Emma seated next to him. My eyes keep scanning the crowd, constantly alert and looking for something out of place. I have men scattered throughout the cemetery.

I refused to leave us open today, no matter how many old-schoolers said that no one would dare do anything during the funeral of a boss.

Dumb fucks don't have a clue what they're talking about.

That's exactly when I'd strike.

When no one was paying attention.

When everyone was preoccupied with other things.

My eyes keep returning to Amelia's beautiful face, her pale cheeks tinged pink from the frigid air. She's dressed in a long, dark-gray wool coat with a pale-pink scarf wrapped around the collar. Her black stockings are showing beneath the coat, and her shiny black heels are getting buried in the snow. At least she's tucked under an oversized umbrella that Declan Sinclair holds for her and his wife. He's keeping the two of them dry while he's getting pelted with snow.

The quarterback's a good guy.

When he catches me watching them, he nods his head in understanding.

I took care of his woman, now it's his turn to help mine.

As the priest drones on about what a good man my father was, something in the distance catches my eye.

A man who doesn't belong here.

A man who belongs in another country.

But he vanishes as quickly as he appeared, leaving me to wonder if I imagined him.

As the service ends and my father is lowered into the ground, the reality of that action closes in on me. I'll never again be his second-in-command. I'll never again have him to defer to or rely on.

It's time to take the seat.

To own it.

It's time to wear the crown.

Once the service ends and the flowers have been dropped into the grave, Bash and I escort Nonna and Emma through the snow back to the limo. I send a message off to Mike and grab Nick.

Sam: Louis Tremblay was just at the cemetery. Pull whatever you can from any surrounding cameras. I want to know what the hell he's up to.

Mike: Give me an hour and I'll get you everything you need.

Getting Nick's attention isn't as easy. He's talking to Thomasso Darpino, the head of the five families in New York. The head of the Commission. He's arguably the most powerful boss in the country. The FBI lining the streets of the cemetery today and taking more pictures than a wedding photographer would call him the *capo di tutti capi*.

The boss of all bosses.

They'd be right.

When I approach, he immediately turns from Nick and reaches out his hand for me to kiss his ring. "Samuel, he was a good man. Have you found the person who set the bomb yet?"

"Thank you for coming today, Thomasso. We may have found him. I'm expecting the final piece of information soon." This man is a legend, and he and I have spoken more than once this week. His agreement was crucial to my plan for Sabatini.

"I look forward to hearing from you later." He shakes my hand, then Nick's, before walking away, surrounded by a group of his loyal soldiers.

Turning my attention to Nick, I tell him, "Louis Tremblay was here."

Nick starts to speak, but I cut him off. "Make sure every man we have has a picture. If they're not guarding the house today, they need to be looking for him. I'll have something to go on as soon as Mike gets back to me."

Nick looks skeptical. "Sammy . . ." He grabs my shoulders, and I step back, breaking his grip.

"That's an order. Fucking find him. And when you do, bring him to the goddamn warehouse alive. If you're not up for this, I'll find someone who is. But let me know now, Nick, because this is the last time you get to question me. This is the last time you hesitate. I love you, Uncle. But you do it again, and I'll put you in the ground next to my father. Do we understand each other?" He's hesitated twice now. I get it. I'm not Pops. I'm not who he's used to. But I know he never would have questioned my father and lived to see his wife that night.

"This ends now. Go. Make sure everyone knows who we're looking for, and make sure Marco has eyes on Amelia wherever she goes."

I turn without another word and see Declan walking the girls back to their cars.

I want to go to her.

I want to tell her that she should be by my side.

But I've got to deal with the rest of this fucking day before that can fucking happen.

Back at the house, Bash, Emma, and I follow Nonna inside together before everyone else arrives. I take my grandmother's coat and am stopped when she takes my hand in hers, then Bash's. "Get through today with spines of steel." She glances at Emma, then adds, "Do what you've got to do, then get everyone the hell out of my house. I'm tired."

Knowing what I have to do, I look at my brother. "I'll be in my office. Dean will grab you when we're ready."

"Sammy . . ." Emma's voice shakes, underscoring the fear she's doing a shit job of hiding, but Sebastian can deal with that.

It's not my job to coddle her.

Once the door to my father's office closes, I take stock. Over the past week, I had more security cameras installed around the compound, and an additional monitor sits on the desk, split into nine windows showing various locations around the house and grounds, twenty-four/seven.

The cars are beginning to line the driveway.

The men are in place.

It's time for the show to begin.

When my brother walks into the office an hour later, it's finally time to extinguish the first fire. "I thought you'd want to be in here for this, Bash. You earned it. If you hadn't remembered what Emma told you, we'd still be trying to figure out a way to deal with this shit." I pour us both a glass of scotch and pass one to Bash. "I'm crossing a line by allowing you to sit in on this conversation, but it's your life, and you deserve to hear this." A knock on the door has me checking the security display. "Showtime."

Carlo Sabatini walks in alone, having no idea what's about to happen, and an eerie calm settles over me.

"Carlo, please take a seat." I gesture toward the leather chair across from Pop's oversized desk, feeling more comfortable in this seat than ever before.

Carlo glares across the room to the couch Bash is slouched on, his black tie hanging loose and his scotch in one hand while the other grips his thigh. Bash looks like a string that's strung too tightly, fraying at the edges and waiting to snap. The discomfort he's causing is evident on Carlo's face. "What's he doing in here?"

Leaning forward, I rest my elbows on the manilla envelope sitting on the desktop. A knowing smile spreads across my lips. This isn't something I'd typically enjoy. But my hatred for this piece of shit runs deep enough that I'll make an exception. "He's here as a witness. After all, it's his life you bargained my father for years ago. And it's his life I'm about to give back to him."

Sabatini chuffs at the statement. "What the hell are you talking about, Beneventi? That was an agreement made between men. You can't break it now," he declares, spittle flying from his fucking lips.

All I can think is *"Watch me."*

With bone-deep satisfaction coursing through my veins, I pass the envelope to Carlo Sabatini. "Open it."

He flips through the evidence in front of him.

Pictures of him standing next to a dead man.

A gun in his hand, hanging down by his side.

A look of shock crosses his face before a mask slides firmly into place.

But I don't miss it. The *oh, shit* moment. He knows he's caught when he finally works up the nerve to ask, "Why am I looking at a picture of a dead man, Beneventi?"

I pick up one of the cigars that sat in my father's case on this desk all week and roll it between my fingers. "Because that's not just any dead man, Carlo. That's Thomasso Darpino's grandson. Funny. I'd think you'd recognize the Don of New York's heir, especially since he died in Atlantic City. Your city. If memory serves me correctly, you helped find the Russian who killed him. But that's not the Russian standing next to that body holding a gun." I wait a moment for realization to sink in, for the mouse to know he's in the trap. "It's you."

Sabatini throws the envelope back across the desk. "A conveniently photoshopped picture proves nothing."

He fucking wishes.

I clip the edge of the cigar and imagine how good it would feel to clip his trigger finger instead. "You and I both know that photo is the original. You should also know I have copies, as well as the other photos taken that night."

Carlo throws his chair back as he stands, his round face turning purple in anger.

Matching his excitement with calmness, I hold his stare. "Do you think the grieving Don will care to investigate whether that photo is faked? Do you think he'll listen when you lie? Or do you think Thomasso Darpino will take one look at the body of the heir to his empire, lying dead on the floor of one of your casinos—with you standing next to him, holding the gun—and then order your death and the deaths of your entire family without question or care?"

My question is met with silence.

Carlo has no answer because he knows he's caught.

When he sits back down, his anger is gone, replaced now with a friendlier smile.

The smile of a desperate man who knows there's no way out. "I assume you have an offer to make me, Beneventi."

Yes, death.

"As far as you're concerned, there will be no engagement between my brother and your daughter. That's my only demand tonight. But when I call, Carlo, you need to answer. Don't get any ideas. If something happens to me or those who are mine, the Don will have the photos in minutes, and you'll be dead before dawn."

Carlo Sabatini says nothing.

He sits before me, a defeated man, waiting to be dismissed.

"Go, Carlo. Go get your wife. Get your daughter. And get the fuck out of my house."

When he stands with a snarl on his face, I know I made

the right decision. Carlo Sabatini attempts to storm out of the office but is stopped by Dean, who's waiting on the other side of the door. Dean escorts Carlo out and follows his earlier instructions to stay with him while he grabs his wife and Emma. Then he escorts them to their car.

Meanwhile, Bash sits up on the couch, elbows on his knees, head hung low. "Is it over, Sammy? The engagement? The shit from this week?"

"Go get your girl, Bash." This may be over, but there's still another fire burning hot. But Bash has made his choice. That fire won't burn my brother, so he doesn't get to know about it.

"You didn't answer my question, Sam." My little brother is too smart for his own good.

I swallow what's left of my scotch and look at the man Bash has grown in to. "I already gave you more today than you should have gotten, Sebastian. Now, check on Nonna. Help me get everyone out of here in an hour. Then go get your girl."

Bash grabs the bottle of scotch and refills our glasses. "Is that what you're gonna do? You gonna go get Amelia?"

I lift my glass in the air toward him. "To the future Beneventi principessas."

Bash clinks his glass with mine. "To the future Beneventi principessas."

I wait until Sebastian leaves my office before I make the call I need to make.

Once the door shuts, I walk over and lock it before sliding my finger across one of my contacts and pressing dial.

Thomasso Darpino answers on the first ring. "What do you have for me, Samuel?"

"It's done. Thank you for allowing me to meet with him first. I'll pay you back one day."

"Thank you for finding my grandson's killer, Sam. You owe me nothing."

The call ends.

I light Pop's cigar and sip my scotch, knowing Carlo Sabatini won't be alive to see tomorrow.

AMELIA

Annabelle insisted I come back with them to their house after the services earlier. When I got here, the snow was coming down, but it was drivable. A few hours later, Nattie and I have finished off two bottles of wine and possibly joined the boys for a shot or two of scotch.

It tastes like a Christmas tree.

Declan has declared that no one is leaving tonight because there's a foot of snow on the ground, and it's supposed to keep coming down.

I could walk home if I really wanted to. It's not that far. But Declan laughed at my drunk self and said no. When Cooper pointed out that my bodyguard is probably freezing to death, sitting outside in his car, I went out, followed by Cooper, and asked poor Marco if he wanted to come in. Marco declined.

It doesn't matter that I can protect myself or that my favorite gun is sitting in my purse on top of Annabelle's fridge because it's not like I can keep it on the table with little hands all around their house. It didn't matter that Cooper is a Navy SEAL, and he promised he'd keep an eye on me. Marco didn't look impressed, and hours later, he was still parked in the same damn spot.

Declan and Belles took Gracie and Evie upstairs to go to bed while Nattie, Brady, Cooper, and I sit around a big bleached-wood dining room table. A Monopoly board sits in front of us, surrounded by chips, dip, salsa, and popcorn.

Belle's brother, Tommy, is watching *Godzilla vs. King Kong* in the other room, having had no interest in our board game. According to him, "Monopoly is boring."

"Do you really have to leave tomorrow, Coop?" I've learned over the last few years, drunk Nattie is always one of two extremes. She's either really happy and hyper or incredibly sappy and sad. Tonight, sappy and sad seem to have won. "What if you just say you missed your flight? What would the Navy do? Tell them it's my fault. Tell them it's a twin thing. Tell them anything. Just don't go back so soon." She wipes away the tears threatening to spill from her pretty blue eyes.

Brady pulls her from her chair and sits her on his lap, wrapping her up in a bear hug.

"Oh, God. Come on. I'm here for a day. Ya think you can keep your hands to yourself for a few more hours, man?" Coop closes his eyes as he dramatically scrunches up his face. Swear to God, I've seen Evie make the same face when Belles tries to get her to eat a vegetable.

When I met Cooper Sinclair, he was nineteen years old and had just finished Navy bootcamp. He was about to start training to become a Navy SEAL. That was two years ago. Since then, he's put on twenty pounds of muscle, lost any baby fat that he still had on his handsome face, and transformed from an attractive teenager into a beautiful man.

These Sinclair genes run strong. Coop and Nattie are both stunning, blue-eyed blondes. However, Nattie's hair is a whiter blonde than Coop's dirty blonde. And Declan may take after his father with his darker complexion and hair, but he's no less stunning.

"Such a manly face, Coop. Do your SEAL buddies know you make that face when you think about your sister having sex?" I know I'm egging him on. But in my defense, it's fun. And bonus points, it keeps my mind off other things, like Sam.

"Whatever you say, Amelia. Just because you're not getting any tonight doesn't mean my sister needs to." Oh, that little shithead.

I take the chip I just dipped in queso and throw it at Coop's face. "Who said I was getting any at all, Coop?"

He grabs the chip mid-air, then eats it before looking across the table at Brady and tips his beer bottle at him, giving him up as the rat.

I point my finger at said rat. "You've got a big mouth, Brady Ryan."

Nattie giggles, hiding her face against Brady's chest. "You have an even bigger mouth, Natalie. If Brady knows anything, it's because you told him."

Annabelle comes back into the dining room, rubbing her baby bump and yawning like she'd rather be in bed with the twins than down here with the adults. "Amelia, you're part of the family. And after the hospital last week, I'm pretty sure everyone knows something is going on with you and Sam. So suck it up, buttercup."

Declan joins the group, sitting down next to his wife. His hand automatically going to her belly just to rest there.

Family.

The people in this room have been the closest thing I've had to family in all the years since my mom died.

I'm not sure why I do what I do next, but I blurt it out before changing my mind. "So, speaking of family, could I get your unbiased opinions on something?"

I take a few minutes and explain everything about the insane Kingston situation, then realize I've accomplished the impossible . . . I've left Natalie Sinclair speechless.

I scan the five people surrounding me when I realize not a soul is speaking.

Instead, they're all just staring.

Cooper blows out a long, low whistle. "Well damn,

Amelia. You really know how to go big or go home, don't you?"

Nattie kicks him under the table.

Well, she tries to, I think. But she manages to kick me instead.

"Children." Declan looks between his siblings. "No fighting. If you wake a twin, you get to put them back to bed."

Belles links her hand with mine and squeezes. "You didn't tell me." She looks hurt.

"I only just found out this week, Belles. I've barely had time to process it, and I have absolutely no idea what to do with any of it." My eyes dart around the room, not sure what to expect.

"Well." Nattie smiles a tentative smile. "Lenny is awesome. I think you'd really like her if you got the chance to know her. Plus, in all honesty, if you're in this thing with Sam Beneventi for the long haul, I think you and Lenny are going to be in each other's lives anyway. She and Bash are the total endgame."

Brady, whose lap Nat moved off a few minutes into my story, wraps his arm around her shoulder. "She's right. That girl is Bash's girl. We've met a few of her brothers. Sawyer owns a bar in Old City called Kingdom. Hudson is an MMA fighter. They're both pretty cool."

"I know Max, Beckett, and Scarlet," Declan offers. "They run the Kings organization. Max is a typical oldest child. Total type A. Worries about everyone. In charge of everything." Dec looks at his siblings. "All the responsibility. None of the accolades. He's a really good guy. Beckett is a lawyer. He's a bit of a goofball, but he's crazy smart."

Annabelle squeezes my hand again. "I know I had my issues with Scarlet when we first met, but once you get to know her, she's loyal to a fault. She's a good person to have in your corner."

I turn my head to look at Cooper. "What . . . ? Don't you know any of the Kingstons, Coop?"

"No. But I know a hundred and twenty-three ways to kill a man without leaving a trace of evidence. If any of them or Sam Beneventi hurts you, all you need to do is call."

That's when it happens.

That's when the tears fall.

That's when my walls come crashing down.

That's when I realize that inviting the Kingstons into my life doesn't have to be scary because I already have a man who loves me and will stand by my side. And I already have a family surrounding me and supporting me.

That's when the pieces of my fucked-up puzzle start to finally fit into place.

SAM

THE PHONE IN MY POCKET VIBRATES HOURS LATER, JUST AS THE last of the mourners have finally cleared out of the house. I'm expecting it to be Dean with an update, but instead, I open the screen to a text from Declan Sinclair.

Declan: Just wanted you to know Amelia is sleeping at our house tonight.
Declan: Your guy is going to turn into a popsicle outside.
Declan: Or would that make him an Italian water ice?
Sam: Thanks for looking out for her today Quarterback. I'll come get her as soon as I can.
Declan: There's a foot of snow outside.
Sam: One of these guys has to have a truck I can borrow.
Sam: It's not like you live far. This town is 5 miles wide.
Declan: You wake a twin - you take them home.
Sam: You talking about your sister or your kids? Cause that sister of yours is a talker. I can definitely see you wanting to let her sleep.
Declan: You're not wrong. Text when you're here. Don't knock.
Sam: Gotcha.

Bash passes by with a grocery bag full of leftovers. "Hey, man. I'm heading to Len's. When Dean asks for his keys later, tell him I've got them."

"How'd you end up with Dean's keys?" I doubt he gave them up willingly.

Sebastian winks and opens the side door leading to the garage. Now that his non-engagement has ended, the weight he carries on his shoulders has lifted. "Don't worry about that. Just tell him I've got his car. If he needs to get home tonight, have him ask one of the guys for a ride. I won't be back."

The door closes behind him, and the phone in my hand rings before I have time to give a shit about how pissed Dean's going to be. Mike's name is flashing across my screen. "Tell me you've got something for me." I make my way down the hall and into the office, closing the door behind me.

"It was Louis Tremblay at the cemetery today. I was able to tap into some of the local security feeds and catch him coming and going. But the trail stops both ways about two blocks out. There's a dead zone I lost him in. I tracked him flying into the small private airport in Northeast Philly yesterday. He's got to still be in town. All flights in and out of the city have been grounded." There's a hesitation in his voice, like there's more he's not telling me.

"Spit it out, Mike. What aren't you saying?"

Mike blows out a long breath before I hear the tap of his fingers on the keyboard. "He flew in and out of the same airport last week, Sam. In on Sunday morning. Out that night."

"Fuck," I roar. Finally, the reality of what he's telling me hits home, and I put my fist through the wall. "It was him."

"I don't think he was alone, Sam. Think about it. He wouldn't have had access to your car. He wouldn't have known where you were."

There's a knock at my door before I hear Dean and Nick's voices yelling.

"Get me evidence, Mike. Get me everything you can." I

hang up the phone and pull open the door to see Dean and Nick standing on the other side. Opening the door wider, I step aside as I try to center myself from the sucker punch I just took to the gut. "Come in."

They both stand there, staring. Waiting for an explanation. An explanation they're only getting one piece of tonight. "Mike got Louis Tremblay on camera. He's here in Philly. He flew into the airport in Northeast Philly. He can't have flown home because the planes have been grounded. He can't have gotten far because he wouldn't know where to fucking go. Mike's got him flying in and out last Sunday too."

I look at my two closest men.

My best friend and my mentor.

My cousin and my uncle.

I don't want to believe one of them is a traitor.

"I want every man we have on this. I want every door knocked down. I want every favor called in. I want every fucking junkie who owes us money looking for this man. I want him found, and I want him found alive. I want to look this man in the eyes before he dies."

It's late by the time I pull up in front of Declan and Annabelle Sinclair's house. They moved into this house a few weeks after the shooting that introduced me to Amelia. In some ways, she saved Annabelle's life that day.

But I think, without knowing it, she might have also saved mine.

She certainly changed it for the better.

There's a high price to pay when you're the man wearing the crown. Humanity is a slippery slope. If someone isn't there pulling you back and anchoring you, it's easy to forget your humanity and become the monster some people think is needed to run an organization like *The Family*. Amelia's my anchor. She has been for a long time. I'll never be what most people would consider a good man. But because of her, I'll try my damnedest not to be a monster.

I shake off that maudlin thought and shoot off a text to Declan, letting him know I'm here. After a quick conversation with Marco, I trudge through the foot of snow to Declan's front door. Just as I make it to the front step, the door opens, and Cooper Sinclair stands there, staring me down. The kid has grown since the last time I saw him. There's something in his eyes that tells me he's seen and done things since then too. "Hey, Cooper. I'm sure it meant a lot to Bash to have you there today. You're a good friend." I offer him my hand, and he eyes it for a moment before shaking it and letting me in.

"Amelia, Nattie, and Belles are watching something in the family room. Amelia is falling asleep on the couch. They're pretty drunk." He laughs at what he just said, then adds, "Well, Nattie and Amelia are. Belle just kept eyeing the wine and telling Dec he's never allowed to knock her up again." Cooper leads me into the kitchen where Declan and Brady are sitting with a bottle of Macallan between them.

They both rise from the chairs. "Sorry for your loss, Sam." Brady Ryan is no longer the scrawny little kid he was the first time Bash brought him home over ten years ago. Fucker's gonna win the Heisman this year.

"Thanks, man." I nod at Declan. "I really just need to get Amelia and get home. It's been a long day."

Annabelle walks in and smiles at me. The ballerina is constantly smiling. I don't know if I've ever met anyone as happy with their life as this woman.

I wonder if I can give that to Amelia?

She walks up to me and wraps her arms around me in a

hug. "Sorry, Sam. I think you might end up holding Amelia's hair tonight."

I look over her head at her husband, who shrugs like his wife hugging another man is no big deal and pat her back awkwardly. "Thanks, ballerina."

"Take care of our girl, Sammy. She's one of the good ones," Annabelle sniffs like she's going to cry, and I look back over at Declan, my eyes begging him to save me.

Before he can step forward, Snow appears in the doorway of the kitchen. She's in black leggings and a loose white sweatshirt that's hanging off one shoulder. Definitely not hers. I like seeing the bare skin, but it's not her style. "If you get to hug mine, I get to feel up yours, Belles."

"Go ahead. But be careful. He has magical fertility powers and can knock women up with the blink of an eye." Annabelle smiles and grabs my hand, pushing down on her big belly. "Feel that?" she asks.

"What is that?" Jesus. It's like that scene in *Alien* when the monster is about to rip its way out of the chick.

"That's a foot. This one's going to be a little football player," she beams.

Amelia joins us, placing her hand over mine. "That will never get old, Belles."

"That's because he's not practicing his touchdown dance on your bladder all night. Trust me, it gets old."

Amelia wraps her arm around my waist and rests her head against my chest. "You ready to go home?"

"I'm ready." I kiss the crown of her head, then thank everyone. After what feels like ten more minutes of Snow hugging everyone goodbye, and Cooper Sinclair giving me the side-eye again, we finally get back in the truck I borrowed from one of the guards tonight.

"Hey, wait . . . Where's Marco?" Amelia looks around frantically, like his car disappeared into the snow.

"I let him leave when I got here."

"Oh," she giggles, and I pull her against me, needing to feel her warmth. Needing to hold her and know she's okay. Needing her to help me be okay. "I might be a little drunk, Sam."

"That's okay, Snow. Let's go home."

She buckles her seatbelt and lays her hand in mine. "I like the sound of that."

"Hmm?"

"Home. You're my home, Sam. I want to come home to you." I glance over at her. Her head is leaning back against the seat. Eyes closed and a smile on her beautiful face.

"My home is where you are, Amelia. We can talk about what that looks like tomorrow."

She answers me with a loud snore.

AMELIA

"What are you doing down here, Snow?" Sam's voice is hoarse when he walks into the kitchen a few hours after we finally went to bed. "It's four a.m."

His arms wrap around me from behind while I finish icing the last of the peanut butter fudge cupcakes he loves so much. Turning my head, I can't help but smile at the sleepy expression on his face. "I couldn't sleep. My internal alarm goes off every day by three, whether I want it to or not."

Sam leans his chin on my shoulder and peeks over at the counter. "So you thought you'd start baking?"

"I figured I might as well bake since I was awake. Thought you might appreciate some cupcakes today." He doesn't need to know this happens to me all the time. That I rarely sleep through the night. That I don't even mind getting up at three a.m.

"I'll never turn down one of your cupcakes, but I'd rather you'd have woken me up if you couldn't sleep. I'm sure I could've come up with a way to tire you out."

Once the last cupcake is iced, I hold it up for him to taste, but Sam has other plans. Turning me in his arms, he sits me on the counter and moves between my legs. Black pajama pants hang from his lean hips and his bare chest is beautifully on display in the low light of the kitchen. Hot and heavy eyes stare back at me with an intensity I love.

"I've dreamt of this for years, Snow." Strong hands trace

up my bare thighs under the t-shirt I threw on before coming down here earlier.

As his hands slide my shirt over my head, I admit, "In my fantasy, we were in the shop."

"Oh, yeah? Tell me more about your fantasy." He swipes a finger through the frosting and trails it down my chest, circling one nipple and then the other before pushing me back to rest on my elbows.

Once he spots the piping bag I used to frost the cupcakes, I confess, "You licked icing from every inch of my body."

He pipes a line of chocolate down my stomach, stopping at the waistband of my panties. "Let's see if the fantasy lives up to the reality."

My toes curl as his hot tongue licks its way up the lines of my body, while his fingers play with my pussy through my panties. Sam takes his time, his blue eyes holding me hostage while he destroys me.

I always wanted to be that finger he'd suck the frosting from.

I couldn't imagine anything hotter.

I was wrong.

This is better.

By the time he's licked, sucked, and nibbled my body clean, Sam doesn't even remove my panties. Just moves them to the side and slides his pajamas down. Then he pulls me to the edge of the counter and cages me in with his palms pressed flat on either side of my body.

The leisurely pace of a few minutes ago is gone.

Burying his face in my neck, Sam fucks me hard.

A low moan escapes me as he tilts his hips and slows his pace.

"I need you so bad, Snow, but you've got to be quiet. We wouldn't want to wake anyone up."

I'd give him anything he needed.

I should have been standing next to this man today, telling the rest of the world to go to hell. I couldn't give him that, but I can give him this. Digging my feet into his ass, I wrap my arms around his strong shoulders and suck on his bottom lip.

"Take what you need, Sam."

His tortured eyes lock with mine.

"You're not hurting me. Take it. Take everything."

Strong lips seal over mine. Owning me. Loving me.

My walls tighten, and I know I can't hold back. "I'm right there, Sam."

Strong hands lift me from the counter, anchoring me in his arms as he slams me down on his cock. "Come now, Snow."

Sam's tongue drives into my mouth, muffling my moan as his thrusts begin to slow, prolonging my orgasm. Once he's come, he doesn't put me back on my feet. No, not this crazy man. Instead, he takes two steps and leans me against the wall. "Are you okay, Amelia? Did I hurt you?"

"You would never hurt me, Sam. But you should put me down before you hurt yourself."

One hand slides up to the back of my neck, holding my head. "Never, Amelia. I'll never let anyone hurt you."

We managed to make it back upstairs and into bed for a few more hours of sleep. But once Sam's phone started ringing, it wouldn't stop. So we gave up and jumped in the shower, deciding it was time to meet the day. I was going to shower on my own so we could move a little faster, but Sam would have none of that.

"We'll save water," he said.

"We'll save time," he claimed.

Well, he lied. But it was the best damn shower of my life.

As we dry off, I realize I don't know what his plans are for the day. "Are you planning on working today?"

Before he has a chance to respond, his phone rings. Grabbing it from the nightstand, he answers, "What?"

I can't completely hear the other side of the call. It's just a muffled male voice saying something about Nick before Sam tells him he'll be right down. Cupping my face in both hands, he brushes his lips over mine. "Come on. Let me feed you, and I can show you what I plan on doing all day today."

Yes, please.

Downstairs, Nick is waiting for us in the kitchen, having helped himself to a cup of Nonna's coffee. "Sit," I'm told while Sam places bread in the toaster, pours me a cup of coffee, and hands me the creamer.

A girl could get used to this.

Once he's got me settled, he finally acknowledges Nick.

"You got something for me?"

Nick's eyes dart between Sam and me, contemplating his next move. "Nothing yet, Sam. The men have been looking all night."

Sam nods and butters my toast.

Ha ha. *Butters my toast.* That sounds so dirty. If only I had the energy to act on it.

When I look up, I see the two of them staring at me and realize I must have laughed out loud. "Why don't I leave you two alone?" I start to rise from the table, but Sam's big hand on my shoulder stops me.

"Sit, Snow. This is your home too," he adds.

"It is?" I ask, having no clue when that happened, but the idea warms my insides.

"It is?" Nick echoes.

Sam's glare would stop most men in their tracks. Not

Nick though. "When did this happen? Where was she yesterday?"

"Why are you here, Nick? You've got nothing for me. Get out until you do."

Sam's phone rings again, the shrill tone making my brain hurt.

"Tell me you've got something, Dean." Sam walks out of the kitchen and down toward the office before he stops in his tracks. "I want him alive. Nobody touches him until I get there. Got it?" A moment later, satisfied with whatever response he received, he hangs up and walks back into the kitchen.

"Dean's got him." Sam's talking to Nick, not me. "Wait here. I need you to drive me to the old warehouse."

Before Nick can say anything, Sam turns around, giving him his back.

Uh-oh . . . *Trouble in paradise?*

"Snow, come upstairs with me for a minute." His hand extends in front of me, and without so much as a bat of an eyelash, I take it and stand. We don't speak until we're in his room with the door closed.

"I need you to sit down and listen to me, Amelia." Sam's blue eyes have lost the sparkle they held earlier.

The caring man who worshipped me this morning is gone.

The warmth of that man has been replaced by ice.

"Just tell me. Whatever it is, we've already established I can handle it. And you're better off telling me now rather than beating around the bush." Instead of sitting, I rest my hands on his hips and step into him. "I won't break, Sam. You've always told me I need to trust you. Now, it's your turn. You need to trust me."

One strong hand tips my chin up to him. "I don't know what I've done to deserve you, but I'm never letting you go."

"Good. Now, what's going on?"

He strips out of his sweats, kicks them to the corner of the room, and walks into his closet I assume to put on a suit. "Sam . . ." I'm interrupted by his phone ringing. *Again.*

"Sam . . . your phone." I reach across the bed and grab it from where he tossed it as he walks out of the closet. Pants on but unbuttoned. Shirt on but hanging open.

It's like he's my very own Ken doll this morning, and I'm seeing all the outfits he has to play with. Unbuttoned, sexy businessman may just be my favorite.

"Snow," He looks at me, waiting. "The phone?"

Oops. I toss it across the room, not wanting him to miss the call, but it falls through his hands and lands on the rug. I guess my aim sucked.

A voice echoes through the speaker of the phone. "You've got my brother, Beneventi."

A familiar voice.

A voice from another lifetime.

SAM

"I DON'T KNOW WHAT YOU'RE TALKING ABOUT. WE BURIED MY father yesterday. I assure you, I haven't seen your brother since our meeting last month. Hold on." I mute the phone and hold it down by my side while stepping closer to Amelia, who's seated on the bed, her face drained of all color.

She must have figured out this has something to do with her.

I planned to fill her in as much as I could. Eventually. When it was safe.

I didn't plan to blindside her with this.

Cupping her face in my hand, I kiss her lips quickly. "Stay here until I get back." When she raises her brown eyes to mine, I add, "Don't go anywhere until I'm home. I promise I'll explain everything I can then." I take a step back, but she grabs my hand, her eyes darting between the phone and my face.

"Sam . . ." She swallows, then looks back at the phone.

"When I get back, Amelia. Just wait for me. Don't leave. I need you to promise me that. I need to focus right now and can't be worried you won't stay here."

She stands on shaky feet and kisses me. "Come home, Sam. Do what you've got to do, then come home to me."

"Always." I step out of the room, closing the door behind me and tucking in my shirt. I'm about to head downstairs, but I think better of it and walk into Sebastian's old room for some privacy to finish this conversation. "What do you want, Tremblay?"

The voice coming through the phone is calm.

Rational.

Not at all like the unhinged brother he sat next to that night in Canada. Yet again proving by his actions that although his words may say he and his brother share control, he's the one in charge. "I want to discuss terms, Sam."

"Why would I discuss anything with you? Seems to me you and your brother made your own terms with no regard to our agreement." It may have only been a month ago, but it feels like another lifetime.

"Sam." There's a hitch in his voice, a crack in the façade. "Ask me how I know you have my brother. Ask me," he pushes harder. "You want to know my answer."

I wish I didn't want to know what he's talking about.

But as I replay the last few days in my mind, I know I have to ask.

"Tell me why you think I have your brother," I demand. Fuck him.

"You've got a rat, Sam. I got a call a few minutes ago. They called a number only a few people have access to. They told me Louis was in Philadelphia, that he was in trouble, and you have him." He waits after that, letting those words sink in.

I don't know how many people know we've got Louis Tremblay.

I don't know who was involved in getting him from the motel where they found him.

Or how many men it took.

Fuck.

"You have no proof." I consider how to play this when George speaks up.

"You're young, Sam. You're in a new position of power. And you've got to show strength to keep the respect of your men. I know what happens next. And I fear I know why. I'm not calling you—"

I cut him off. "I don't know who the fuck you think you are, but I don't need some wannabe-wise, old Canadian fuck who didn't even know not to cross the Mexicans telling me how to run my business. So you can crawl back into the hole you came out of and find your brother yourself. I'm sure someone as smart as you doesn't need my help."

"I want his body, Sam." There's a pause. "Once it's done, I want his body." His voice is detached. Cold. Emotionless. "He has a wife and two daughters. I need to bring him home for them."

What the fuck? "You're assuming I have him."

"You have him. You have him because *I'm assuming* he's the reason you buried your father. If he was, he acted without consulting me. He acted without permission. He acted alone. He went rogue. And then, *I'm assuming* he was idiotic enough to fly back there to watch your father's body be lowered into the ground. He likes to know it's done." Another sigh. "You're within your rights to do what you've got to do. My brother is impulsive. He's trouble. He's brought us more trouble lately. He hated you because you came here calmly. You came here ready to deal, and you had us by the balls because of something he fucked up. He hated you on sight, Sam. But even more, he hated that I liked you. That I respected what you came here to do and how you did it."

Having heard enough, I cut him off. "And if I find your brother for you and make sure you have something to bring home, what do I get in return?"

"I'll send you the information on the phone that was used to call me." George Tremblay must think I'm stupid.

I scoff. "A burner phone won't tell me shit, Tremblay. And anyone worth their salt would have used a burner phone."

"And if I tell you the person whose pockets you need to check for the burner phone?" There's a pause before he adds, "I recognized the voice, Sam."

Having heard enough to understand what he's telling me, I end the call and dial Sebastian.

"Whatever it is, make it quick, Sammy. I'm a little busy." Lenny is laughing in the background, and I know he's gonna be pissed.

"I need a favor."

AMELIA

THE BEDROOM DOOR SHUTS BEHIND SAM, AND A SHUDDER wracks my body.

My mother used to say it meant someone was dancing over your grave.

That voice.

That was his voice—George's voice. There's no way I could forget his voice.

But it can't be. I mean, how could it be? Why could it be? I must be wrong.

Aren't I?

Why would George be calling Sam?

He told me to cut ties. That it was the only way to keep us all safe. I did it. As hard as it was to leave the only people I had left in the world, I did it. I never looked back. I never called, no matter how much I wanted to. I did what he told me to do.

Can it really be him calling now?

Maybe I'm crazy.

It's been years since I've heard his voice, so maybe it just sounded like him. Maybe I just need to crawl back in bed, wrap myself up in sheets that smell like Sam, and go back to sleep.

After deciding sleep is the way to go, I climb back in bed and close my eyes, hoping when I wake up, Sam will be home and ready to explain what the hell just happened.

A loud banging nearby stirs me from sleep. My hand slides across the cool sheets to Sam's side of the bed, but it's empty. The events of the morning begin to trickle back into my mind. I groan and cover my head with the pillow. He's not back yet, and staying right here in this bed until he gets back sounds like the perfect way to spend this day.

The light peeking through the curtains makes me think that I haven't been asleep for long. I bet I could get a few more hours in if that incessant knocking would just stop.

"Come on, Amelia." Ugh. It's Bash. "We drove over here in a foot of snow so you wouldn't be stuck in this house alone all day. The least you can do is come downstairs so we can be alone together."

What the heck is Sebastian doing here?

"Go away, Bash. I'm trying to sleep."

He knocks again. "No can do. Sammy asked me to come over and keep you company. And I'm not in a position to piss off my brother right now."

I swing my legs over the side of the bed and take a moment to fully wake up. Padding across the floor, I open the door just as Bash's hand raises to knock again. "Why are you raging against my door, Sebastian?"

He leans against the door frame and crosses his arms over that broad Beneventi chest both of these brothers share. "Your door? When did it become your door?"

"Whatever." I walk through the door and push by him, deciding I could use some ibuprofen and something to drink. "I meant Sam's door, boy genius. I'm half asleep and wasn't prepared to get the third degree over one word."

Taking the rubber band from my wrist, I throw my hair up in a ponytail and head down the stairs with Sebastian on my heels. "Hold up, Amelia."

219

"Cut me a break, Bash. It's been a weird morning, and I need something for this headache and a glass of water before you can expect me to be fit to spar with you." The Beneventi boys love to rile me up, but they're both so damn smart, I need to always bring my A-game. And I'm pretty sure my A-game went into hiding after a few too many glasses of wine last night, my complete lack of sleep, and this weird-as-hell morning.

However, when I come to a stop at the bottom of the steps, I rethink my decision to get out of bed, ignoring Sebastian.

Because standing there, staring back at me, is Eleanor Kingston.

My sister.

This morning just got a whole lot weirder and definitely more complicated.

I turn and look behind me to make sure Sebastian knows how fortunate he is that I left my gun upstairs.

Because I'm going to kill him.

"Sorry, Amelia," Bash offers sheepishly as he runs his fingers through his dark hair. "I tried to give you a heads-up. You've met Lenny before. I was at her house when Sammy called, so I brought her with me."

Just as I turn back around, Lenny adds, "And Jace."

Confused, I ask, "Who's Jace?"

Bash moves past me and wraps his arm around Lenny. "Jace is Lenny's little brother. He slept at her house last night because of the snow. I figured I'd let him tag along so Nonna could feed him."

Oh. *That Jace.*

The one from the funeral.

The one from my shop.

I don't know if it's the hangover from hell or that this morning keeps getting stranger by the minute, but I need some caffeine and ibuprofen now or this dull throb in the front of my head will go from an annoyance to a full-blown migraine at any minute. Deciding coffee needs to happen first, I walk past the two of them and head for the kitchen and the smell of Nonna's freshly ground beans.

You've got to love a woman who appreciates excellent coffee.

When I step through the entrance of the kitchen, Nonna is placing a piece of strata on a plate and handing it to Jace. "Good morning, principessa. Did Sebastian introduce you to our guests?" She glances my way with a warm smile on her face. I'm not surprised that feeding and taking care of people would be what brought her smile back.

"Good morning, Nonna." I move next to her and lean in to kiss her cheek, having already settled into a routine with my new honorary grandmother. "We actually met yesterday."

She passes me the pot of coffee and then a mug before turning to grab me the cream. This woman lives to take care of people. And I take it, thankful to be counted among the people she cares for.

I turn, leaning against the counter and let the piping hot goodness slide down my throat as I observe the room. Jace sits at the table while Bash and Lenny each make a plate and then sit down with him.

I guess we might as well deal with the elephant in the room. They had to know it was coming. As if she knows exactly what I'm thinking, Nonna pats my hand with hers. "Family comes in many shapes, dear. Give them a chance."

When I stare back into her blue eyes in shock, her lips tilt up knowingly. "There are worse things in this world." She shrugs her shoulders and walks over to Bash. A weathered hand traces his cheek before she places a kiss there. "Don't leave without saying goodbye, prupetta."

When I sit down at the table, I allow my gaze to travel

over Jace Kingston. His dirty blonde hair, a little too shaggy, brushes his hoodie. Broad shoulders stretch it tight. Definitely an athlete. His eyes are the same shade of gray as Lenny's. But where her face has sharp features, Jace hasn't lost his baby fat yet. You can see the beginning of the handsome man he'll become one day though.

My thoughts are interrupted when Bash elbows me.

"Did I hear my grandmother say, 'We have guests, principessa'? So, are you officially living here, Amelia?" There's a sarcastic tone in his voice I recognize.

Sam has that tone.

The two brothers share the same teasing sense of humor.

We all do.

This is comfortable for us.

Sarcasm is our love language.

I make sure Nonna is out of earshot before I turn to Jace. Sebastian knew what he was doing bringing the Kingstons here today. I may not be able to kill him for ambushing me because I love his brother, but I'm absolutely not going to give them the upper hand. He forgets who he's dealing with. Silly man. "So Jace, yesterday wasn't exactly the first time we met, was it?" I ask, laying it on thick with sugary sweetness.

Jace chokes on his breakfast, then looks from Lenny to me. "Umm, I guess not." He clears his throat, then adds, "I mean, I was at the hospital last week when Sebastian was brought in. So technically, we were in the same room that night too."

"Oh, no." Resting my elbows on the table, I bring my coffee mug up to my lips and peer over the top at him. "I meant the two times you were in my shop last week." Luckily, the mug hides my smile when Lenny slaps her hand against his leg.

"I told you, you stand out, jack off," she mutters, annoyed as she tries to smack the back of Jace's head.

Jace manages to duck and grabs her wrist. "Don't call me 'jack off,' Lenny Lou. It was your idea to tag along with Bash today. I just came along for the ride."

Lenny pales, then glances my way. "Well . . . why wouldn't I want to take advantage of the chance to get to know Sebastian's brother's girlfriend?"

"Guys." Bash shakes his head. "I told you this was a bad move."

This is just painful.

I should put them all out of their misery.

Turning toward Lenny and Jace, I decide to go for it. "It's okay. I know. I've known for a few days. Not as long as you've known, according to Sam. But he told me a few days ago. So we don't need to pretend there isn't a giant freaking pink elephant in the room."

"Did you know that the pink elephants in that movie were pink because the guy who wrote it was trippin' on acid?" Jace looks proud of his random fact, and I'm not sure whether to laugh or be disturbed that he just ruined one of my favorite childhood movies.

"Jesus Christ, Jace. Shut up." Lenny angles herself away from her brother and toward me. "I'm sorry if you feel ambushed, Amelia. It's just that when Sam called this morning, it felt like a chance. It felt like a sign. We've been looking for you for so long, and we finally found you. But then everything happened with the bombing. We've wanted so badly to reach out, but it didn't feel like the right time. I forced Sebastian to bring me with him, and the moron over there tagged along."

"Hey . . ." Jace whines exaggeratedly.

Lenny ignores him and continues. "Max is going to kill us when he finds out what we did. But it's just so crazy. I mean, we only found out recently that we even had a sister. So, when we found out it was you and that a few of us had actually met you before at Kings games . . . Then we realized you're with Sam Beneventi, and I'm in love with his brother."

Bash's hand moves under the table, I'm guessing to lend strength to his girlfriend.

But I don't think she needs the help.

She seems to be doing just fine on her own.

"I just didn't want to pass up the opportunity to spend time with you. To get to know you." She chews on her bottom lip. "And to be perfectly honest, there's a lot of us. It might actually be easier on you if you meet us in small doses."

Eleanor Kingston is beautiful. Her long, wavy, dark hair hangs around her shoulders. Sparkling gray eyes dance as she tells me her reasons for coming here today. She looks from me to Bash, nerves breaking through her calm façade. "Please say something, Amelia."

Jace has hung on her every word. His eyes never straying from his sister until now. Now he looks at me like my answer will save the world.

And I realize we have something in common besides DNA.

Everyone sitting at this table is an orphan.

Our parents are dead.

Maybe everything really does happen for a reason.

Trying to lighten the tension hanging thick in the room, I ask, "How many of you are there?"

Really? I mean, really?

That was the best I could come up with?

Why didn't I just ask if I could carry a watermelon?

Jace smiles, showing off perfectly straight, perfectly white teeth.

Yup. He's going to be a heartbreaker one day.

Then he answers me and manages to add another crack to the walls I've spent years building. "Counting you, Amelia, there are nine Kingston kids."

Counting me.

Well, hell.

SAM

NICK DRIVES THROUGH THE SNOW-COVERED CITY STREETS with ease, shifting his SUV into four-by-four mode and not slowing down at all. He's amped-up this morning. Talking a mile a minute. It's not like him. Nick is an opinionated fucker, but he's generally more intentional. This feels like talking for the sake of filling the quiet vehicle and the silent streets. "You need to make an example of him, Sammy. Don't let him beg for mercy. Don't listen to him. Fuck this cock-sucker. He needs to die." He turns the corner and speeds up again. "I worked for your father for thirty years. He deserved better than this."

Nick loves this.

Vengeance.

He has no mercy.

He kills without remorse.

Nick is able to do what all good killers do.

He kills without allowing humanity to get in his way.

If it makes *The Family* stronger . . . If it needs to be done . . . He does it.

He always has.

When we pull up to the old, abandoned warehouse on the outskirts of the city, I think back to the first time my uncle brought me here. The first time I was told to kill a man. My mother's killer. There was no hesitation that day.

We're met outside by one of Dean's men, who tells us Dean is inside, dealing with the trash.

"It's cold as a fucking witch's tit out here, Sammy. Let's make this fast and get on with it," Nick vibrates as he rubs his hands together, blowing out his cold breath.

I was hoping this one time my gut was wrong.

When Mike told me to look at the people who knew my schedule.

The people who had access to my car.

Fuck. I wanted to be wrong.

We walk through the maze of the old steel factory, back to where I know they've stashed Louis Tremblay, and I'm not disappointed.

There he is.

The fat fuck.

His hands are tied above his head, hanging from a hook on the ceiling so just the tips of his toes scrape the ground. A rag is shoved in his mouth, keeping him quiet. He's beaten and bruised, his eyes nearly swollen shut.

Without thought, I pull the gun from its holster and turn to Dean, "Didn't I say no one touches him but me?"

"That's from when we grabbed him at the motel, Sammy." His hands go up in front of himself in defense. "No one's touched him since. I swear it on my life."

Dean steps forward and pulls the gag from Louis's mouth, tossing it aside.

Before the rag hits the floor, a spray of red blood coats Dean's face.

The echo of the gunshot bounces deafeningly off the old steel walls.

Nick doesn't believe in silencers. Never has.

His gun is held out in front of him.

No longer pointing at Louis Tremblay, who's dangling lifelessly from the ceiling.

Now it's pointed at me.

I wanted to be wrong.

When Mike told me to look at the people closest to me, I wanted to be wrong.

I wanted him to be wrong.

But I knew I wasn't.

"It was supposed to be you too. What the fuck was the point of getting rid of the old man, if I didn't get rid of you both?" Nick explains with his gun cocked and aimed at my head. "I told your father you weren't ready to lead this family. You were never going to be the guy to take us where we need to be. You don't see the big picture, Sam. If you did, we wouldn't have wasted our time going to Canada. We wouldn't have been taking care of pussy instead of business." He sucks in air through his teeth. "I hope it was good pussy, Sammy, because I'm gonna be tryin' that shit out later tonight."

He's angry. But his anger is making him careless. Because now he's flustered.

I'm angry too. But unlike him, I don't get sloppy.

My anger is fueling my calm.

I've been waiting for this. Anticipating this.

I step into the gun. Closer. "How could you do this to *The Family?* To my dad?" On the inside, I'm raging. But on the outside, I stay cool. I stay calm. Just like this cocksucker always taught me. "He loved you. He took care of you your whole worthless life." My voice booms through the building while everyone looks on.

Their guns are all drawn.

Waiting.

Not knowing what to do.

But I know.

With one glance over Nick's shoulder, I confirm that Marco's in place.

Last night, after my phone call with Mike, I thought about what he said.

About who had known where I was.

About who had access to my car.

When I got to Declan Sinclair's house, I stopped to talk to Marco before I let him leave for the night. I told him I was going to need his skills today and that he needed to answer when I called. That he needed to be ready. I'd tell him when and where, and he needed to be there.

No questions asked.

I hope this kid's as good as they say he is.

"It was supposed to be my turn," Nick yells, spit flying from his mouth. "The old man was dying anyway. But if I could get you out of the way too, then I could take control. I've been his right hand our entire fucking lives. It should have been mine." He smiles. He actually fucking smiles. "I thought I'd hidden my thoughts well enough, but Louis saw it. He saw how you couldn't get out of your own way. He saw what your father didn't. If he saw it . . . If he knew we'd be better off with me leading *The Family*, everyone else will see it too."

"Well, Louis is dead now, isn't he, Nick? You just killed your ally. And if you think George is your ally, you're dead fucking wrong. He called me this morning. He wants no part of your fucked-up agenda."

One step to my left gets us where I need us to be.

I smile and wrap my hands around the barrel of his gun, holding it up against my forehead. "Never underestimate your enemy, Nick."

I overpower him and angle the gun up to the ceiling, while he struggles to get back control.

"Fuck you, Sam." Those are Nick's last words.

For one split-second, he looks confused.

Surprised.

That doesn't last long.

The barely audible whizz of a bullet is drowned out by

the clang of the metal shell hitting the concrete floor. Nick's head snaps to the side from the momentum of the bullet shot into his brain. A perfectly round hole appears on the left side of his temple before the bullet makes its way through the right side of his head, taking half of Nick's head with it.

In the corner of the open second-floor catwalk, Marco is lying on his stomach, his McMillan TAC-338 rifle fitted with a custom suppresser in his hands, having just made the perfect shot.

The silence only lasts as long as it takes for reality to kick in. Then everyone starts talking at once. Guns are out. Men scatter around the scene, trying to figure out what just happened, and if we're being attacked.

I ignore them all and take Dean aside. "Listen to me very carefully. I want Tremblay put on ice. I've made arrangements for him."

Dean wipes the blood from his face. "What do you want done with Nick? We need to make sure everyone knows he was a traitor. Are we giving him a traitor's death?"

I look at my uncle, disgusted by the man on the floor.

The man who helped teach me this business.

Who always preached *The Family* comes first.

"Cut off his cock and shove it in his mouth. Then make sure his body is found. I want his mother to know he was a traitor. I want his wife to know he was a traitor. I want there to be no question where his loyalties lay."

The men stand there, staring at me.

"Make sure we leave no doubt about what we do to traitors. Now clean this shit up."

Later, once we feel like Dean's crew has it under control, he and I leave. I climb into the snow truck he opens, trying to figure out why the hell he's driving this beast. "What's up with the ride?"

"Your fuck-wit brother stole my keys yesterday. We need to get you and Bash new cars." He starts the old-as-fuck truck and jacks the heat up. "How'd you know what was going on? When did you find out about Nick? And why the fuck didn't you tell me?" He glances over before he starts driving us home.

"Yeah. I already ordered the car last week. I pick it up after my follow-up with the surgeon Monday." I fucking hate having to depend on people to drive me around. "As for the rest, I had a feeling but couldn't figure it out. Then I talked to Mike after the funeral, and he said something that clicked. I really fucking hoped he was wrong, but I knew he wasn't."

Maybe a plow truck isn't the worst thing to be driving after the biggest November snowstorm Philly's ever seen hit the city. Dean maneuvers us through the back streets to Kroydon Hills without issue. "Have you ever considered bringing Mike on in a more official role? I mean, he's pretty fucking useful to have on the payroll."

"No. Mike does better as a lone wolf. This way he gets to do his thing, and I can pay him well to do my thing. Works for now." I've considered it before, but Mike fucking hates authority. He'd never work well as part of *The Family*.

Dean slams on the brakes, and we slide up to the stop sign. "So why are we keeping Canada's body on ice? What's your plan for that fat fuck?"

I tell him about the call I got this morning that confirmed my suspicions about Nick, then throw up a quick prayer that this ass doesn't kill us before we get home.

"No shit? He fucking ratted us out? A traitor and a rat. Fuck." Dean looks sick.

I nod my head and grab the *oh-shit* handle as we slide around a corner on what feels like two wheels. "I managed not to die today. Or last week. Can you not kill me on the ice, asshole?"

Dean's laughter stops when we skid again. "Whatever. Man up."

"If I'm dead, you can't be my underboss." I planned to move him into the position after the funeral. I just hadn't had a chance to deal with the moves yet.

"Hey, you gotta take a guy to dinner before you ask him to marry ya, man." This fucker.

I watch the snow-covered streets pass us by.

The pristine white of yesterday is gone.

Now it's brown from the salt and sand the plows dropped on the roads.

Messy.

Real life.

Pristine doesn't last. Dirty does.

"Position is yours, Dean. Don't fuck it up."

AMELIA

"Okay, so tell me more about Scarlet. I mean, she can't really be as bitchy as you make her sound, can she?" Sebastian, Lenny, Jace, and I are gathered around a fireplace in the family room. The fire is burning hot, warming the room and the atmosphere. The awkward start to the visit has faded slowly, leaving curiosity in its place.

"Come on, Amelia. Bitchy knows bitchy. You two should get along just fine." Sebastian throws a pillow from across the room at me.

"You're just pissed I shot you down when we first met." I think back to that night a few years ago when Belle took me to my first Kings game and how nervous I was to meet her friends.

"Shot me down?" he mocks.

"I believe I told you, 'Nice try, little boy.'"

We all laugh at the grouchy look on Bash's face.

Lenny screeches, "Oh my God, Sebastian. You hit on my sister," and all laughing stops.

The three of them turn to look at me, probably to see how I'd take that slip of the tongue, which is not so much a slip as it is the truth. "Well, I guess you could say the Beneventi brothers definitely have a type."

Lenny seems to like that answer. "So, Amelia. What do you like to do in your free time? I mean, besides bake?"

Bash pulls Lenny closer to him. "She likes to shoot."

I glare.

"Come on, it's been two years. It can't be too soon to go there." One of Bash's blue eyes winks at me, and I think I'm gonna kill him.

"Be careful, Bash. You don't want to piss me off. I'm still a better shot than you."

Holy shit. I never thought I'd joke about this.

What has happened to me?

A door creaks down the hall, and Bash stands. "I'm just gonna go see who that is."

"Maybe take Amelia with you, just to be safe, Bashy boy," Jace tells him.

Bash shoots him a *What the fuck?* look. "What did you just call me?"

"Kingstons do nicknames, dude. You better get used to it." Jace shrugs like it's no big deal. Like he didn't just call a six-foot-five mountain of a man "Bashy boy."

"Dude, you're not even out of high school yet. Seriously, are you even out of diapers? Don't call me 'Bashy.' I'm not scared to throw down with a hockey player." Sebastian grabs a pillow from the couch and whacks him with it.

"You might want to graduate college before you start picking on a high schooler." And just like that, I feel like I can truly let go of the breath I've been holding since Sam left this morning. He looks the same, but his beautiful blue eyes look weary. I'm not sure if it's coming home to see Lenny and Jace in his house or if it's because of whatever he left to deal with this morning.

Sebastian stops beating Jace up with a pillow and turns to his brother. The smile falls from his face. "Hey, man. Everything alright?"

Sam doesn't take his eyes from mine as he answers Bash. "Yeah. Thanks for coming over to keep Amelia company today." If I had to guess, I'd say he's trying to figure out whether we're talking about the whole long-lost sibling thing. But I'm not sure. He finally tears his eyes away from mine, and there's a look crossing those crystal blues I'm not so sure about.

Is it sympathy?

Sorrow?

Pain?

"Listen, we need to talk. But not tonight. You gonna be around tomorrow?" Sam's asking Bash, but it's Jace who answers him.

"There's a Kings home game tomorrow at four. Why don't you guys come?"

Lenny moves to stand next to Bash and turns to me. "You know, that's not a bad idea, Amelia. A few more Kingstons are guaranteed to be there. But there'll be other people around as buffers. Plus, we behave better when we're in public."

Knowing how Sam and I left things this morning, I give the best answer I can for the moment. "That sounds like it could work. Can I let you know tomorrow though?" Sam's shoulders are tense. He's stressed. I can see what he's not showing, and I need to know what's going on here before I worry about when I'm going to meet anyone else.

Disappointment crosses Lenny's face, but she masks it well. "Of course." She pulls her phone from her pocket. "Can I have your number? I'll text you mine."

Butterflies float around inside my stomach. I'm really doing this. I'm going to willingly put myself out there.

"Yeah. Me too," Jace adds.

Bash looks at me with a mix of laughter and pity in his eyes. "Bad news, Amelia. Their family brings codependency to a whole new level. Have fun with that."

Lenny, Jace, and I exchange numbers before we hug awkwardly and say our goodbyes.

Once it's just Sam and me left, I lace my fingers through his. "Are you alright?"

He turns and tugs me behind him, quietly leading me up the stairs and into his room. Once the door is shut and the light turned on, he peels off his wool coat, and I get a glimpse of what looks like tiny spots of blood on his white dress shirt. "Sam," I gasp as my heart speeds up. "Are you okay?" I reach toward him only for him to step back.

"Yeah. I'm alright." His voice is tired. Defeated.

"Sam . . ." I plead, letting his name hang in the air. "You're not alright. You may be able to fool everyone else, but I'm not them."

He starts unbuttoning his shirt. "Shower with me, Snow. Help me wash away this day." The lines on his face show the toll that's been taken.

"Tell me what's going on." I place my hands over his and finish unbuttoning his shirt. "No hiding. No more lies. Remember?" I need to lessen this load for him. Take care of him. "Let me help you."

His hands stop mine. "No more lies. I promise. But there are certain things I can't tell you. It's for your safety as much as it's for mine."

"Should I be scared?" I ask coyly, batting my lashes as I push his white shirt over his shoulders and watch it fall to the floor.

My hand moves to the buckle of his leather belt before he stops me. "You will never need to be scared, Snow. Never again. But there are things we can't discuss. Not yet. Not legally."

I step back and pull my shirt over my head, adding it to the growing pile. "Then when can we discuss them?" Turning, I begin to walk away.

Sam follows me into the bathroom, watching me strip out of my leggings and underwear. He reaches into the shower and turns on all the showerheads, allowing steam to start filling the room. "We can discuss more after you're my wife, Amelia. Right now, they could force you to testify against me."

"Then marry me, Sam. A piece of paper means nothing to me. It doesn't change anything between us." I trace the stitches above his eye and slide my lips over his. "I love you. Nothing is going to change that."

Backing me into the shower, he deepens our kiss.

My hips grind against him helplessly, wanting more.

He bites my lip then sucks it into his mouth as he picks me up.

My arms circle his shoulders as my nails score his skin.

My legs automatically circle his waist when he leans me up against the cool tile.

His tongue dances over my pulse point before his teeth graze my skin. "That piece of paper means something to me. We're not getting married because I watched a man die. When we get married, it's going to be because I got down on one knee and asked you to be my wife. I'm not going to marry you so you don't have to testify against me, Amelia. I'm going to marry you so I can spend the rest of my life making you smile." Hot water rushes over the tension in his face, washing away the weariness I saw earlier. Sam lines his cock up and slowly lowers me onto him as he thrusts. "Call me old-fashioned, but I want to marry you in a church. I want to stand in front of God and promise to love you every day until I take my last breath." One hand smooths my wet hair from my eyes as the water beats down on us, and his lips graze mine. His slow pace picks up in intensity until he's fucking me like it's the last night of our lives. My stomach tightens, and the room begins to close in around us as my orgasm sits just out of reach.

237

Sam kisses a trail up to my ear, then whispers, "Because I do love you, Amelia. And I'm going to ask soon."

How did I ever live without this man?

Sam's blue eyes turn molten before his mouth is back on mine and he fucks me hard.

Consuming me.

And I'm lost and found all at once.

His tongue claiming mine as hungry hands grip my ass tightly.

Holding me to him.

Filling me completely. Loving me completely.

"Tell me you're mine, Snow."

"I'm yours, Sam. I've only ever been yours."

He bites down on my lip, and I come, chanting his name.

Thanking God this man is mine.

SAM

ONCE THE WATER BEGAN TO RUN COLD, SNOW AND I GOT OUT of the shower and climbed into bed. She's lying naked in my arms, and for the first time in my life, I feel like the king everyone has always told me I'd become. Not because of business. Because of the woman in my arms. My fingers trace the ridges of her spine as she lies with her head on my chest.

For so many years, I wondered what my life would look like when I took over control of *The Family*. It wasn't until I met this woman that I finally knew what I wanted that life to be. "So, Snow . . . When I ask, you'll say yes?"

The hand that had been tracing my tattoo stops. She doesn't move. Doesn't look at me. But I'm not worried because this woman is mine. She's everything, and for two years, I haven't doubted that she felt the same way. I was just biding my time, waiting for her to be ready.

"I guess you better ask and find out," is whispered into the dark night.

I kiss the top of her head and skim my hand over the smooth curves of her body. "Guess I'm not finding out tonight then."

"Sam Beneventi." She sits up, bringing the sheet with her. Fire colors her chest, moving up her neck and to her face. "That is not a nice thing to do to a woman."

There's that spark I love.

There's the fire.

239

"I don't have your ring here. It's in the condo." I sit up and take her hand in mine, tracing where my ring will sit. "I can't ask without a ring."

"Sam." The word comes out barely a breath from her lips. "You have a ring? But how? We weren't even really together before all of this."

Holding her head in my hands, I kiss her lips. "We've been together for two years, Snow. I don't know how many times I can tell you that you've been all I've seen since the day we met, but one of these days, you're going to listen to me, woman. You'll listen, and you'll believe it."

She moves one leg over my hips and straddles my lap, her arms going around my neck. She runs her fingers through my hair and smiles. It's the smile I want to wake up to every day for the rest of my life. "Ask me, Sam. I don't need a ring. You're the one who wants all the formalities. I just want you." She leans in, so close her breath caresses my lips. "Ask me, Sam."

I wrap my arms around her back and hold her to me. "Marry me, Amelia."

"That didn't sound like a question, Sam."

I close the inch between us and run my tongue over her lips. "That's because it wasn't. Marry me, Amelia. Let me love you. Let me keep you safe. Let me give you a family. You'll always hold all the real power in this relationship. The whole city will kneel down to me, but I'll only ever kneel for you. Marry me."

Her glassy eyes hold mine before she whispers, "You want babies? You want to give me a family?" A lone tear slides down her beautiful face.

"I want to give you everything."

Amelia rocks back, and I know she's not oblivious to what she's doing to me as my cock grows hard, snuggled against her perfect ass. "Amelia," I warn.

She rocks back again. "Yes, Sam."

I look up at her, unsure whether she's answering me or heeding my warning until that smile takes over her entire face.

"Yes, Sam. I'll marry you," she murmurs against my lips as her mouth seals over mine.

I wrap an arm around her waist, ready to seal the deal when my cell phone rings.

"I'm naked and in your arms. I just agreed to marry you, Sam Beneventi. Please tell me you're not going to answer that."

I lean my forehead against her chest, wishing I didn't have to. "The ringtone is for the guards, Snow. I have to answer."

She climbs off my lap and places a kiss on my shoulder blade when I lean away to grab the phone from the nightstand. "What?" I answer and lean back against the headboard.

Snow's nails skim down over my chest, causing my cock to jump.

"There's someone here to see you, boss. Says his name is George Tremblay. He says you'll want to see him. He's alone."

Jesus. Fucking. Christ.

"Make sure he's clean. No weapons. Make sure he's alone. Then bring him to the front door. Wait with him until I get there. I'll be down in a minute." I end the call and turn back to Amelia, expecting her to be pissed I took the call. Instead, I'm greeted by a frozen Amelia. She's as pale as a ghost and staring at me in disbelief.

"Who . . . Who's downstairs, Sam?" Her voice shakes as her body trembles.

I rub my hands up and down her arms. "I'm sorry, Snow. I need to take care of this. I'll be back up as soon as I can." I slide my legs off the bed but am stopped by Amelia, grabbing my arm.

"Sam?"

"I'll be back up as soon as I can. Stay here."

I pull on a pair of jeans and a shirt from the closet and grab my Glock from the dresser, checking to ensure the magazine is loaded with one in the chamber. When I turn to check on Amelia, she's still pale. "Is your gun in the nightstand?"

She nods.

"Good." I kiss her quickly. "Stay here."

The house is quiet as I take a calming breath before I open the front door. George Tremblay stands just outside, next to one of my men.

With my gun trained between his eyes, I ask, "What the fuck were you thinking, coming to my house? Tell me why I shouldn't shoot you right here and now."

I hear the creak of footsteps on the staircase behind me before he answers and know it's already too late.

AMELIA

"GO BACK UPSTAIRS, AMELIA." SAM'S VOICE IS SHARP ENOUGH to cut glass, but he never takes his eyes off whoever is on the other side of the door, so I keep moving down the stairs.

Needing to see who it is.

Afraid I already know the answer.

Sam's gun is held high and pointing at the intruder.

Blocking his face.

Until the man moves his head slightly, and my world tilts on its axis.

"I'm here to see her as much as I am you, Beneventi. Are you going to let me in?"

With the hand not holding my revolver, I brace myself against the railing, refusing to let my knees buckle like they're threatening to.

For a minute, I'm a ten-year-old girl again, wanting to know what her mother is doing in the basement. "Sam?"

He never turns his head away from the man standing at the door. "Go back upstairs."

"It's been a long time, Anastasia." That voice . . .

No sooner have the words left George's mouth than Sam's gun is placed flat up against his head. "One more word. One more inch, Tremblay, and you're a dead man."

Forcing my feet to move, I hurry down to the bottom of the stairs and run to Sam's side. It's as if I've been run over by a Mack truck when I see him, up close and unobstructed.

A ghost from a past I left behind.

Sam's angry eyes look from me to George, then back to me. "Are you ever going to do what you're told?"

"No," I tell him honestly.

"Let me in, Beneventi. It's fucking cold out here, and I've come a long way to see you." His eyes scan me from head to toe before adding, "And her."

"He's clean, boss," Sam's man adds.

Sam steps aside, never lowering his gun. "One wrong move, and I will shoot you."

George's lips slowly inch up into a small smile. "I'm more worried about her. She's a better shot than you."

"And why would you think that?" Sam asks as we walk to his office.

"Because I taught her."

That one single sentence brings back a lifetime of memories, while also adding so much hurt and confusion.

Sam stops dead in his tracks with concern lacing his eyes. Eyes that look at me, into me, and ask me if I'm okay without ever opening his mouth.

Once we enter Sam's office, he waits for George to sit in one of the chairs across from his desk, then sits behind the desk. I lean against the wall next to the door.

A silent observer.

For now.

"Explain to me why you thought it would be a good idea to come to my house in the middle of the night, uninvited." He lays his gun down on the desk but keeps his hand on it. His eyes never stray from George. They don't so much as look an inch in my direction. "Explain to me why you don't think you deserve to die for that."

"I told you I was coming to claim my brother's body." George turns from Sam and looks at me. He's older. Heavier. With more lines and wrinkles marring his face than when I left Washington. But there's no doubt it's him. "And I needed to see you, Anastasia. I needed to explain."

Sam stands and bangs his gun against the desk threateningly. "You do not speak to her. You do not get to so much as fucking look at her." Sam finally looks my way, but the anger is still there, coursing through his veins. "Explain it to me."

"Do you remember me telling you about the man who taught me to shoot? The man who helped me get a new identity? The man who helped me escape?" I move next to Sam, across from George, trying desperately to figure this all out. "That was him," I tell him before turning back to George. "What are you doing here? You told me never to contact you again, to cut all ties and never look back. I don't understand why you're here, and what any of this has to do with Sam."

Before George can answer, Sam does. "Let me make sure I'm getting this right. This man, who came to our house in the middle of the fucking night, like only a killer would have the balls to do, is the man who helped you get away from who? The Canadian drug cartel that your mother and stepfather were running drugs for? The cartel you were scared would find you and kill you because you stole their money? He let you think he was helping you? Keeping you safe?"

"Anastasia . . ." George interrupts.

Sam startles me when he rounds his desk and pistol-whips George across the face, splitting his cheek and leaving a small trickle of red blood dripping down toward his jaw. "What did I say? Do not fucking speak to her. Sit there, shut up, and I may let you leave here alive." Sam's gun is still in his hand, and if I know this man at all, I know he's nearing the end of his patience.

"He was helping me, Sam. I don't know what he's doing here now, but I wouldn't be here if it wasn't for him helping me three years ago."

He looks at me with pity in his eyes, and my blood boils.

"I'm not sure what he was doing, Amelia, but he wasn't helping you. That man, there, *is* the Canadian cartel. He runs it. He's who you stole the money from." Sam's voice is cold. Hard. I'm not sure who he's angrier with. Me for not listening to him, or George for coming here. "He had the power to do whatever he wanted. He runs the whole fucking thing."

"You're wrong." He's wrong. He has to be wrong. "No. George helped me. He helped us. My mom and me." I look over at George, knowing Sam would never lie to me, and the pieces of the riddle become clearer. "Tell him he's wrong, George. Tell him you don't know what he's talking about. Tell him you were like a father to me." When George looks at me with pity in his eyes, much the same way Sam did earlier, I decide that's enough pity for one night.

Raising my gun, I aim at his T-zone like he taught me to do all those years ago. "I'm a good shot, old man. I was taught by the best. Tell me Sam's wrong."

"He's not wrong, Anastasia." George's eyes flick toward Sam, silently asking for permission to answer. The two men stay locked in a death stare until Sam finally nods his head once, allowing George to speak.

The dumb man doesn't realize he should be more worried about me right now than the man standing next to me.

If I kill him tonight, Sam would gladly clean up my mess.

"You were so young, Anastasia. There was never a need to tell you what we were doing. Why would we? I was always vigilant to keep my professional and personal lives very separate. But your mother was different. There was always something about her. I promised her if you ever needed it, you'd have my protection. I tried to make sure you'd never need it, that you were prepared to defend yourself in any situation. Watching you grow up, and helping you learn how to protect yourself was one thing. But then one day, you weren't a little girl anymore. You were a beautiful young woman, and you needed me, Anastasia. She died, and your stepfather attacked you. And I wanted to protect you so badly, but keeping you wrapped up in my life wasn't the answer. If you'd given me any inclination you wanted to stay . . . that you wanted to stay with me, I'd have told you everything. But you kept saying you wanted to get away, so I waited until the time was right and hid the money in your mother's closet. I left it there for you to find, for you to start a new life with."

My heart is in my throat as he unloads all his truths. "Oh my God. I was a child. You were the closest thing I ever had to a father. I feel sick."

"No one was ever coming after you. Because I never told anyone you had the money. I said I didn't know what your mother and stepfather did with it before she died, and he went to prison. I told them to leave it be. You were safe. You were gone. And you were living your new life. That's all I wanted for you." George hasn't moved a muscle since he started speaking. His eyes are locked on mine while my gun remains trained on him . . . until I turn to Sam.

"Did you know? Were you keeping this from me?" Please, God, don't let that be the case.

Sam flinches infinitesimally at my question.

George wouldn't have noticed it.

But I did.

"No, Amelia. I knew George was the head of the cartel because he's who I met with to clear your debt. To make you safe. To make it so you never felt like you had to look over your shoulder again. I had no idea he was the man you told me about until now." The cool distance in Sam's voice hurts worse than knowing George betrayed me, but what should I expect when I basically just asked him if he betrayed me too.

"Why are you here now, George? Why tell me now? I need to know the whys if I'm going to wrap my head around this. I need to know why you were so willing to push me away before but needed me to know the truth now," I demand.

"That's not up to me. That's up to Sam." George crosses his leg at the knees and waits for the explosion, knowing he just lit a bomb.

I turn to Sam. "What's he talking about?"

Sam's jaw clenches tightly.

Fury rolls off him in red hot waves.

Maybe George didn't light the bomb.

Maybe I did.

SAM

Amelia has no idea the situation she's put me in. We just killed this man's brother, and there's no way there's any doubt left in his mind what my biggest weakness is.

Her.

What was she thinking leaving that room?

What part of "stay here" did she not understand?

I made a promise to her, and myself, that I'd keep her safe.

So how do I get her the hell out of this situation?

"Why did you come here, Tremblay? What did you think you would accomplish?" I lean back against the desk and cross my arms so my gun is still there, pointed in his face. Meanwhile, this guy looks calm as a fucking cucumber, sitting relaxed in that chair.

He nods his head toward Amelia. "Think you could put that gun down, Anastasia?"

"Nope. You taught me better than that, asshole." She straightens her stance and keeps her arms held strong. "Why are you here, George?"

"Your boyfriend killed my brother today."

I knew it was coming but still hoped this wouldn't have to be discussed in front of Amelia. She might be better equipped to handle this than most women, but that doesn't mean I want her to know any part of this. I have to give her credit though. She doesn't give any kind of reaction. No shock. No horror. She remains standing without a single emotion crossing her beautiful face.

Waiting for an explanation.

One she's not getting from me.

Not now.

Not in front of this man.

"We made a deal this morning. I gave him information, and now he needs to give me Louis's body." George shifts, his eyes looking anywhere but at Amelia. "And I decided it was a good time to check in on you, Anastasia."

"After three fucking years?" I asked, ready to disembowel him for hurting her.

Snow lowers her gun to her side and loosens her stance. "You've got to stop calling me that." Her strong voice softens, giving him what he wanted. "That girl died in Washington. I left her behind. I made a new life. I'd say I appreciate everything you've done for me, but I don't know how I feel now. Did you really do it for me? Or did you do it as a way to get rid of me because I was a problem for you? Either way, I don't care what your business with Sam is." She briefly turns her head toward me, but her face gives nothing away. "That's between you and him. And I don't appreciate you trying to drag me into the middle of it." She steps in closer to him and waits.

George stands hesitantly from his chair.

I swear to God if he touches her, I'm going to kill him.

Amelia takes one small step forward before she rests her palm on his chest and I flex my fist. "Thank you for teaching me how to take care of myself." Then, in a move that surprises the hell out of me, she stomps down on his foot before driving her knee into his balls, causing him to double over in pain. Once he's gasping for breath, she takes the handle of her gun and slams it down into the back of his head, adding, "You taught me well. Now get the hell out of my house."

This woman was born to be my queen.

With her head held high, she walks slowly out of my office and closes the door behind her.

Gasping for breath, George sits back down on the edge of his seat, groaning in pain, with blood still dripping from the cut on his face.

I can't figure him out.

"Did you get what you came here for? Did you think she was going to say 'Thank you'?"

When he's finally able to look at me, the look of pain is replaced with hostility. He cracks his neck and adjusts himself. "Have you ever loved something you had to set free, Beneventi? It's not beautiful the way poets make it sound. I loved that girl for most of her life. When I let her go, I thought it was to build a better life than what she had. A safer life. Then you show up in my city, ready to pay off her debt and put yourself at risk for her. She didn't build a safer life. She flew from one dangerous life to another. Though, in my world, no one knew who she was. She was hidden. By your side, she'll always be a brightly shining target."

"Why come here and expose the truth? You had to know she wouldn't thank you." Christ, she's going to be pissed when I get upstairs.

George stands and straightens his coat. "I needed to see for myself that you'd protect her. I needed to know she'd let you. I needed to see she was safe and that she could handle herself the way I taught her to." He offers me his hand, adding, "I'm sorry for the loss of your father and the part my family played in it. When your uncle called me this morning, I'd like to say I was shocked. But I wasn't. I wasn't surprised by Louis's actions, and I wasn't surprised your uncle had turned on you. Watch your back, Sam. Family will always cause the most problems."

"I think that about wraps us up here. I'll have my men escort you to your brother and then back to your plane. After that, we'll be good if you stay the fuck out of my city." I shake his hand, sealing our earlier deal.

George Tremblay agrees and adds, "Don't let this world touch her."

"Done."

After having Tremblay escorted out of the house and giving instructions to my men on where to take him, I call Dean and fill him in on everything that just went down.

"She really kneed him in the nuts then cracked him in the head with the butt of her gun?" Dean whistles. "Damn, Sammy boy. Remind me not to ever piss your woman off. She's lethal. Not that we didn't know that already. But seriously, guard your balls when you come home late."

"Thanks, asshole. I'll try to remember that. So, Nick's taken care of?"

A car door slams shut on Dean's end, and the engine roars to life. Guess Dean got his car back from Bash. "Yeah. That's handled. They'll find him at some point tomorrow. Everyone will know he was a traitor."

"We'll announce your new position as underboss at Tribute this week. Let me know who you think can step up and take over your crew. We'll need to figure out who's the best fit for my advisor without Nick here now." My head hurts just thinking about it.

"Yeah. I gotcha. Want to go over it tomorrow?"

We're going to have to deal with this sooner rather than later, but . . . "Not tomorrow. Let's do it Monday. I've got some things I need to do tomorrow."

"Sounds good, boss. Talk later."

I end the call and look around the room.
It's time to make some changes.
In this room.
In this house.
With my life.

SAM

IT'S HOURS LATER THAT I OPEN MY BEDROOM DOOR, EQUALLY hoping like hell Amelia is on the other side and concerned she won't be there.

That she'll have run.

Scared in a way I'll never admit to another soul.

The vice around my heart loosens when I find her on the bed.

She's curled up in a ball, lying on her side, facing me.

She's bathed in the moonlight.

She's breathtaking.

And she's crying.

In two steps, I'm next to the bed and on my knees in front of her, moving her hair out of her face. My lips brush over her forehead and whisper, "What can I do, Snow? How do I make this better for you?"

She sniffs and wipes her face with her sleeve. "Just don't yell at me right now. I know you want to. I know I should have listened to you and stayed up here. But I didn't. I'm not sure why or how, but I knew who was at that door. I heard his voice this morning. I tried to tell myself I was crazy." She sits up and tucks her legs underneath herself. "But I knew I wasn't. I knew that voice. Then when you answered the phone tonight, I heard his name and thought it couldn't be him." She laughs a sad laugh at herself. "I mean, why would George be in Philly? I was wrong. I had to be. But the further you got from this room, the more something pulled at me to follow you."

"I'm not going to yell at you. But babe, you can't ever do that again. If he had hurt you, I'd have killed him. No questions. No second chances. No hesitation. That move would have started a war. And wars mean people die. I wouldn't think twice about doing it for you. I wouldn't have thought at all. I would have reacted. So, you coming down those stairs when I specifically told you not to would have cost people their lives. I don't want that on your conscience. But you need to understand that if you're going to live this life. You have to listen. You have to do what I say. For your safety and everyone else's."

She reaches out for my hand, then clasps it to her chest. "I'm sorry, Sam."

"You showed someone my weakness tonight. You showed Tremblay what you mean to me. If he ever wants to come at me now, he knows to do it through you." She shivers, but I keep going. "I'll never let that happen, Snow. But you've got to help me." She tugs harder on my arm until I rise and sit next to her on the bed. With my arms wrapped around her, she cries against my chest.

"I just don't understand how many times I'm going to be told my life is a lie. First, by my mother when she told me we were in witness protection. Then, by the Kingstons telling me that my father is dead and I'm their sister, even though I was raised as an only child with no family. And tonight, by George, the closest thing I ever had to a father. He may have helped me, but at what cost? I've lived the last three years in fear, constantly looking over my shoulder. Always worrying that I would have to run. Scared to ever let anyone close because I didn't want to risk putting them in the cross-hairs."

"Amelia, look at me." I wait for her to tilt her head up and wipe the tears from her eyes with my thumbs. "Are you done?"

Her head snaps back, and her shoulders tighten at the harsh tone of my question. "What?"

I stand up, pulling her with me. Then turn her around so she's looking at our reflection in the large mirror over the dresser. "Are you done crying? Are you done feeling sorry for yourself? Yeah, it sucks. People you cared about lied to you. But you're here now. You're with me now. And I will never fucking lie to you. So now you're free to make whatever decisions you want without being worried there are people coming after you." I stand behind her with my hands holding her shoulders, watching her reflection in front of me.

Those brown eyes harden as she steels her spine. "Your mom lied to protect you. And she did it. You grew up safe. It might not have been the idyllic childhood you wish you had, but you were loved. Fuck, George Tremblay. He lied, but his lie brought you here. And I'm so fucking thankful you're here. And you're the one in control of what happens now. You want an entire football team of brothers and sisters? You got 'em. I was a little surprised to see them here earlier, but if that's what you want, then we can have them for Sunday fucking dinner for all I care. Your whole life is in front of you, Snow. You hold all the power."

She turns slowly in my arms. "You'd really do that? You'd invite that entire family to your house for dinner?" A hint of a smile graces her face, and I know I'd destroy the entire city if that's what it took to keep it there.

"Of course, I would. But you have to sit next to Max. He's a pompous pain in the ass."

Warm hands close around my face before those lips make me forget why I was mad. "We could always do it at one of the restaurants. We own enough of them. We really don't have to do it here."

She pulls away from me and leads me to our bed where she slowly removes her leggings and her shirt. Then she wags her finger in front of me. "Uh-uh. You said we could have them here. No take-backs now."

Standing in front of me in a white silk bra and panties, she's as pure as her name.

And I want nothing more than to dirty her up.

"You said something earlier, Snow." I pull my shirt off and add it to her pile.

Slim fingers play with the button of my jeans. "Oh, yeah? What did I say? Because I said a lot of things earlier." She pops the button, and I grab both of her hands in mine and turn her toward the bed.

"You told Tremblay to get out of *your* house." I bend her over the bed so her chest is flat against the comforter. "Your house, Snow. Do you have any idea what hearing that did to me?" I let go of her hands and run my knuckle down her spine before shucking off my pants.

Snow starts to push up off the bed. "Hands on the bed. If you move, this ends."

"What ends?" she asks breathlessly.

I drop to my knees and run my nose along the inside of her thigh.

She smells like heaven.

And I'm about to crash the gates.

Slipping her panties to the side, I slide my tongue along the seam of her lips and feel a tremor skirt down her body as she moans. Her tart taste covers my tongue while I devour her but never give her what she really wants. Instead, I circle her clit, over and over. First with my tongue, then with my finger. Not letting either give her more than I'm ready to allow.

"Sam . . ." she whines. "I need . . . I need more."

Sitting back on my heels, I smack her ass. "You'll get what you're given tonight, Amelia."

"Oh, God." She shivers and starts to rise from the bed.

"Yeah, baby. I knew you'd like that." I stand and rip her panties from her body and admire my handprint on her ass, bright red on her perfect porcelain skin. My palm runs over my mark and rubs it gently as I lean over her body and whisper in her ear, "Are you ready for me, Amelia?"

"God, yes," she whimpers. But she never moves, being the good girl she needs to be right now.

When I stand back up, I smack her beautiful ass again, and she cries out.

"Yes. Oh, yes." I fucking knew she'd love this.

This woman is perfect.

My woman.

Mine.

I take the head of my cock in my hand in rub it through her soaking wet cunt before bottoming out in one strong move, my fingers gripping her hips and pulling her against me. "Mine, Amelia. You're all fucking mine."

Her hands stretch out in front of her, fisting the sheets. "So good, Sam. Don't stop. Give me more."

I smack the other cheek of her ass, adding another red print, and she screams and comes, pulsing around my cock. Milking me. I couldn't pull out now if I wanted to. And I don't want to. I want to mark her, inside and out.

"Oh God, Sam. Don't stop. Come inside me. Let me feel you."

With her body still flat on the bed and her head turned to look at me, I come with a roar that reverberates off the walls of the room. Then I blanket her body with mine, peppering kisses along her spine. "I love you, Snow."

"Thank God. Because I'm gonna need to do that again."

Yeah. This woman is everything.

AMELIA

Sam and I are sitting at the kitchen table the following day when my phone vibrates with a text.

Belles: Are you coming to the Kings game today?
Amelia: I'm not sure what we're doing.
Belles: Woo Hoo. You're finally a WE!!!
Amelia: You are too much.
Belles: Nope. I'm just enough.
Belles: So are you AND Sam coming to the Kings game today? It's at 4 pm.
Amelia: Well . . . Lenny kind of asked me to meet her there.
Amelia: But I think I like the idea of being in your box better. I think I'd feel more comfortable there. Would you be okay with that?

Sam leans over my shoulder and skims through the texts. "I like the idea of you being in her box too. It paints a pretty picture." He smirks, and I'm embarrassed to admit I'm confused.

"What the hell are you talking about?" When his eyebrows waggle like a stupid cartoon character, it clicks. "You're a pig."

A kiss is pressed against my lips. "Yup. But I'm *your* pig."

Belles: Wait. I'm confused.
Belles: Are you telling me you talked to Lenny about the

whole long-lost sibling thing, and I'm only just hearing about it?

Amelia: Sorry. It was yesterday. And there was too much going on.

Belles: I expect the down and dirty on this one day next week.

Amelia: Works for me. So can I use your box as a buffer?

Amelia: Is everyone going to the game?

Belles: Of course you can! And yup – we'll all be there. Coop is even going. His flight got pushed back until later tonight. So you'll be getting all sorts of Sinclairs.

Amelia: You're the best, Belles.

Belles: Of course I am.

Belles: See you at 4!

When I put the phone down and look up, it's to find Sam sitting with his arms crossed over his chest. Waiting. "So, are we going to the Kings game today?"

"Is that okay with you? We can be in Belle's box and then either stop by the Kingston's box or ask them to stop by Belle's. What do you think?" I ask, not sure which way I think would be less awful. I suck at meeting new people. With the amount of moving around I've done, I should be better at it. But I've made a career out of trying not to get close to people. And I'm not even sure how I feel about all this yet, but I know I want to take the next step.

Sam sips his coffee as Nonna walks into the room. "Of course, it's okay with him. He just wants you to be happy. You met two of them yesterday, meet the rest today and get it over with. Then you bring them all here, and I will cook a feast. My boys are in love with sisters." She kisses each of us and walks right back out of the room.

I turn back to Sam. "How did she know?"

"The walls have ears, principessa," is yelled back into the room, and the two of us burst into laughter.

When Sam and I stop at my apartment that afternoon so I can change clothes, I realize something.

As I slide my Watkins jersey over my head, Sam sits on my bed, watching. "What are you thinking so hard about over there, Snow?"

"I was just thinking this doesn't feel like home anymore. I love it here. I love the life that I built inside these walls. But it doesn't feel like home because I know this isn't going to be where you are at the end of the day. Where are we going to live, Sam?"

Sam stands and prowls my way. When his strong hand cups my cheek, I lean into its warmth. "Wherever you want, principessa."

"It sounds so different when you say it."

Sam drops down to one knee and pulls a red box out of his jeans pocket, and I gasp.

"Snow, you're the center of my world. You're going to be the center of our family. The fire to my ice. I've loved you since the first minute I saw you, and I'll spend the rest of my life loving you, trying to be the man you deserve to have standing by your side. Marry me." He cracks open the box, and there, sitting nestled in black velvet, is the most stunning ruby with pear-shaped diamonds on either side. "The color reminded me of you, so I bought it. But if you want a diamond instead, we can get you that too."

"It's my favorite color," I tell him with tears in my eyes. "Please stand up."

"You haven't answered me."

Kneeling down in front of him, I wrap my arms around

his neck and kiss his lips. I'm full of so much love for this man. "Because you never asked, silly man. Of course, I'll marry you. But I don't want to wait forever, Sam. I want to marry you as soon as we can. I want you. I want the life we're going to build. I want to give our babies your last name."

Sam pulls the ring out and slips it on my finger.

"When did you get this? I thought you said it was at your place?" I hold my hand out in front of me and admire this exquisite ring.

"If you're asking when I got it today, I had Dean pick it up and drop it off earlier. If you're asking when I bought it, the answer is thirteen months ago." And my mind is blown.

"Thirteen months ago?" My voice squeaks. "You've had this for a year?"

Sam stands, pulling me with him. "You've always been mine, Snow. I just needed you to catch up."

For the first time in my life, I feel like the Disney princess he's named me after. "Thanks for being patient, Sam."

"I'd wait forever for you, Snow."

AMELIA

"I messaged Lenny earlier to let her know Sam and I would be at the game and we'd be in the suite with you guys." I try to contain my nerves as I stand next to Bash in the suite while we watch Declan throw a perfect spiral downfield for a fifty-yard gain.

"Go, Daddy," Belle's daughter, Evie shouts while she and Gracie jump up and down, dressed in their little Sinclair jerseys and matching pink tutus. Before either girl sees it coming, Callen Sinclair—Coach Sinclair's youngest son, who's technically their uncle but also only one week older than the girls and over twenty years younger than Declan, Nattie, and Cooper—plows both twins down while he runs with a football the size of his head in his hands.

"Touchdown!" He spikes his ball as the girls start to cry. Both Belle and Katherine, Coach's wife and Callen's mother, run for the kids.

Bash and I move over to the bar in the back of the box where Sam is talking to Brady and Cooper. Beers are passed out as we approach, and Sam's arm circles my waist, pulling me in close to him.

Belle walks over, looking frustrated with her kids until something catches her eye and her entire expression changes. "Oh my God. What is that on your finger?"

Blushing, I smile up at Sam before turning back to Belle and holding my hand out.

Bash slaps Sam on the back. "Way to go, Sammy." Then he wraps me up in a hug. "You're way too good for him, Amelia."

Belle pulls him off me and holds my hand up in front of her. "Amelia . . ." she squeals and looks from me to Sam, then back. "I'm so happy for you!" She squeezes me tightly before I'm passed to Brady and Cooper.

Everyone is smiling. Celebrating. It's a good day.

This is what family is supposed to be.

Maybe I made a mistake, and I should back out of my plans with the Kingstons today.

Quit while I'm ahead.

I hate to even admit to myself that I'm letting my nerves get the better of me, but it's true. Momentarily lost in my own world, I missed whatever caused Sam's grip on me to tighten, but when Bash moves towards the door, I know my chance to back out is gone. Standing in the door of the suite is Lenny with Scarlet by her side and a group of ridiculously tall men behind them.

One of the tall guys maneuvers around the women and heads in our direction. "Prince!" he bellows.

"King," Sam answers a little less obnoxiously. Then he whispers in my ear, "This is Becket Kingston. I've known him for years."

Taking a deep breath, I square my shoulders and turn to face the first of what's bound to be a full-blown pack of Kingstons.

Brady and Cooper make room for Becket, and he slides into our small circle as if this isn't at all uncomfortable for him. "Gentlemen." He nods. "So Prince, aren't you going to introduce us?"

Sam's grip on my hip tightens. "Amelia, this is Becket. He's a dick, but he means well."

Becket laughs, and his smile lights up the room like fireworks on the Fourth of July. Incredible blue eyes, the color of the ocean, dance with excitement, and I find myself relaxing a bit. When I reach my hand out to him, he takes it gently, and I think, *"Okay, I can handle this."* But then he pulls me toward him and embraces me in a hug, and I know I'm in over my head.

"Hands off, Becks," Sam orders, but there's no malice in his voice.

Becket is well over six feet tall with light brown hair and chiseled features that don't match the sheepish smile he gives me when he lets go. "I'm sorry. It's just that we've been searching for you for three years. After the first year of not being able to find anything, we were worried something had happened to you. But this last year . . . finding out you were alive but could be in trouble . . . We all wanted to be able to do something to help you if you needed it, and we couldn't."

Oh wow.

The tears build behind my eyes before I force them down. "You didn't even know me."

It's then I realize that we've been joined by more Kingstons. A man I've seen in this box before takes a confident step forward. "It didn't matter if we knew you. You're one of us."

Damnit. I don't know whether I wanted to actually like these people, but they're making it very hard not to.

Becket shakes his head at his brother. "You were supposed to wait your turn, Max."

A strikingly beautiful woman who I have no doubt is Scarlet Kingston steps in front of both of her brothers. "You are all idiots." She offers me her hand. "Scarlet. It's nice to finally meet you, Amelia. Ignore our brothers. They're like puppies. Obnoxious. Sometimes overly excitable. But they're trainable, for the most part. Just don't let them pee on your rug."

They all stare at me with a *Holy shit, she did not just say that*

265

look on their faces, waiting to see how I react. But when I smile and take Scarlet's hand with a laugh, everyone breathes a sigh of relief. "Nice to meet you, Scarlet. I've heard a lot about you."

"From Lenny?" she asks, glancing toward her sister.

Belle moves next to me with Gracie on her hip. "Nope. From me," she tells the group with a tilt of her head.

"I'm not that bad," Scarlet denies at the same time, and a few of her brothers groan.

"Yes, you are," adds the biggest man in this insanely attractive group of people who somehow share my DNA. He's tall and broad with muscles stretching the sleeves of his long-sleeved t-shirt.

"Shut up, Huddy," Scarlet snaps.

"Can we not bust out the nicknames until we've at least told our sister our actual names?" I think I'm going to call this one Hulk instead of Huddy. He's freaking huge. "I'm Hudson, Amelia. Welcome to the family."

Jesus. The words "sister," "brothers," and "family" roll off their tongues as if it were natural. Normal. As if I'm not the first long-lost sister they've found. "Umm, thanks. I guess."

When Lenny finally makes her way over to us with Jace and another brother I haven't met, I start counting the siblings.

How many of them did they say there are?

"Hey, Amelia." Lenny stands sandwiched between Sebastian and the unknown brother.

He looks around at everyone crowded into the corner of the suite. "Well, if these guys haven't scared you away yet, I'm Sawyer."

Lenny smacks his shoulder. "We're not scary,"

"Speak for yourself, Lenny Lou. I'm scary," Scarlet owns it, and I think I may have a girl-crush on my sister.

"You are scary, Scar. I'm still not convinced you don't

suck the life out of your dates when you're done with them," Becket laughs at his own joke as Scarlet scowls.

"Go fuck a cheerleader, Becks." She takes my hand and Lenny's and starts tugging us along behind her. "We're going to have some girl time. Bye, boys."

Sam lets go of me and pats my ass as I'm pulled away.

I hear Jace groan. "Dude, that's my sister."

Okay. That's going to take some getting used to.

"Well, she's going to be my wife very soon, so I outrank you, high schooler."

When Lenny, Scarlet, and I sit down at one of the high-top tables, they're both staring at me, waiting. "Did I just hear Sam say you're going to be his wife?" Len asks.

Heat crawls up my face as I switch the hands holding my bottle of beer to show off my new engagement ring. "He did."

Lenny squeals, and Scarlet pulls my hand toward her, drawing the attention of Annabelle and every other woman in this suite. "That is stunning. He has good taste," Scarlet approves.

"Of course, he does. He's marrying her," Belle tells the women as she joins us, handing me Gracie while she pulls up a chair. "He's a lucky man." Her eyes trail over my face, shimmering with unshed tears. She's such a crier. "You're all lucky to have this woman in your lives."

Gracie lays her head down on my shoulder and starts twirling my hair as she sucks her finger.

That's totally her tell. This kid is going to be out like a light at any minute. I pat her back as I listen to these women talk, and I realize I had nothing to be nervous about.

The Kingstons are as crazy as the family I've already found.

This kind of crazy creates my kind of people.

My kind of family.

SAM

Watching Amelia getting comfortable with the Kingstons is a strange thing. She's been passed around from one Kingston to the next the entire game. She's been laughing and smiling the whole time, so they get to live for now.

"Have you set a date yet?" Bash asks as Max Kingston joins us at the bar.

Max asks the bartender to get five bottles of champagne and leans back against the bar, watching the room.

His empire.

His family.

"No date yet. Amelia would be happy to just go down to city hall and get married in front of a judge. I had to convince her to get married in a church. Nothing big. Just our family." Bash nods, knowing that I mean this won't be an event for *The Family*. Even if, as the head of *The Family*, it's expected of me. That's not what Snow would want, and I plan on giving her everything she's ever wanted.

Max looks at me, torn.

"What's on your mind, Max?" We've never been close. I wouldn't call him a friend. But for Amelia, I'll fucking try.

The bartender begins filling crystal champagne flutes behind us with Max watching him out of the corner of his eye. "Just wondering if she'll consider us family by then. If she'll want a relationship after today."

"She'll come around. She's used to being on her own. But

she'll come around. Just give her time and the space she needs to get there." The bartender hands me a flute as Scarlet joins the three of us.

"The two of you are taking two of my sisters. Know someone who wants to take number three off my hands?" Max tips his glass toward Scarlet.

"Fuck off, Maxie pad. You wouldn't know what to do without me." A waiter begins moving around the room, passing out flutes of champagne, and Scarlet looks tempted to pour hers over her brother's head.

Max raises his glass. "I'd like to make a toast."

The box quiets, and everyone turns in our direction. "I know we're a loud, and sometimes an obnoxious and over-whelming bunch. I know we take a little getting used to. But I hope you're willing to take a chance on us, Amelia, because we love hard. We have each other's backs. And we'd be lucky to have yours too, if you'll let us."

If I know my girl, she hates all this attention.

The way she's chewing her thumbnail tells me I'm right. Becks must notice it too because he cuts off his brother's next words, "To old friends, and new family."

The entire stadium erupts as Declan Sinclair runs the ball into the end zone.

Amelia raises her glass. "To the Kings."

"To the Kings," is echoed throughout the suite.

After placing my glass on the bar, I move next to my bride-to-be and hold her face in my hands. "I love you."

Her answering smile is everything.

When our lips meet, a high-pitched peel of laughter comes zooming toward us before one of the twins pushes in-between our legs. "Kisses," she demands.

Bash picks her up and kisses her head.

She smooshes her lips to his cheeks. "Kisses, Bashy."

"Told you it was a good nickname, asshole," Jace flips

Bash off just before Annabelle marches over in full momma-bear mode and flicks his ear.

"Welcome to the family, baby Kingston. Don't curse in front of my kids." She takes Evie away from Bash and hands her to Jace. "Here. Your turn," she says and walks away without a backward glance.

"What the fu—" Jace gets cut off by Scarlet.

"I wouldn't mess with Annabelle Sinclair, Jace. You'll lose."

Jace watches his sister walk away before turning back to us. "That woman is scarier than Scarlet. And her punishment smells like it needs her diaper changed." He scrunches up his nose and holds Evie away from his body. "Help?"

Amelia runs her hands down Evie's back. "Have fun with that. The diaper bag is over there." She laces her fingers with mine. "Come on, Sam. Let's go watch the fourth quarter."

"Whatever you want, Snow."

After the Kings pulled out a hard-fought victory over the Bears, everyone said their goodnights and goodbyes. The majority of the Kingstons watched Amelia like she was a deer that was going to bolt. They underestimate her strength right now. But that's okay. After they get to know her, they'll realize she's a force to be reckoned with. It takes a whole lot more than that to scare my girl.

Once we're both tucked into her piece-of-shit car, we wait in the stadium traffic to get home. "Can I please order you a car as a wedding present? Seriously, Snow. This car is one oil change away from dying while you're driving it."

"Hey." She rubs her steering wheel. "I like my car. And you're not normal. You realize that, right? People don't just order cars like groceries, Sam. You go to the dealer. You offer them less than they're asking for. You test-drive the thing."

"I order cars, Snow. And I'm ordering you one. You need to be safe. Our kids will need to be safe."

"Sam Beneventi, I just said I'd marry you. You're not allowed to guilt me into getting a new car because of kids we might have one day." She sits on her side of the car, pouting as we inch along. "How many do you want?"

"Cars? I don't know. Three, I guess." That's not what she was asking, and I know it. But watching the fiery red color blossom on her face makes it all worth it.

"You're a dumbass, Sam. Who needs three cars? I meant kids. But seriously, three cars? We're two people. Aren't two cars good enough?"

"I don't know how many kids I want, Snow. I just know I want them. I want to watch you hold our babies. I want to fill the house with kids and laughter and cookies." I lean over and crush my lips to hers. Her hands cup my face as my tongue traces her perfect lips. "And you're going to need to pick a wedding date so that can all happen."

"Call the priest, Sam." She rubs her fingers along my jaw. "See how fast we can get this scheduled. I can't wait to be Amelia Beneventi."

"I'll call him tomorrow morning. Right after I order your car."

Amelia tugs on my hair. "Sam . . ."

I kiss her lips again, and she melts against me.

A horn honks behind us.

"Let's go home, Snow." I try to pull back, but she grabs my face and holds my lips to hers, kissing me. Loving me.

"Let's go home, Sam."

AMELIA

ONE YEAR LATER

Belle and I are sitting on the sofa in the corner of Coach's suite at the Kings stadium when my phone vibrates on the table, alerting me to a text on the Kingston family group text chain.

Lenny: Amelia – are you here?
Jace: Where's here? Because none of you were at my hockey game this afternoon.
Hudson: Aww. Poor baby. Is somebody feeling neglected?
Amelia: I'm here. I'm in Coach's suite with Belle.
Lenny: On it. I'll be there in a minute.
Max: You're supposed to be working.
Lenny: Becks isn't even here.
Sawyer: He's probably with his girlfriend.
Hudson: She's fucking awful.
Becks: I'm on the damn text asshole.
Hudson: Sorry. She's perfect for you. Love her.
Scarlet: She sucks. Get a new one.
Becks: At least I have a woman.
Sawyer: Nope. I'd rather be single.
Jace: Yup. Me too.
Hudson: Me three.
Max: You're supposed to be working.
Becks: Whatever assholes.

Gracie and Evie decide now is the perfect time to make a run for Aunt Amelia's gigantic belly, but my sexy husband cuts them off at the pass, picking both girls up under their arms and turning them back to face the field where we're watching Declan and Sebastian kick some Sentinel ass. Belles is sitting across from me, rocking her son, Nixon, to sleep in her arms. "Why is it, that as I get bigger and bigger, my sex drive gets more out of control than ever?"

She takes a big sip of wine as a smug smile settles over her face. "It's almost over. Just a few more weeks. Find whatever position is the least uncomfortable, and go for it. Just make him do all the work."

"I second that." I hadn't heard Scarlet come in, looking as fashionable as ever in a gorgeous winter-white pants suit and matching heels, but apparently, she heard enough of our conversation to agree. She's tall and thin, and not a single strand of her dark hair is out of place. And I might hate her a little bit right now, while I sit here like a beached whale, feeling like I'm nineteen months pregnant instead of nine. "You've got two more weeks. Let him do all the work, and make sure he gets you off first. I mean, how long do you have to wait after you birth my perfect niece or nephew?"

"Six weeks," Belles and I say in sync, to which Scarlet makes a horrified face.

"Yet another reason I'll be their favorite aunt but do not want any of my own." She reaches over and rubs my belly. "Repeat after me, little Kingston. Auntie Scarlet is your favorite."

My husband moves behind me and squeezes my shoulders. "Baby Beneventi, Scarlet."

"Whatever, Sam. You and Bash have stolen both of my sisters. I think I should get to name the baby." She leans closer to my belly. "What do you think about that? I'll name you. I'll be your favorite. And then I'll buy you your very first car." Scarlet throws a half-hearted glare in Sam's direction when he attempts to cut her off. "Fine." Then her eyes light up. "I'll buy you your first pony."

Belle giggles, and baby Nixon whines from the interruption. "I swear this kid only wants to sleep when he's being walked around."

I push up from the chair. "Give him to me. My back hurts. I need to move around." But as I reach for Nixon, water gushes down my legs, and I stare in horror as I see the puddle I've left on the floor, as well as all over Scarlet's pristine white pants and shoes. "Oh my God."

"Amelia, please tell me you didn't just pee on me. Please, please, please." Everyone ignores Scarlet as a flurry of activity starts around me. It seems like everyone starts speaking at once, making it hard to catch who's saying what.

"Your water broke." That was Belles . . . I think.

"Breathe, baby." Sam. Definitely Sam.

I reach out, knowing Sam is there. "It's time."

He wraps me in his arms, whispering, "I love you, Snow. Let's go have a baby," as he begins to usher me out of the box.

As Brady opens the door, Scarlet follows us out. "I'm coming too. Someone will have to keep the family updated."

Sam looks at me, silently asking if I'm alright with this, and I agree.

It doesn't take long to get to Kroydon Hills Hospital, but in the span of the thirty minutes, my contractions have started coming fast and strong. By the time I'm wheeled into a delivery room and checked out by my doctor, I'm fully dilated and 100 percent effaced. "Oh my God. This is really happening. I thought the first time it took hours. Days even. I'm not even due for another two weeks."

Scarlet is on one side of me, and Sam is on the other when the doctor comes back in, looking like she means business in her gown and gloves.

"Okay, Amelia. It's time to push. Are you ready?"

Scarlet lets go of my hand. "I'm just going to . . ."

"Oh no, you don't." I grab her hand and squeeze while Sam holds my other hand. "Nobody is going anywhere."

I lean my head against Sam's arm, scared. "I don't think I can do this."

"You're the strongest woman I've ever known, Snow. You've got this, and we've got you."

"Okay, Amelia. I need you to push," The doctor smiles, and I kinda want to tell her to fuck off.

"I'm scared," I announce.

Sam holds my hand to his chest. "I love you. Now push."

Four hours later, Lenny and Bash are the first family members from the waiting room that we let in my hospital room. Sam and I took an hour to ourselves and then let Scarlet back in. She was a trooper during my labor. She never complained once. Even though, according to her, I may have broken her hand, and she's definitely throwing out her suit and shoes. She's curled up in a chair with hospital socks on her feet, cradling our son, Maddox, close to her while she watches him sleep.

Sam is sitting on the bed next to me. His arm is wrapped around me as my head rests on his chest, and I lie there exhausted but elated.

When Lenny enters the room, she makes a beeline over to Scarlet then makes grabby hands. "Gimme."

"Nope," our sister tells her. "He's mine. Go make your own."

While Lenny and Scarlet fight sweetly over Maddox, Bash leans down and kisses my forehead before he shakes his brother's hand. "Congratulations, brother."

After Scarlet finally relents and shares my son with his other aunt, Lenny happily brings him over to introduce him to Bash. Beaming, she asks him, "Do you want to meet your nephew?"

Bash gently lifts him from her arms and holds him close to his chest. "You did so good, Amelia."

Maddox begins rooting around Sebastian's chest, appearing to be hungry and looking for a source of food Bash won't be able to provide. "I think he wants his momma, Snow."

As Bash passes Maddox to me, Scarlet stands and joins us.

"Scar, where are your shoes?" Len asks with a quizzical look on her face.

Scarlet's eyes never stray from Maddox. "In the trash." Once she finally looks up, she proclaims to Len and Bash, "He likes me better. Just telling you now. I was there when this little man was born." She runs the tip of her finger down his nose. "And I will be his favorite." She kisses his head softly, then squeezes my hand. "I guess I can't hog him any longer. Annabelle's been blowing up my phone, claiming it's her turn. I'll be back tomorrow. Call me if you need anything." Then she moves to the other side of the bed and hugs Sam. "Take care of our girl, Sammy." She whispers something to my husband that I can't hear before turning back to Len and Bash. "I think Amelia may want a little privacy."

Lenny leans down and kisses Maddox's cheek, then whispers, "She might have met you first, but I'm your auntie on both sides, so I get extra time with you, little man."

Bash places his hand on Lenny's back, and they follow Scarlet out of the room.

My eyes start to get heavy as I lean back against Sam and let Maddox get comfortable while he latches on.

"He's so perfect, Snow." The back of a single finger gets

dragged down the bare skin of his little back, causing him to wiggle before he finds his comfy spot and starts sucking like a little champion.

"I never knew life could be this good, Sam."

His arm tightens around me. "It's just the beginning, Snow. It's just the beginning."

The End

WHAT COMES NEXT?

Not ready to say goodbye to Kroydon Hills just yet? Don't fret. Follow the Kingston family as they each figure out what comes next while falling in love in the new series, Restless Kings.

Scarlet Kingston's book, Broken King, will be releasing March 9th.

Pre-order it here - https://books2read.com/RK2

Want a glimpse into Scarlet and Cade?

CHAPTER 1 — SCARLET

"Amelia, I've got to go. I'm in the parking lot and need to go inside before I'm late." I love my sister. Although we only officially met her a year and a half ago, she turned out to be the true missing piece of our fucked up family. However, since my nephew was born a few months ago, she's so thrilled to talk to someone who isn't babbling nonsensically back at her, she's pretty hard to get off the phone.

"Okay. Are you still coming over after?" Maddox, my nephew begins whining in the background, causing Amelia to jostle the phone.

It's been a long Friday. But I already cut out of work early for this appointment and am definitely looking forward to drinks with my sisters. "Wouldn't miss it. See you then." I tell her, then end the call. Amelia helps our sister Lenny and I even out the estrogen to testosterone ratio in our family.

It will never be even.

There are five guys to three women and one five-year-old diva.

But at least now, we're a little closer to it.

Max and Becket are older than me. Sawyer and Hudson are next after me. Amelia is between Hudson and Lenny, with Jace rounding out the semi-adult Kingstons. Our youngest sister, Madeline, is the baby of the family.

We all share the same father with a mix of five different mothers. I never had any illusions that the late, great John Joseph Kingston was a saint. But it sure shocked the hell out of all of us when we found out that there was a missing Kingston sister out there somewhere. It turns out, dear old Dad didn't know she existed either. But once he died, and the search was left to us, we spared no resource in our quest to find our missing sister.

We protect what's ours, and Amelia was ours.

Luckily for us, fate turned out not to be the fickle bitch she usually is. Amelia had started her new life in Kroydon Hills, just minutes away from our late father's estate, where a few of my siblings still live. Lenny, Amelia, and I try to get together at least once a week. Tonight, Len and I are going to Amelia's house. Apparently, someone gave her and her husband, Sam, a fruit-and-cheese-of-the-month-club membership, and as lame as it sounds, the three of us love devouring it each month.

Plus, this woman makes a charcuterie board like no one I've ever met.

And it's the perfect way to end a long week.

TGI freaking F.

I enter my doctor's office, sign in, and take a seat to wait. The sea of pregnant women surrounding me seems to be closing in. When I switched from the pill to the shot three months ago, I was looking for something a little more user-friendly. I'd tried a few different birth control pills over the last few years, and the side effects weren't for me.

The shot, however, has been great.

Less migraines to deal with, and I'm a much happier woman.

It would be even better if I didn't have to come back in every three months.

But for now, it'll do.

When a woman, who appears to be about a hundred years pregnant, sits down next to me with a toddler covered in peanut butter and jelly by her side, I hug the opposite side of my chair and pray the nurse calls me quickly.

Don't get me wrong, kids are great. I love my nephew and my little sister.

But I love when I give them back too.

I'm not a woman who gushes over other people's kids.

Most babies look more like small aliens than perfect little angels.

This . . . I take stock of the waiting room around me and grimace.

This madhouse surrounding me today is just not for me.

***

Thirty minutes later, I'm sitting on the exam table in a pale pink paper robe, when my doctor finally walks in. "How are we doing today, Scarlet?" She pulls up my chart on her tablet, then sits down on her little stool on wheels.

"I'm fine, Doctor Esher. No complaints. Just ready to get this exam over with and get on with my night." Unless you count how damn cold it is in this room. It's not like they don't know their patients are going to get naked in here. Would it kill them to turn the heat up just a tad?

Doctor Esher scrolls through what I'm guessing is my chart before rolling over toward the table. The smile that was on her face moments ago is gone, replaced by a purposefully blank expression. "Scarlet, have you had any issues in the past ninety days?"

"No issues. Not so much as a cough. Why? Is something wrong with my bloodwork? I wasn't supposed to be fasting, was I? Because I had coffee before I had it done the other day. I thought you said it didn't matter. We just needed to make sure the hormones from the shot didn't throw off anything else." I get migraines. Bad migraines. Sometimes debilitating migraines. They started a few years ago. I've tried every pill out there, and they all exacerbate the crippling headaches. The shot was my next best option. And as far as I'm concerned, so far, so good.

Doctor Esher clears her throat. "Scarlet, according to your bloodwork, you're pregnant."

I tilt my head to the side and study her. I don't think she'd kid about something so serious. But . . . "Is this a bad joke? I mean honestly, that really isn't funny."

Her face stays unmoving.

No reaction.

She's not laughing.

"Scarlet." Her tone has dropped an octave, no longer light and airy like it was when she greeted me. "This isn't a joke. I wouldn't do that to you. According to your bloodwork, you're pregnant. Judging by your HCG levels, I'd guess you're about ten weeks along."

"I don't know what to tell you, Doc. But the draft was last month. I've barely had time to sleep, let alone sleep with anyone . . ." I trail off as I run through my mental calendar.

The draft was last month, yes.

But Hudson's title fight in Las Vegas was the month before that.

Son of a bitch.

I wasn't concerned with a broken condom.

I was covered with the shot.

What are the odds that both forms of birth control would fail?

Apparently, higher than I knew.

"I can't be pregnant." I meet Doctor Esher's knowing brown eyes and cringe.

I am Scarlet fucking Kingston.

I am stronger than this.

I do not panic in public.

"Could you please run the test again? I have to believe there was a mistake." There. I sounded in control. Inside, I might be hyperventilating, but she doesn't need to know that.

Slow deep breaths.

That's better.

A mistake.

This has to be a mistake.

But even as I say it to myself, I think back to that night in Las Vegas, and know there's no mistake. If ever there was a man whose sperm could leap tall buildings and blow their way past all hormones in one bound, it would be his.

***

"I'm sorry, but you're going to have to repeat that," Lenny

all but yells at me after I've walked into Amelia's house in shock this evening.

"You asked me why I'm late, and I'm telling you why. My doctor's appointment ran a little late because they wanted to do an ultrasound and confirm that I am, indeed, pregnant." We all walk into the kitchen, where the table is covered with enough meat, cheese, and fruit to feed all nine siblings, not just the three of us. I pop a green grape into my mouth and point across the table between Lenny and Amelia, whose mouths both appear to be unhinged at the moment as they stand, staring at me in shock. "That's pretty much what I looked like when I was finally alone in my car for the proper fucking freak-out that was building the entire time I was in the doctor's office."

Lenny is younger than me by six years.

We weren't close growing up. My little sister never met a problem she couldn't run away from. We couldn't possibly have been more different. She had a luxury most of us never knew. She grew up with two parents who loved each other and adored Jace and her. She was never a bargaining chip for more alimony, like the rest of us were.

She was never part of a transaction.

But once she came back to Philadelphia, she and I worked through some of our differences.

After she finished her master's degree, Lenny moved home and started working for the professional football team our family owns, right around the time she met her fiancé, Sebastian. She's engaged to Amelia's brother-in-law. Go fucking figure. "Holy shit, Scar. What are you going to do?" Len's voice is loud and carries throughout the kitchen.

She knows I've never wanted kids.

I love my life.

I love my career.

I love my family.

I never felt like anything was missing.

Amelia's son, Maddox, who was previously content, sleeping in his swing, startles and begins to fuss.

"You really don't need to yell, Len. I'm freaking out enough right now. And I'd say you both know me well enough to know . . . I. Don't. Freak. The. Fuck. Out." The words may come out a little harsher than I intended, but I'm holding on by a thin string right now, and Lennie losing her cool is not going to help me stay calm.

My family likes to call me the "ice queen" because I'm not a fan of overt displays of emotion. I'm a private person, and I prefer to keep it that way. I also don't care for being involved in messy situations. Once the shock wears off, they'll have a field day with this.

Lenny drops down in a chair across from me while Amelia picks Maddox up from his swing and holds him close to her as she lulls him back to sleep. In a soft voice, Amelia asks, "Do you know when it happened, Scar?"

"Forget when." Lenny reaches for a bottle of wine, then glances at me sheepishly and places it back on the table. "Who's the father, and are you going to keep it?"

One night.

I let myself have one night with him.

I've avoided him for years.

But apparently, one night was all it took for history to repeat itself.

Damnit.

ACKNOWLEDGMENTS

M ~ Without you none of it is possible.

Deana ~ Thank you for believing in me, even when I'm doubting myself. Love you!

K. ~ No bigger cheerleader ever existed. You are the Nattie to my Belles.

Savy ~ Words are hard, and there aren't enough of them to adequately thank you for everything you do for me.

To my very own Coop ~ There are no words that can do justice for how thankful I am for every aspect of our forced friendship. Thank you just isn't enough.

Tammy ~ I am so incredibly grateful for you. You are Superwoman.

Jen W. ~ Thank you for pushing me through this book. Sammy would be a big old softy if it wasn't for you.

My Betas, Brittany, Vicki, Kelly & Heather ~ I cannot thank you enough for taking the time out of your own hectic lives to read this book. Your notes are EVERYTHING.

My Street Team, Kelly, Shawna, Vicki, Ashley, Heather, Oriana, Shannon, Nichole, Tash, Nicole, Hannah, Meghan,

Amy, Christy, Emma, Brianna, Adanna, Jennifer, Lissete, Poppy & Jacqueline ~ Thank you, ladies, for loving these characters and this world. Our group is my safe place, and I'm so thankful for every one of you in it. Family Meetings Rock!

Sarah ~ I'm so grateful to have you in my corner. Thank you so much for all the late-night texts, and all the guidance.

My editors, Jess & Dena. You both take such good care of my words. Thank you for pushing me harder, and making me better.

Gemma – Thanks for giving it that finishing touch.

Jena ~ you are so talented! This cover is EVERYTHING!

To all of the Indie authors out there who have helped me along the way – you are amazing! This community is so incredibly supportive, and I am so lucky to be a part of it!

Thank you to all of the bloggers who took the time to read, review, and promote Rise of the King.

And finally, the biggest thank you to you, the reader. I hope you enjoyed reading Sam and Amelia's love story as much as I enjoyed writing it.

ABOUT THE AUTHOR

Bella Matthews is a Jersey girl at heart. She is married to her very own Alpha Male and raising three little ones. You can typically find her running from one sporting event to another. When she is home, she is usually hiding in her home office with the only other female in her house, her rescue dog Tinker Bell by her side. She likes to write swoon-worthy heroes and sassy, smart heroines with a healthy dose of laughter thrown and all the feels.

Stay Connected

Amazon Author Page: https://amzn.to/2UWU7Xs

Facebook Page: https://bit.ly/3kHi8ip

Reader Group: https://bit.ly/Game--Changers

Instagram: @bellamatthews.author

Bookbub: https://bit.ly/3kKNCEp

Goodreads: https://bit.ly/327Yl5j

TikTok: https://bit.ly/3meOrGX

Newsletter: https://bit.ly/38eBKVF

ALSO BY BELLA MATTHEWS

Kings of Kroydon Hills

All In

More Than A Game

Always Earned, Never Given

Under Pressure

Restless Kings

Rise of the King

Broken King